Eden

Redefined

Kyle Hunter

ISBN 979-8-9856352-3-2

More novels by Kyle Hunter that take you places

Circle Back Around

One December

Provence Series

Prodigals in Provence

A Promise in Provence

The Second Chance Series

Marissa Rewritten (A Novella)

Julia Redesigned

Sydney Rewound

Eden Redefined

Chapter One

Eden Godfrey shifted in her window seat to gaze down at the landscape and coastline coming into view. The plane's revving engine and the sound of tray tables being folded signaled preparation for landing. As the plane descended and pressure built in her ears, buildings took the place of water through the smudged glass. Wilmington, North Carolina, was only a short distance away.

"Are you visiting or going home?" A male voice drew her attention from the sun-drenched view.

She turned to the older man seated beside her who'd been absorbed in his iPad for the duration of the trip. How easy it was for people to be friendly in the last ten minutes of a flight. He'd perched his glasses on his balding scalp and looked at her with weathered blue eyes.

Eden smiled. "I live in Indiana, but I'm going to Wilmington for a wedding. The wedding isn't until Saturday, but my college girlfriends and I are renting a beach house for a few days beforehand."

Even as she spoke, a flush of embarrassment heated her face. How confusing that must be for the man, since he could likely tell that she, at age fifty, was hardly a college student. She laughed. "I mean, I was in college over twenty-five years ago, but I get together with three women from my college days about twice a year. One of them is getting married. It's her second marriage." Why did she feel the need to explain why a woman nearing fifty was getting married? Happened all the time, though it hadn't happened to her since becoming a widow twelve years earlier. Not that she'd tried. But it *was* a statistical possibility and likely not much more than that for her.

"And you? Is this home?" She hoped her forced statement would steer her from the sudden turn of her thoughts, which lately, had been more frequent.

"Yes, I'm going home after a visit to see my daughter and grandchildren in Lafayette. When I retired, I moved to Emerald Isle, which is just north of here."

Eden nodded. "Sounds nice. I like the name." Would she want to live at the beach all year round? Sydney, the bride-to-be, had grown up in a beach town and ended up moving back the previous year. And *that* decision changed her entire future.

The roar of the engine intensified, cutting off further communication. The cabin shuddered as the plane's wheels bounced once on the tarmac, then rolled smoothly to a halt.

Eden unlatched her seatbelt and reached for her purse. She rejoiced to soon see her friends and was happy about how their lives were turning out. Yet, a thread of tension lay just beneath the surface when she thought of her own. Still adrift, she was like a marble on a Chinese checkerboard sliding around each hole, but not finding the right one. For the last three years since, at her instigation, the four of them—Sydney, Marissa, and Julia—began meeting twice annually for a fun and supportive girls' weekend, Eden had watched each woman's life unfold and flourish, both professionally and romantically. Would that change the bond they all had and gradually phase out the special weekends she looked forward to all year? And would *she* remain the only one whose life sat securely in a rut?

"Enjoy your visit and your friend's wedding," the man said once he'd pulled a weekend bag from the overhead compartment.

"Thank you. I'm sure it'll be a great time." No doubt, it would.

She stood, unsteady in the narrow space between the seats and the crowded aisle. As usual, she'd worn wedge heels, a style adopted many years earlier to compensate for being five foot four.

With a smile and parting nod, the man melded into the thicket of passengers. Minutes later, at baggage claim, Eden tapped her toe as she scanned the stream of bags. She yanked her suitcase from the carousel.

Outside, a blanket of humid air enveloped her. She could almost smell the salt and hear the waves.

"There she is! Eden, over here!"

She shoved darker thoughts aside as she released her suitcase and spread her arms wide to Sydney, who bounded down the sidewalk from where she'd parallel parked. Sydney bent and hugged Eden, swaying her side to side. Close behind her were Marissa and Julia, each one in her turn offering *it's been too long* hugs.

"You're all a sight for sore eyes." Eden grinned, buoyant with joy as soon as she saw them. "How is it that you all, quite unfairly, look more gorgeous than the last time we saw each other?" Seemed like ages since they'd been together, but it was only the previous October. "I've got airplane hair and feel like a folded envelope."

Sydney, looking like an elegant hippie, wore a faded denim mini skirt and a lime green tank top, her thick braid hanging over one shoulder. Matching bangle bracelets adorned one wrist. She laughed and slid one suntanned arm around Eden. "You look great to me. And we have *many* ways of unfolding you this week."

"How did you plan anything at all for us when you had a wedding to prepare, Sydney?" Dark-haired Julia walked beside Marissa as the women moved en masse toward Sydney's SUV.

"It's been planned for a while, so not much more to do. Plus, we weren't aiming for the gala of the century. Something simple with my best friends, you all, of course, and family." Sydney pushed the button on her key fob and the back of the SUV opened.

"Are your brothers coming? I remember you fell out with them last year." Marissa took Eden's canvas bag against her protest and slipped it into the car. She pushed a wavy strand of dark hair from her face and waited as Eden settled her suitcase in the trunk.

They all slid in, and Sydney pulled away from the curb. "My brother, Kevin, and I made up. He and his family'll be at the wedding. Chet is still nursing imaginary wounds, so I don't expect him there. Nor did I invite him."

"His loss," murmured Julia.

"Got that right. Here we go, ladies. Onward to the beach!"

When they entered the condo Sydney had found for their week, each woman stopped and looked around, oohing and murmuring in appreciation.

"Wow, this is beautiful. Sydney, you've outdone yourself." Eden took in the luxury. Surrounded by beachy furnishings in off-white and turquoise, with waves and sand meeting her direct gaze through the balcony window, Eden relaxed her shoulders and eased into vacation mode.

Sydney preened. "Only the best wow-worthy digs for my girls." She stretched one arm toward a hallway to her right. "There are four bedrooms and baths, which we'll all enjoy until Saturday morning. Then *I'll* be whisked away by my groom to a romantic island and you three can have it to yourselves for a couple more days."

"That is definitely an acceptable plan," said Eden, who'd ventured close to the sliding glass door. "Especially for you, Sydney. As for me, I could just park myself here and look at this stunning view for a while." She pulled open the door and allowed a balmy breeze to stroke her face. Mesmerized by the rhythmic sound of gentle waves below, she closed her eyes and breathed deeply.

"Or park yourself with the rest of us on this roomy balcony." Marissa joined Eden at the door, her soft southern lilt adding warmth to the inviting scene. "Looks big enough for us *and* our snacks." The two women gazed out in silence. Julia and Sydney crowded alongside to see the view.

"It's lovely, isn't it?" Marissa said. "I miss being an easy drive from the ocean, but the Asheville mountains are stunning too."

"So much to catch up on." Julia sighed, likely thinking of Marissa's recent move from Raleigh to Asheville. She turned then, her clear blue eyes panning the small group. "We'd better get started, ladies."

In a matter of minutes, they'd all deposited their suitcases into their respective bedrooms and changed into comfortable clothes. According to their tradition, they carried the usual overload of snacks and beverages to the balcony and settled in. The space was well furnished for meals and relaxing, though the women would surely hit the beach that beckoned them from five stories below. Eden could almost feel cool waves foaming around her bare feet. April in North Carolina was more like summer up north.

"Oh, this is heavenly. Just the break I needed." Julia's slight New York accent flavored her words as she sighed and leaned her head against the plump cushion of her chair. "My work has been so pressured lately by two clients in particular. Picky, picky. Thankfully, I'll finish their projects soon."

"Individuals or hotels?" asked Marissa.

"One of each. Business is good in D. C." Julia reached for a plate of crackers that Eden had unwrapped.

"And *you* have a wedding to plan too. It's not just mine we should talk about." Sydney's voice carried a mischievous inflection. "Aside from it taking place in Florence, Italy, I know *no* details." She flicked her braid from her shoulder.

"Except that you're all invited. That's the main thing you need to know." Julia took on a secretive smile, her olive skin illuminated by clear blue eyes.

"Must be nice to have relatives in Italy." Eden placed a slice of cheese on a cracker. "And so very convenient that you met your handsome hubby-to-be there too."

"They're the only relatives I've got, even if they're across the world," Julia said.

"Ha, you wouldn't hear *me* complaining." Sydney gave an emphatic nod then mimicked, "Oh, gotta go see the fam in *Florence*."

The women laughed. Julia reached out and poured a glass of sparkling water. "Some details even I don't know. My cousin Valentina is handling a lot of it, since she lives in Florence. It's her gift to us."

"Molto Fantastico," Sydney said, reaching for the corkscrew. "Jessie was a big help with mine, although she's a senior, in the throes of college applications and other senior-y things. She made time and enjoyed the heck out of it."

"I'm glad she's supportive. That's so sweet," Eden said. Sydney and her daughter Jessie had always been so close. It was a blessing that Jessie wasn't jealous of Sydney's new-old love. Or renewed love might be a better term.

Eden sighed happily on Sydney's behalf. Her friend had known past struggles but now sat glowing and peaceful across the balcony table from her.

"How long did you take off from your job, Sydney?" Marissa asked.

"Two full weeks. I have a very cool boss who told me to take as much time as I needed. I tell you, after eighteen years teaching high school math, this analyst job is almost a breeze. It has its moments, but it's a good fit for me. And I get to work from home."

"That sounds perfect." Marissa took the plate of cold cuts Julia passed to her. "And to be available to your mom and to Jessie is a huge advantage."

"Yes, absolutely."

"I want to hear more about your new life, Marissa." Eden leaned her elbows on her knees. She knew the basics, since the two of them talked often on the phone, but it wasn't the same as in person.

"Have you enjoyed living in Asheville? Be honest, does it measure up to Raleigh?" Julia asked as attention went to Marissa.

"Oh, yes. It's been just over a year now, so I'm fully settled in. You all probably remember when I sold my house in Raleigh. I bought the Asheville condo and moved soon after. I wanted to be closer to Jarrod but have my own space too. It's been good for us. He'd been doing most of the driving from Asheville to Raleigh, so I think he was relieved."

"Aw, Jarrod would climb mountains for you, Marissa," Sydney said. "He'd cross oceans, he'd scale—"

"Alright, alright." Marissa laughed. "I thought I'd miss Raleigh, and I do a little, but Asheville is different and fun. It's beautiful there too. I love it. I should have sold that money pit—I mean that historic house—long ago." Her smile faded. "I think it kept me stuck in grieving Robert. I feel freer now, and I think Robert would want that."

"Absolutely, he would. Now you're beginning a new life, a new love. So exciting." Eden clasped her hands. "Any talk of marriage? Let's see, you've known him almost two years, moved to Asheville a year ago . . ."

A delicate flush crossed Marissa's pale face. "Yes, we've talked about it. It's not official, but we're talking. Probably won't be long before I have an announcement for you."

"Oh, my, that's exciting news. My goodness, I need a dedicated calendar just for weddings." Eden sent them all a wide-eyed expression of glee, despite a faint weight inside her that screamed, *you're being left behind.* She swallowed and blinked but held onto her congratulatory smile. The other women murmured their enthusiasm for Marissa's news.

"Keep us posted. That's not an option." Sydney shot Marissa a pointed stare with a fake scowl as everyone murmured their agreement.

"What about you, Eden? Anything new and different? Oh, I'm sorry for how that sounded." Julia's ivory face pinkened. "I didn't mean—"

"No offense taken *ever* from you, dear sisters, and that's for all of you. We can speak the truth here. You and I all know I'm stuck. Let's admit it. I'm the aimless widow. That's what I am."

Sydney set her glass on the table and stared at her. "For once in my life, I don't know what to say."

Maybe she was trying to be humorous, as was her style, but Eden didn't think so. Sydney's gaze was compassionate, solemn, her voice soft.

"The question is," Sydney continued, "How do *you* feel about being *stuck*, as you say? Are you peaceful with it or do you long for something else? Are you chafing or resting?"

Eden forced out a light chuckle as a nearby seagull shrieked. "Wow, Sydney, you've changed. No more snarky one-liners? You could preach a sermon on that thought." Her outburst drew some soft laughter, but everyone fell silent again, awaiting her response. She took a breath as they all stared at her. *No reason to be intimidated. They love you and want your best.* "Okay, I guess since selling my restaurant over a year and a half ago, I've dabbled in this and that. It was nice for a while, and I needed the break. No stress, time to work on my house, volunteer at church, take up painting, find myself. But the last part hasn't worked that well. I haven't found myself, or what I want to do next."

Sydney leaned forward and grabbed one of Eden's hands. "The point I wanted to make was if you're happy with your life, who's to say you're stuck or should be doing something else? How *you* feel is what matters."

Eden pressed her lips together and nodded. "That's true, I guess. I, uh, I was content for a long time. I learned to enjoy running the restaurant after Gerry died. He didn't involve me all that much when he was alive, so it was nice having that opportunity. Not that I'm glad he's gone, of course." She smoothed an imaginary wrinkle from her shorts. "I'm not unhappy, but now with the kids out of the house and the restaurant gone, I'd like a new challenge to focus on. Something . . . meaningful."

Marissa and Julia nodded in her peripheral vision, waiting for her to go on.

"And . . ." She moistened her lips, "I'd like to . . ." She shrugged and splayed her hands. ". . . not be alone anymore. It was always too hard to think of that with everything else I had to do. And I honestly haven't met anyone for years. *And years.* I'm satisfied in some ways. You know, I don't really like change. Things are stable and boring. No one's at home getting on my nerves or telling me what to do. I'm not desperate or needy. But it would be nice to talk to someone in the evening. To travel with someone. And seeing you all settled in your love lives—"

"Which we didn't have only two years ago," Sydney added.

Eden gave them a crooked smile. "Yeah, it can happen quickly, I guess. I'm so pleased for each of you. I hope it won't change what we all have together."

"Of course, we'd never give us up voluntarily, either." The old Sydney was back.

Eden laughed. "Amen to that!" She shot a jubilant fist into the air.

"Well, there's that concern out of the way, Eden. But at least you're identifying that you'd like companionship." Marissa's dark eyebrows lifted as she made her point. "I think that's healthy because I've never heard you say that before." Maybe Marissa had missed her calling by becoming a successful novelist instead of a counselor.

"Let's not waste our week feeling bad for lonely old Eden, okay? I'll be fine. We want to share Sydney's happiness and being together. And of course, Julia's happiness and Marissa's happiness." She ignored the doubtful expressions on her friends' faces as she realized how pathetic she sounded.

Eden reached for a bowl of crackers and dip. "How 'bout some of that dip? Looks tasty."

Marissa had hit on something. Something that had hovered quietly in her mind for the last few months and was growing louder with every passing day.

ʘ   ʘ   ʘ

Eden dug her toes into the sand, chuckling at the paradox of a barefoot beach wedding. Knowing Sydney, it seemed a perfectly natural decision. Rows of folding chairs formed a semi-circle around an arched pergola festooned with flowers and vines. Behind it, waves lapped, providing gentle and fitting music prior to the ceremony. Overhead, the sky stretched an endless velvet blue.

Surprisingly, the days at the beach had been a relaxed vacation for all the women, rarely interrupted by last-minute wedding tasks or crises. Sydney had made a few phone calls and beginning on Friday, out-of-town guests began to arrive followed by a festive rehearsal dinner. *This is our time*, the bride had said to them on that first day. *Time for our extended bachelorette party, but I'm not the focus. We all are.*

Eden savored each day walking on the beach, taking part in a gab session that seemed to ebb and flow but never end, sampling local restaurants, cooking in the condo, and embracing the circle of love surrounding her. She desperately hoped Sydney's earlier proclamation would be true, that they'd stay close friends even as each woman married and began a different type of life.

Today, they'd witness the first among them step into her new future with a second chance at a loving relationship.

Sydney appeared beside her, a fairy princess in an off-white calf-length dress, its uneven hem flowing around her like whipped cream. Her thick, highlighted hair hung to her shoulders, and a crown of tiny flowers encircled her head. And, of course, her feet were bare. "Eden, this is my dad, Richard, and his wife, Melody."

Eden shook hands with the older man and woman standing beside Sydney. She saw a resemblance between the distinguished-looking man and his daughter. "It's very nice meeting you both." She'd said the same thing numerous times already but was glad to see a good turnout for Sydney and Tyler's special day.

Apparently, Sydney wasn't the type of bride to hide out until the start of the ceremony. She left Eden's side to escort her father and his wife to meet other guests. Nearby, the groom, Tyler, talked with a cluster of people dressed in casual suits, elegant dresses, and bare feet. Being the owner of two golf courses, he likely had hundreds of friends and acquaintances in town, though a more modest number were present that day, since he and Sydney had wanted a smaller event.

Julia and Marissa were already seated in the second row and beside them were their fiancés, Craig and Jarrod, who'd arrived the previous day. Eden had been glad she could finally meet the men she'd only heard about for the last two years. Her next encounter with them would be at Julia's August wedding in Florence.

Eden sighed as her eyes panned the group. Near the pergola, Sydney's blonde daughter, Jessic, was discussing something with a young dark-haired man she guessed was Tyler's son, Zach. Next to them, two guitars were perched on stands.

Sydney was again beside her. "My mom is here, Eden. Do you remember her?" Sydney seemed slightly breathless from so many introductions and pre-wedding excitement.

"How do you stay so serene with all this going on?" Eden laughed. "You don't have to personally introduce me to everyone with all that's on your plate, wedding girl."

"Just my mom, Carolyn. You haven't seen her since we were in college."

"With pleasure. How is her health?"

Sydney clasped her hands together. "I'm so grateful. She's been in remission now for about six months. Let's pray it continues."

"Absolutely."

Sydney led Eden to where an older woman sat at the end of a row. Though she was thin and her short hair pure white, her eyes exuded a youthfulness and an intelligent spark. "It's nice to see you again, Eden," she said, lifting a bony hand to grasp hers. "I'd recognize you anywhere, with that golden-blond hair. You haven't changed since you were nineteen."

Eden laughed. "You're so kind, but exaggerating ever so slightly, Mrs. Davis."

"Call me Carolyn. Everyone does, even my own kids sometimes. Have you met my son, Kevin, and his family?" She extended her other hand toward a group of six that took up an entire row.

"Yes, I met them a while ago," she said with a tight little wave in their direction.

"Please take your seats, everyone," Zach said into the microphone on the pergola. "Thank you all for coming to our parents' wedding."

Eden settled into a chair next to Carolyn. What a remarkable day it was. Sydney was finally marrying her high school sweetheart. So much had happened in the intervening years, but at the perfect time, those pieces had come together for her. Evidence that it was never too late.

Zach's father was marrying Jessie's mother that day, but Zach and Jessie seemed to be a couple as well, or at least excellent friends. Jessie stood next to him, and he handed her a guitar. He picked up the second one and slid the strap around his neck.

"Welcome to everyone on this very important day," Jessie called over the shush of waves and the hum of conversation. "We'd like to start our ceremony with a special song dedicated to our parents."

She and Zach exchanged a glance, plucked a string twice to tune, then strummed. With an impish expression, Zach leaned toward the microphone. "This is a song we wrote called, *It Took You Long Enough.*"

He and Jessie bestowed angelic grins on the audience as laughter rippled through the rows. A light wind fluffed Jessie's hair as she cradled her guitar. "Here goes . .

> *People always say*
> *Good things are worth the wait*
> *And thirty years is long enough*
> *To see that truth today*
>
> *As teenagers who fell in love*
> *So very long ago*
> *We're glad they finally got a clue*
> *As they're about to show."*

Eden giggled along with the other guests as some leaned forward to hear the lyrics over the waves. Jessie and Zach exchanged a laugh as they continued singing. Not a very solemn beginning to a wedding procession, but considering Sydney and Tyler's history, so fitting.

> *"Took you long enough*
> *To recognize your love*
> *To see that you belong as two*

And all that mushy stuff.

*We're happy, Syd and Tyler
To witness this great day
We never thought you'd figure out
It should have always been this way.
It should have always been this way."*

When they finished, everyone erupted in applause as Jessie and Zach took a bow. Jessie leaned toward the microphone. "If you don't know the background of their story, I guess the song filled you in. Now we'll get into the more serious stuff as we honor our parents on this sacred occasion."

They kept their guitars strapped to their necks and began strumming a non-traditional but beautiful tune. Tyler took his place at the pergola next to the pastor and turned toward the sandy aisle where Sydney approached in small steps. She kept time with the guitar music, one hand curled around her father's arm, her eyes riveted on Tyler's.

Eden's gaze shifted from Sydney to Tyler. She drew in a sharp breath and her throat tightened at the look on his face as he watched his bride approach. Eden's eyes stung as both joy and loss tumbled over her. Was she thinking of Gerry, with whom she'd exchanged the same vows so many years ago? And who she'd lost so young? Or was she longing for someone to love her the same way Tyler obviously loved Sydney?

No, she couldn't think about that. She wouldn't be selfish enough to think of her own pain while her friends had found love and a new future. And before her, as Sydney and Tyler faced each other and joined their hands, oblivious of all but one another, they finally entered a life, as Jessie had sung, which should have always been theirs.

Chapter Two

The flight from Wilmington to Indianapolis via Charlotte on Sunday afternoon went smoothly and Eden arrived at her two-story brick home by six p.m. It took under an hour to drive to Wadesboro, the mid-sized town where she'd lived for nearly twenty-five years. That time provided needed margin to prepare herself for the transition. A transition from spring temperatures, loving friends, and a stunning coastline to, well, to an empty house.

An abrupt shift of setting, but she'd get through it. Wadesboro, with its linear blocks, flat landscape, predictable subdivisions, and strip malls, was familiar, comfortable. The home she and Gerry had bought when she was pregnant with Brent was welcoming in its familiarity as well, though unexciting, despite her kitchen renovation the previous year. Since selling the restaurant, she'd thought about downsizing. It was a lot of house for just her. But as she'd told her friends that weekend, change was hard. And where else would she go? She needed a plan, a destination, a reason before selling her home. She didn't have those yet. A plan would come along eventually. Somehow.

She emptied the contents of her suitcase onto her bed and returned downstairs to make a light dinner in the bright, updated kitchen. By this time, Sydney and Tyler were enjoying their honeymoon in Barbados. Their wedding had been unique, touching and, at moments, humorous. The memory of it lingered in Eden's mind as if she couldn't bear to let it go and end her trip for real. During the weekend, she'd occasionally felt like a fifth wheel, one of the few guests not paired up. Yet, joy for Sydney, Marissa, and Julia bubbled up and filled her. Filled the yawning gaps in her own life.

She hadn't been unhappy over the last two years, as she'd told her friends. She'd needed the break following her intense involvement in the restaurant and had loved having the time to complete overdue projects as well as increase her involvement in her church. She'd be fine continuing those things into the future, but lately, the concerns she'd voiced at the beach had begun tugging at her. A bigger story and someone to share it with. How would a bigger story look? The absence of a clear picture felt unfocused, hollow.

She chewed absently on a grilled cheese sandwich, having lacked motivation to make anything more complex, and mentally rewound the trip. Weddings were solemn and joyful all at one time, and Sydney's was no different.

A vague recollection of her own wedding filtered through her thoughts like an old movie. On impulse, Eden rose from the island stool where she ate, leaving bread crusts on her plate as she'd done all her life. She went to the living room, where a faded photo of her wedding day with Gerry sat on an end table in an ornate but tarnished frame. In the photo, she looked even younger than her twins, Claire and Jordan. Like a child playing dress-up, her youthful face smiled out from rows of ruffles and lace of a dress she must have loved at the time, but now made her cringe. She'd kept the frame there on the bookshelf for Gerry's memory at first, then for the kids. With a wave of guilt, she realized she didn't look at it anymore and should tuck it away in a box of mementos.

At age twenty-two, she'd been so young when she married him, and he'd been nine years older. Years later, she understood that she'd loved Gerry, but had married him in part to escape her parents' alcoholic home. He had a restaurant, and she'd worked there as a college student. But that was another story, another lifetime ago.

It had been a decent marriage, though not perfect. Gerry hadn't been a drinker, but ironically had been killed by one in a car accident as he returned from a late weekend night at the restaurant. In the blink of an eye, Eden had to raise three teenagers and run a restaurant alone. Somehow, she did it. Only God's strength and provision had pulled her through some tough days, but her belief in herself had also bumped up a few levels. At times she'd look to the sky and say, *See what I did, Gerry? Bet you're surprised.* For years her role had been the little woman maintaining the house and kids while he did the important work of running Godfrey Gourmet, a popular landmark in Wadesboro.

With a long sigh, Eden returned to the renovated kitchen, one of her aimless widow projects, though she appreciated the outcome, bringing the room into the current fashion with its off-white cupboards, a coordinating backsplash, and stainless-steel appliances.

She put her dishes into the dishwasher as a wave of melancholy swept through her. Back to normal life, a life starting to feel like a too-tight bra. Before she left Wilmington, she'd promised Marissa and Julia she'd redouble her efforts to find a compelling purpose for the immediate future.

A buzz sounded from her phone on the granite island in the center of her kitchen. She picked it up to read the message and let out a squeal. *Are you home yet? Jordan and I are planning to come visit you next weekend. Hope that's okay.*

Eden slid onto the barstool and punched her daughter's number. "Hi, Claire. I'm glad to hear from you. I got your text."

"Yeah, Mom, I just sent it, like one minute ago. Are you home now?"

Just hearing Claire's voice pumped fresh energy into Eden's sagging spirits.

"I got here an hour or so ago. I'm so glad you girls are coming next weekend. I had to laugh when you said, 'hope that's okay'. It's always okay for my girls to come." The prospect of their visit would pull her through the coming week. After that, she'd address the deeper issues of surrounding the rest of her life.

"We were talking about it the other day, and we realized it was a good time to get away. Besides that, we haven't visited in a while."

That was true, but Eden wouldn't agree or put Claire on a guilt trip. "I've missed you, but I know you girls are busy with your jobs and lives. At least you're good about keeping in touch." Her twins both worked full time, Claire as a nurse, and Jordan as a marketing guru for a small company. They shared an apartment in Indianapolis.

"We try. It'll be a crazy week between now and then, but we'll plan to be there by supper on Friday, okay?"

"Yes, perfect. I'll take you to dinner wherever you want."

She hung up and fingered a small escaping tear. She didn't want to be a clingy mom with her grown daughters but was immensely grateful they were coming. Soon, she'd have her own life more developed, but for now, a visit from Claire and Jordan was exactly what she needed. She'd regroup over the next few days until they arrived.

Eden didn't have the same closeness with her son as she had with her girls. She and Brent got along fine, but he lived in California where he'd just finished college and had settled for the near future, thanks to a serious girlfriend. As a guy, he didn't call regularly and share about his latest haircut or a weekend away like her girls did. Sons didn't keep in touch like that, she supposed.

A bigger reason was that his personality was like his father's. More categorical, a black and white thinker. He was less sensitive and often looked mystified when his mother and sisters shared tears after a movie or a touching story they'd heard. As long as he was happy and fulfilled where he was, that was fine. And he kept in touch in his own sporadic way.

Eden texted him, knowing from experience that was the best method of reaching him. He likely wouldn't respond for a couple of days. Then she texted Julia and Marissa. *Got home safely and miss you already! It was wonderful to see you both and share in Sydney's joy. Now it's back to real life.*

She hadn't wanted to sound pathetic. *My girls are coming next weekend for a visit, so maybe they can give me some ideas to help me find myself.* She reread her words. They still sounded needy and lost. But she planned to brainstorm with Claire and Jordan once they arrived. So far, that was the only plan she had.

⁍ ⁍ ⁍

"You'll enjoy this place I found," Eden told her daughters as they entered a brightly lit restaurant under a colorful awning. "Tex-Mex."

The twins had arrived thirty minutes earlier. Their presence and banter in the house and car were music to Eden's soul after a productive but unexciting week. She'd kept busy with house tasks, attended her weekly Bible study, prepared a meal for a woman who'd just had surgery, and effectively pushed out her troubling thoughts to the determined best of her ability.

"I skipped lunch today, so I'm starved." Jordan shoved a rogue lock of dark blond bangs from her forehead.

Cheerful colors surrounded them, orange on the walls with red and yellow lamps hanging over each table. The enticing aroma of cheese and peppers permeated the air. The hostess led them to a booth.

Eden slid in one side. "Why'd you skip lunch? That's not good, Jordan."

"I had a deadline, so I munched on an energy bar and an apple. So, technically, I didn't skip lunch, but I'm still starved."

"I can top that." Claire straightened. "A gunshot wound, an overdose, a broken tibia . . . Not boring at all."

"Yes, yes, you win." Jordan's voice was indulgent. "Maybe I should trade places with you and whip that ER into shape."

"Is your job still a challenge for you right now?" Eden asked Jordan.

Her daughter shrugged. "I like the marketing stuff, but there are way too many deadlines. And my boss is developing an alternate personality that I'm afraid is her new default. Demanding, impatient, critical. She used to be pretty cool, but not anymore."

"Sounds like she's going through a personal crisis and taking it out on her staff." Claire snagged a tortilla chip from the bowl placed in front of them. "Since it's not her usual behavior." She looked up at the waitress. "Can we have some guac and queso too?"

"I'm glad you're thinking that way, Claire," Eden said. "It's always good to look beyond the obnoxious behavior of someone and think about other stresses in their lives that might drive them. Gives us more patience with them."

Jordan snorted. "Like you did with Dad all those years. I miss him, but he could be tough sometimes. And you were such a saint."

Eden rolled her eyes and laughed. "Thanks for that." Yes, Gerry could be tough. Demanding at times, generous and loving at others. In other words, human. But the girls remembered the frequent tension, and she did too. "He had a high-stress job, so some of it spilled out on us at times."

"We shouldn't talk about Dad that way." Claire's brows gathered on her smooth forehead. "He's gone, after all."

Jordan grimaced at her sister. "Just because we're honest doesn't mean we don't love and miss him." She scooped a handful of chips and smiled at the server who'd just brought the queso and guacamole. "On another topic, tell us about the wedding, Mom."

"Gladly. It was a lovely week." Eden recounted the things she and her friends did during their bachelorette week and supplied descriptive details from the wedding. She filled them in on Marissa and Julia's interesting lives as well. "Sydney's daughter, Jessie, sang this funny song she'd written. It wasn't a solemn, boring wedding at all. It was so . . . so Sydney."

"You met them in college, right?"

"Yes, but we'd mostly lost touch over the years as our lives unfolded in different ways. Then later, when we were all single again, we started meeting." Eden smiled at the memory, the moment she'd reached out to each of them to suggest a girls' weekend. The rest was history.

"I wanna meet these girls one day." Claire dipped a chip into the steaming queso and lifted it, a strand of cheese extending from the bowl to her hand. "You always have a glow when you come back from a weekend with them."

Eden's smile emerged unbidden at the memory just as their server arrived with a large tray of hot, tantalizing dishes. "Fajitas, enchiladas . . ." Their tangy aroma and sizzle filled the air around them.

After a brief prayer for the meal, Eden added her silent thanks for her girls who, at twenty-six, were like daughters and friends at the same time.

She smoothed her napkin in her lap. "It was hard to leave the weather, the beach, and, of course, my girlfriends."

"I'm sure it was more fun than working in the yard and helping out at the church nursery," Claire said.

"Mom." Jordan leaned forward to face Eden across the table. "Do you mean to tell me that all three of your friends are engaged or married now? Just two or so years ago, you were all single. That's the reason you got everyone together as a support group, you told us."

Eden shrugged. "Things change. They all met someone special since that time. I'm happy for them. Especially Sydney. She fell in love with Tyler when they were seventeen but didn't marry him until last week. Long story, but it's sweet that they finally got together."

"True, very sweet for them, but what about you, Mom? It's been, what, twelve years since Dad died?" Claire's voice held an edge of impatience.

"Yeah, Mom," Jordan said. "You need to get on with your life. Don't you want to meet somebody?"

Eden wiped her mouth. "Hey, are you two ganging up on me?" True, she wouldn't mind meeting someone, but how to avoid getting ensnared and at the mercy of someone else? Was it possible? An involuntary shudder passed through her chest.

"Don't change the subject. Are you happy being alone for so long?" Claire cocked her head to one side. Though her hair was an identical color to her sister's, her shoulder-length bob contrasted with Jordan's longer layers. And Jordan's round glasses and bohemian clothing styles distinguished the twins even further. Claire's personality was more serious and quieter, but when the three of them were together, she could be just as sassy.

"I *was* happy, or happy enough for a long time," Eden began, flustered by the sudden turn of the conversation. Seemed everyone wanted to pair her up with someone. And even *she* felt tugs of longing more often than before. "Happy isn't the right word. Imagine having three teens at home and being suddenly alone to care for them and run a restaurant, which, I remind you, I'd never done in my life. My plate was full, no pun intended."

"You did great with the restaurant, no argument there. You were a natural, though it helped that you'd worked in one for years," Jordan offered. "And you're smart, of course."

"Beside the point." Claire's voice rose. "You did a good job with the restaurant and with us three. You were a wonderful single mom, even though I'm sure it was hard sometimes. But now is now. What do you want *now*?"

Eden drew a breath. She looked at the intense expressions on her daughters' faces and knew she needed to yield to this discussion. Again. All the people who cared about her were pounding on this subject. She blinked and stared back and forth at the twins. "During those years, I wasn't very interested in dating because I had a lot to deal with."

"So you've said. You had that one date about a year after Dad died. Remember that dude, what was his name?" Jordan asked, turning her head toward her sister.

"Oh, Art or something." Claire said. They both cackled. "Yeah, he was a piece of work."

"I'd even forgotten his name." Eden waved the air dismissively. "His goal was a trophy, not a relationship." After two months or so dating Art, she'd wanted nothing to do with men for years. "Since those days, I'm a little clearer on what I want in a person."

Claire and Jordan seemed to perk up to attention. Eden could finally articulate what had been only impressions and feelings before. She'd given it some thought on the flight from Wilmington to Indianapolis. "I want a companion and a partner," she said. "An equal." She allowed silence for them to respond, but they didn't. Her gaze went to their perplexed faces. "When I married your father, I was a kid, and he was much older. He did his thing in the restaurant, and I was a housewife. I wasn't a partner in his business and back then, I didn't mind. But I don't want that kind of relationship anymore. I want a partnership, like a friendship between equals. We'd enjoy doing things together, challenge each other, share our interests instead of having them be separate and private. You know?"

They did. Eden could tell by the soft expressions of longing that had stolen across their faces. "That sounds great, Mom," Jordan said quietly. "I want that too. That's why I broke up with Ethan last month. He was all into *his* stuff and didn't care about mine. It was all about him."

Eden nodded. She knew that all too well. To some degree, Gerry was the same, as well as the famous Art. After that, she'd wanted to be her own person, or at least try to figure out who that person was. Seemed she was still on that quest.

Jordan's head hitched up. "I know what, Mom. We'll set up an online dating profile for you and you can meet someone."

Eden recoiled against the vinyl seat back as if someone had pushed her. "Oh, no. Not that! I'm not that desperate."

"It's not for desperate people, Mom." Claire pushed her plate aside. "It's for someone who wants to zero in on the kind of person they're looking for but can't meet the normal way. It's not foolproof, of course. You'll make lots of mistakes before you find the right one."

"And you may not meet him for a while, but at least it's a way to be proactive." Jordan turned to her sister with a nod of agreement.

Yes, they were ganging up on their mother.

Eden wrinkled her nose. "It seems so . . . ugh. Like you're putting your photo up on the internet with a sign, *Eden Godfrey, on sale now for $11.99.*"

Claire and Jordan burst into laughter. "No, it's not," Jordan said, still grinning. "Like I said, it's a way for people to meet others in a more focused way. And everyone's doing it. Most people I know are online if they want a relationship."

Eden held up one hand. "That argument doesn't hold much water with me. When have I ever subscribed to that *most people* thinking?" What a ridiculous idea. Not to mention absolutely terrifying.

Two hours later, the three of them had donned pajamas and sat together in the den. The television was on, but the volume was low, providing a muffled background noise. Jordan's legs stretched out to the coffee table as she typed on her laptop. "Okay, got your profile ready, Mom."

Eden sat up. "What? What profile? Is that what you've been doing for the last twenty minutes? I thought you were doing something for work or writing to one of your friends."

Jordan shook her head, a sneaky look on her face. "I text friends. The computer is usually for work, but the laptop is easier to see for creating your dating profile. You'll want to tweak your description and add some photos."

"How about if I don't want to? You can set up the profile, but I don't have to go through with it." Eden knew she sounded like a petulant toddler just then. What a crazy idea.

"Up to you, Mom, but I'll post some photos unless you do. I think you'd rather choose your own, wouldn't you?" Jordan shot her an evil grin. "Here, I'll read the description. *I've lived in Indiana all my life and was married for 16 years before becoming a widow. My three children mean the world to me, but they're adults living their own lives. I'm healthy, energetic, and attractive and want to experience the next half of my life with a fun-loving partner—*"

"Okay, that's enough." A flush of heat filled Eden's face. What had she gotten herself into? "You're blackmailing me." She sniffed. "And I can write my *own* profile, thank you very much."

Claire and Jordan let out a festive whoop. "That's great, Mom," Jordan said. "Send it to me, and I'll give you feedback. And send me the photos you choose too."

Eden frowned. "Who says I'm even doing this crazy thing?"

"*You* just did! Come on, Mom, give it a try." Claire's face was impassioned. "What have you got to lose?"

Eden should prove to them this was a dumb idea. She could only try, against her will, but she'd show them. Jordan, Claire, Sydney, Marissa, and Julia. Then they'd all leave her alone.

Sunday afternoon arrived too quickly. Eden stood at the door and hugged each of her daughters for too long. She pulled back and straightened Jordan's collar. Her daughter was too old for that, but Eden couldn't help herself. "It was a lovely visit, girls. I can't believe it's over already."

"Yup, back to the salt mines. It was nice to see you, Mom. Now, don't forget to send me your edited profile, and I'll let you know what I think." Eden made a face and Jordan chuckled.

"Me too, I want to see it." Claire hugged Eden a second time. "Just because I'm not a marketer doesn't mean I don't have a taste for good, descriptive writing."

Eden sent them her most severe fake frown, and both girls laughed.

"You've blackmailed me, is all I can say. But I'll give it a try." Unless she changed her mind the next day. That was her prerogative.

After they left, the house was silent and still. Eden stood in the foyer without moving for a moment, then glanced up at the wall at a row of pictures displaying photos of her children at various ages. Now they were bossing her around. She laughed aloud. The sound filled the hollow hall.

She made a salad and took it to her office as her mind churned. What should she write in her profile? What photos should she post? Was she crazy to do this at her age?

Curiosity urged her toward the laptop on her desk. She powered it up and found the website that Jordan had noted for her on a swatch of paper, as well as the password. Not all the fields had been completed yet, and the profile needed her scrutiny and editing. Then there were the photos. For years, she'd been the family photographer and consequently, there weren't enough pictures of her on her hard drive. She scanned through family vacation shots and found one or two of her which seemed suitable. She needed something more recent. Marissa had taken one of her against the balcony railing during their week together. That was recent, and the photo wasn't bad.

Eden pulled up the photo on her phone and stared at it. Her blond hair had caught sunlight on the edges, giving her an intriguing glow. A late afternoon shadow covered her face, smoothing out the tiny lines she was too aware of. Still, her gaze seemed bold and there was a gentle curve to her pink lips. It wasn't posed. That's why it was a good photo. She'd been relaxed and happy in that place with her best friends, and it showed on her face. Lately, she guessed she didn't have that look very often.

That could be her profile photo, with a few others added in. In the last year, she'd lost a few pounds and could fit into clothes she hadn't worn in five or six years, which was one of her minor accomplishments since selling the restaurant. Less stress gave her more self-discipline.

Eden turned her attention to the profile and reread what Jordan had written. She shook her head. She'd never have written such things about herself, but admittedly, it wasn't bad. She added, *My Christian faith is important to me, and I'd like to meet a like-minded companion.* That would limit the playing field considerably. And maybe completely.

She spent the next fifteen minutes tweaking her profile and adding photos, chuckling a few times as she did. Of course, she'd cancel the whole thing the following day. She was on the free program, after all. She emailed Jordan her edited profile and photos, imagining her daughter's surprise to see she'd complied with her steamrolling.

After emailing Jordan, Eden navigated to a screen of photos. Staring back at her were faces of men of all different sizes, colors, styles. A lump formed in her throat. She swallowed. All these men were in her age range, lived nearby, and wanted to meet someone. Where had they all come from?

Inhaling deeply, she clicked on the profile of a man who called himself *Funloving*. The man in the photo was scowling, making his chosen moniker unconvincing. Other photos of him were better, but he still looked grim, except for the one with the ten-gallon hat. She looked in the background for a steer but didn't see one. His profile was brief, only a paragraph, listing the things he liked and what he looked for in a woman. Active, in shape, sexy, intelligent. Eden snorted. All about him, apparently. Funloving's profile ended with, *if you want to meet me, send me a note. If not, well, your loss.*

She laughed aloud. "Don't hold your breath, Funloving," she muttered. "Have fun with someone else." She scrolled to another photo. The second man was more attractive, but when she clicked on his profile, nothing was there. Just his age, fifty-three, and his marital status, divorced. Who'd go onto a dating site and not complete a description of himself? No one she'd want to meet.

By the time Eden's eyes grew weary of staring at the screen, she'd spent over an hour poring through photos and profiles. Amazing how quickly the evening had slipped away. There had been plenty of selfies taken in front of the bathroom mirror, lots of guys with dogs, some who were only separated but still on the prowl for someone, and quite a few who had partial custody of small children. She hadn't seen anyone who piqued her interest or shared her beliefs, but her education was only beginning.

Chapter Three

The following morning, Eden nursed a hot cup of coffee while she read her devotional book in the recliner of her downstairs study, as she did every morning. Shafts of early light from the window spilled across her chair. Her mind was like a distracted bird, hopping from one branch to another as the profiles she'd read the previous evening teased at her. But no way would she put that before her spiritual reading.

"Lord, Guide me on this *thing*, please. It's . . ." She took a sip of coffee and her gaze drifted to the window. "It's scary. Scary to get out there and meet men I don't even know. Right now, I want to crawl into a hole and avoid it. But part of me wonders if something good might happen if I can be braver and try. Please tell me if this is a dumb idea and I should bow out before I pay anything."

After her breakfast smoothie, she gathered her courage and settled into her desk chair. She'd read and edit her profile, scan more photos of prospective dates, and find other ways to procrastinate before deciding to either do this online dating thing or not.

When she powered up her computer and opened the website, she gasped. Fifteen messages waited for her. How had that happened? She skimmed her account and saw she had an active membership for six months.

Her gaze flicked through her email inbox searching for a clue and saw a message from Jordan. *Thanks for sending me your personal profile and photos, Mom. You're on the right track! This sounds good! I went ahead and signed you up for 6 months. You should be able to meet some men with potential in that amount of time. I'm so excited to hear how it goes! Love you, Jordan.*

Eden frowned. Jordan had decided *for* her, probably to keep her from backing out. Now she was stuck. She could always waste Jordan's money and do nothing, but for her daughter's sake, she'd try it. A little loving manipulation on Jordan's part, but at that point, Eden didn't know whether to thank her or scold her.

With a sigh, she clicked on the first message. Perspiration broke out on the back of her neck. She looked up for a moment and fixed her gaze on the man's photo. "I'm just reading. That's all, no reason to be afraid."

Her pulse slowed, and she lowered her eyes to read the first message. *Hello, Eden. I liked reading your profile. Have a look at mine and tag me if you want to talk. Bernie.* She went to Bernie's profile. His face was kind, but she didn't find him otherwise attractive. That didn't matter as long as they clicked, right? She read his description and saw healthy activities and interests, but no mention of faith.

She repeated the process six more times and found similar results. No sign of a like-minded believer. Hadn't they read her profile? Some men she found attractive, others less so. Several had only sent an icon response, whereas others had sent a message. Eden logged out of her laptop. That was plenty for one day.

What would Gerry think if he could see her now? Was he looking down from heaven with a frown, shaking his head? Or was he saying, *It's about time, Eden?*

Gerry. Eden met him when she waitressed in his first restaurant, Gathering Place. After having to leave U. N. C. and return to Indiana, she'd worked for him part time to pay her tuition. And escape home.

At first, Gerry treated her like everyone else did, like a teen in her first job. She blamed her bright blond hair and five-foot four height for that but often struggled to shed the feeling that she'd never quite grown up. In time, Gerry noticed her and began spending time with her under the guise of job training. He'd been twenty-nine and lanky, with serious brown eyes and matching wavy hair. At twenty-one, she was flattered by his attention, and pleased to finally be recognized as an adult woman. Eventually, she fell in love with him.

He had a good touch with restaurants. Both Gathering Place and Godfrey Gourmet, known by locals as Godfrey's, had been successful. She'd been relieved that she hadn't ruined Godfrey's as soon as he died, and she had to take over. Those years went by like a whirlwind of responsibilities for the business and her children. She enjoyed running the restaurant and giving it her unique vision until years later when she grew tired of the steady pressures. She sold it and here she stood on the threshold of an empty chapter waiting to be filled. By something. And possibly someone.

Her eyes fell to her phone that sat on the desk. Her girlfriends would never believe this, but they'd likely be proud of her. Or shocked. She sent them a group text. *Good morning, ladies. My girls visited over the weekend and coerced me into starting an online dating account. I knew you'd be pleased, since you were so concerned about my relationship status. I'll let you know how it goes. Hope you're all doing well. Thinking of you, Sydney, as you return from your honeymoon and start your new wife life. Love and miss you all.*

A few minutes later, her phone pinged with a text from Julia. *Got time for a quick phone call? I'm between meetings.* Yes, of course. Eden tapped her friend's number.

"I'm so proud of you, Eden," Julia said. "Though, it sounds like you weren't totally willing." She laughed. "That's okay. It's an experiment." In the background, Eden could hear a murmur of conversation at Julia's urban design store.

Eden chuckled with her. "Yes, my sneaky daughter. An experiment is a good way to think about it. I'm terrified."

"I understand. A whole new world of strange men. I hope they aren't *too* strange, though."

Eden heard the humor in Julia's voice. At least someone was enjoying this.

"Remember, you've done harder things than this, Eden. Just take one small step at a time."

A small step. Among so many she needed to make. "Good advice. You know, meeting someone would be nice, but . . . there's *more* I want right now."

"Sounds like something else might be going on. Spill it."

Eden let out a breath. "Over the last few months, I've realized I want to have a bigger story. I hinted at that when we were at the beach, but there wasn't a lot more I could say. I want my life to *matter* in the sense of helping people. Maybe . . . I don't know, maybe a nonprofit of some kind. I could volunteer in one, then maybe one day even start one. Of course, I'd love to meet a wonderful man too, like you, Marissa, and Sydney have. I want both. The life and the man. Is that too much to ask?" Eden laughed.

"No, it's not. I believe God wants that for you. I think your longing to make an impact comes from him. And your longings for companionship too. I really believe that because it's a legitimate human desire. You've been alone for a long time."

Eden snagged her lip between her teeth. It was comforting to hear Julia say her longings were normal. Could she really have both? "I don't want to be just a nice person, you know, marginally useful, but otherwise unimportant, oblivious to opportunities as the years fly by. And suddenly, I'm ninety-two."

"Marginally useful? You're much more than that already, Eden. Your compassion and energy inspire others in so many ways." Julia's gentle voice had grown insistent. "You've had an positive influence on each one of us. In fact, you're the one who got us all together three years ago. Where would we all be as friends if you hadn't done that?"

Her words stroked a bruised place inside Eden. "Thanks for saying that. I'm so grateful for each of you. The benefit wasn't only yours. I should look at my current status as a transition. That way, it looks hopeful instead of empty." And brimming with possibilities if she could only believe it.

"Yes, exactly. So, you're headed into a new, wonderful chapter. Aren't you excited? The nonprofit idea has huge potential, and you seem gifted for that. Online dating has possibilities too, but whether or not you meet someone right away, it's still out of your comfort zone, and that's a good thing. You've expressed it yourself, in different words, that you're tired of the comfort zone, and you want something more compelling."

Eden paused. "Exactly. The status quo is getting uncomfortable. As comfortable as it *can* also be sometimes. I know I'm meant for *more*. And I've hung out in static mode for almost two years since selling the restaurant. I think God is giving me a boot in the pants."

Julia laughed. "Lovingly, of course."

"When I picture the next part of my life, I have a mixture of dread and excitement. But it's all a blank slate. The unknown has always scared me to death."

"What about when you went to U.N.C.? You left your home state to go where you didn't know anyone. That was a step of faith all those years ago."

"True, but I had reasons. It wasn't just guts and courage. I had to get away from home, plus I had that partial scholarship. I had the perfect opportunity to tell my parents I was leaving the state for college. They couldn't argue with a scholarship." Yet somehow, they'd managed to drag her back home so many years ago. The memory still stirred heaviness in her stomach. "Anyway, I'm a different person now. I hope I can find that determination I used to have. I thought I'd developed more courage out of necessity, but here I am terrified at this new phase."

"It's normal to fear the unknown. How do you think I felt embarking on a trip to Italy last August to see relatives I hadn't seen in *forty* years?"

"I'm sure it was intimidating. But it turned out *great* for you."

"My point exactly. Just because you don't know what's coming doesn't mean God doesn't."

As Eden nodded her agreement, a pang inside told her she'd been hanging in the safe waters even in her faith, clinging to stability and security with both hands. Staying moored at the dock, yet complaining about so few answers, so few whispered instructions. Maybe God was waiting for her to take a step of faith. He was thrusting her away from the dock into wild waters.

Eden disconnected and tiny fingers of courage tickled inside her. Probably temporary courage, so she'd move forward before it evaporated. She sat again at her desk and scrolled her mouse to one man, Paul, who had a flicker of potential. His profile hadn't described his faith in any detail but had mentioned being part of a church men's group. He'd written, *Hey Eden. How are you today? I read your profile and would like to get to know you better.*

That sounded friendly. She responded, *Hello, Paul. I'm fine. Hope you are.* Hmm, what to say next? How to get the ball rolling with a complete stranger?

To her surprise, he responded immediately. He was online at that moment. *Yes, I'm well, thanks. I work at home in IT so that gives me a lot of flexibility. I like that, so I can take my dog, Wally, out for a walk or do some laundry if I need to. What are you up to today?*

This was getting personal already, though she appreciated the sketch of his typical routine. She could do the same, couldn't she? Not that she had specific plans that day. Maybe she should get a dog.

After several exchanges of banal conversation, Eden started to relax. This wasn't so hard. Her tranquility came to an abrupt halt when he wrote, *Would you like to meet for coffee one day this week? As I said, I have a flexible schedule.*

Her neck grew moist and hot. Was she ready for this? May as well get the first one over with. *Sure, that would be nice. I'm free Wednesday through Friday in the late morning.* She'd make it sound like her life was filled with interesting activities. The delay would give her a couple of days to prepare herself mentally.

Let's meet at the Starbucks on Gold Coast Road Wednesday at eleven. Know where that is?

Yes, I know it. Sounds good. See you then, Paul.

Eden fell back against her chair and swallowed. She did it. She had a date with an absolute stranger. Just coffee, but still. The adventure had begun.

ॐ   ॐ   ॐ

Paul didn't look like his photo. In fact, Eden thought she'd been stood up for the first ten minutes as she sat alone in an armchair near the window at Starbucks. She considered leaving when a man approached her. "Eden?"

She looked up at him. "Paul? Hello, I didn't recognize you from your photo." In the photo, he had more hair, and it was darker. And his physique was leaner. *Much* leaner.

He chuckled. "I don't have a good supply of recent photos." With a loud grunt, he sat in the armchair next to her.

"I had the same problem, but I was on vacation the week before, so had at least a couple current photos." He'd probably ask about her vacation, which she'd be happy to describe.

"All of Wally's photos are recent, though."

"Wally?"

"My dog."

An awkward silence ensued. "Can I get you something to drink?" he asked.

39

Good sign. A bit of manners. "Yes, thank you. I'll have a plain iced coffee."

"Coming right up." He rose and joined the line at the counter.

Eden let out a breath. *Don't judge anything. Just live in the moment.*

When Paul returned, he set a paper cup on the table beside Eden. "Thank you." Steam billowed out the top. Of her iced coffee.

"I saw they had raspberry syrup and that sounded good, so I went ahead and got you some in your coffee."

"You did?"

He looked smug, as if he thought she was glad he overrode her request. "I've had it before, and it's good. You'll like it. Try it." He pushed the cup toward her.

"How long have you worked at home in IT?" she asked after a brief silence.

"About four years. I used to go into the office, then went to two days a week at home. Now I'm completely at home. As long as I get my work done, no one cares. I can take the day off and work in the evening if I want. Wally and I like that flexibility."

Eden nodded. Her mind scrambled for something else to say. "Do you have children?"

"Two. They're older, but we don't have a close relationship. In fact, I never hear from them. Busy in their lives. My ex-wife has them wrapped around her finger, so they don't like me too well."

"That's a shame." She suspected she knew why.

He continued talking about his adult children. They lived in another state near their mother, who'd robbed him of his kids as well as a pile of assets. "She's a devil if there ever was one." He took a long sip of his cola.

A strand of discomfort began dangling inside her. Eden's gaze wandered to the wall clock. "I have three children." She'd go ahead and tell him, since he hadn't asked. "Twin daughters, age twenty-six, and a son who lives in California. He's twenty-four and in his first career."

Paul smiled but didn't respond. His eyes wandered over her head for a long moment.

"What do you do for fun?" By this time, she felt like an interview hostess.

His eyes lit up. "After work, I head out to the shed. You see, I've been building this awesome shed for about two years. It's much more than a shed, really. It's a workshop. I do woodworking out there, keep all my lawn equipment in neat condition, all that. I wanted something specific when I started building it. I couldn't find plans I liked, so I designed it myself."

Eden nodded. "Oh, that sounds nice. Is that your man cave?" She chuckled.

Paul didn't. "No, I live alone. The whole house is my man cave. Except for Wally, who's a boy too. Man and dog cave." He laughed then. "Though I'd love a companion of the female persuasion to share my interests."

His pointed stare looked more like a leer. Eden shuddered, but kept a cordial smile affixed to her face. Her eyes drifted again to the clock. He wanted a companion to share his interests. What about hers?

"What other activities do you do?" Last chance to increase his score.

Paul's eyes took on a faraway look. "I love fly-fishing but haven't been in a while. When I retire in a few years, I'm going to do that all the time. With Wally, of course. Right now, I just do some fishing on weekends. I stay gone the whole weekend and come back with enough fish for a few weeks."

Eden blinked. Took a sip of her flavored hot coffee. "Tell me more about your church men's group."

A mystified expression crossed Paul's face.

"You mentioned you were part of a men's group at your church. What's that group like?"

"Oh, that." Paul waved at the air with one hand. "We meet once a month for a pancake breakfast. It's a great time. The women in the church cook for us."

"Do you discuss issues together or study the Bible?" she ventured weakly.

"Nah, we let the women do that kind of stuff." He guffawed. "We go to baseball or hockey games and, of course, we talk during games. And we help each other out if one of us needs to work on an engine or someone needs a ride to the airport. Stuff like that."

"That's nice. It's important to have friends to help us out sometimes."

"Got that right. Especially when the wife walks out and slams the door. Then there's no one to do that stuff. She never worked on engines, but she was a good cook. I miss that." His face closed as a petulant tone entered his voice.

According to the wall clock, it had been nearly an hour. Quite sufficient for a first encounter. And last. "Well, Paul, I'll need to run. It was nice meeting you. Thanks for the coffee." She stood.

His head jerked up. "You're leaving? Oh, okay. When can I see you again?"

Terror swept through her. "Um, I don't . . . know. Uh, I'll be really busy in the next few weeks. I'll let you know online, okay?" With a forced smile, she left the café.

Great. Now she'd have to break up with him online. Just the thing she hadn't wanted to do. She'd need to develop a phrase she could say to indicate that it wasn't a fit and be able to say it while they were still together.

A phrase that would undoubtedly get a lot of use.

Chapter Four

"Not sure this is my thing, Jordan." Eden stood at the kitchen island and hitched her shoulder up to keep from dropping the phone while she prepared her coffee. She stirred milk in, but it looked like mud, so she added more.

"Mom, you can't give up after one date." Jordan's voice was insistent. "I warned you it would take a few dates, maybe even a lot, before you find someone worth seeing a second time. It's a process."

"I know, I know." Eden sighed. "Is there any kind of Christian dating site out there? That would've been easier."

"There are a couple, but this one is the biggest site, so I wanted you to have a lot of choices. And there are Christians on the site. I've seen them, though you have to keep a sharp eye out."

"I'm not finding men with any kind of faith on *this* platform, even though my profile clearly states what I'm looking for. Don't they read it?" She'd searched in vain for an hour and found two who mentioned church involvement and none who talked about a relationship with God.

"Unfortunately, many guys online don't read them carefully. You could list bullet points for everything you are hoping for, but some guys will still just look at your photo, think you're hot, and send you a message."

Eden laughed, but her face grew warm. "Me, *hot*? That's hilarious."

"I know you don't think that way about yourself, but a lot of men will look just at the physical. And you *are* pretty, Mom, whether or not you know it. Of course, lots of women do the same thing, looking at the guys' photos and no further."

Eden felt touched by Jordan's compliment, hoping it was true. "But the typical woman will carefully read the man's profile, won't she? She'll want to know what he's like, how he talks about his kids, and what kind of job he has. Men must know this, because they put a lot of emphasis on their kids and their jobs." And their dogs. Most of them had dogs and plenty of photos of them, as if the dog was a selling point.

"Probably. Women are hard-wired to think instinctively about provision and the care of family."

This was starting to look like a mating ritual on Animal Planet. "I'm sure there are women out there looking for a provider. I suppose the using can go both ways." Even if she had financial need, that would be the furthest thing from her mind. She cringed to think of women going online for that reason. Though she wasn't wealthy, she was stable, thanks to Gerry's insurance policy and the restaurant sale, plus what they'd saved over the years.

"Try again, Mom. That's all I can say. And be patient."

So, she did. The second date occurred at the same coffee shop. Too many more of these and Eden would consider it her new office. Her date's online name was Adventure Man, but his real name was Steve. She preferred real names. She wouldn't tell Steve that his online handle made him sound like a comic book action figure.

Action figure he was not. Steve was an ordinary-looking middle-aged man whose idea of adventure was taking an annual trip to the mountains. Nothing wrong with that, though with the name he'd chosen, she expected whitewater raft trips on the Colorado River, bungee jumping, and African safaris. Steve *did* own a dirt bike. And two dogs.

He bought the correct drink for her and asked appropriate questions about her life. He described his involvement as a deacon in his local church. But she had to admit, there wasn't a spark. She was better prepared for the moment when she had to tell him there'd be no second date. It felt cold, but she'd learned it was the protocol. Jordan had briefed her.

For the third date, Eden decided to be more daring by agreeing to dinner instead of coffee. Dinner with Mark, who'd used his real name. She preferred lunch, but he persuaded her with gentle pressure, describing the restaurant, which he insisted she'd love.

"I'll pick you up at six-thirty. Where do you live?" he asked.

Warning bells sounded in Eden's mind. "I'd rather meet you at the restaurant."

He'd insisted a bit, but she held her ground and he finally gave in. The battle of wills had annoyed her before even meeting him, but decided she'd give him a chance.

She dressed for dinner in a flowing black skirt with a print batwing blouse. She wore matching wedge heels with an open toe and dangly silver earrings and had taken extra effort with her makeup. Felt good to dress up for a proper date for the first time in a decade. She entered the restaurant and scanned the entryway. No sign of the man who matched his photo. "Are you waiting for Mark?" the hostess asked. At Eden's nod, the woman led her to a table.

Mark rose and reached for her hand. He stood almost a foot taller than Eden and was more handsome than in his photo. For a change. His full head of hair was dark but tinted with gray, and his clothes were crisp and stylish. His tanned face was long with a strong, determined jaw. "Eden, I'm so glad to finally meet you. You're lovely. Here, sit down." He pulled out a chair for her. So far, so good, despite the scuffle over coming to her home. Maybe he was just old-school and wanted to treat a lady right by picking her up at her house. Maybe that was a good sign.

"Do you drink wine? I'll order some if you don't mind," he said.

"Yes, I occasionally do. I prefer red."

"I know just the thing." He perused the wine list and ordered a bottle for them. "For dinner, I recommend the grilled Fisherman's

Catch, if you like seafood. And their pasta primavera with chicken is quite good, as well."

She decided on the grilled seafood. As the meal proceeded, Mark asked her questions about her life and family and talked about himself too. A bit too much, but for a first date, Eden didn't mind. He'd been widowed and divorced, two different women, and had two grown kids and a couple of adult step-kids. He owned a business that distributed equipment to hotels and restaurants. That launched a long discussion about the restaurant industry, a topic Eden felt competent to talk about intelligently. Their conversation flowed and time passed quickly. Could this be a partner, an equal? Eden pushed the thought from her mind. Way too early. Besides, he hadn't said a thing about his beliefs. Maybe that would come up during the second date.

Eden rarely ordered dessert, but Mark insisted that the amaretto crème brûlée was the best thing on the menu and she ought to try it. "I'll have some too. You'll love it."

"Okay, I'll try it." She was too full but would make the effort since Mark had raved about it so much. And he'd been so *certain* she would love it.

After Mark paid the bill, he leaned forward. "I want to take you to the Paradise Lounge now. They have a live band and a wonderful drink menu. The night is young. Do you dance?" His face lit up with eagerness.

"It's been a lovely dinner, Mark. It's getting a bit late, though, and I'd rather go on home."

His smile fell. "But it's early. It's just before nine. You'll enjoy it, I promise." Like he promised, she'd enjoy the fish, the wine, the dessert, the restaurant.

She gave him a conciliatory smile. "It's been a wonderful evening, but I'm a little tired. We could go another time."

His jaw hardened, and suddenly it reminded her of Gerry. Panic swept through her, unreasonable, inexplicable panic. She pushed it down. Had to go home. Had to go now.

Mark forced out a smile, though hardness glittered in his dark eyes. "It would make me *very* happy if you'd come with me, Eden." His voice emerged louder, almost carrying an *or else.*

Eden sighed but smiled back, despite the roiling inside her. "How about if we go together *another* time? It sounds very nice, but really, I'm tired and prefer to wait on that. Okay?"

"If you prefer." His tone became frosty. "I guess we're finished here." He stood.

Eden stood also and slipped her purse over her shoulder. "Thank you for dinner."

"You're welcome." Formality overtook his previous warmth. "I'll go ahead to the club without you. Maybe next time."

"Yes, of course. Goodbye, Mark."

As Eden drove home, she replayed the evening in her mind. Subtle, but unrelentingly insistent. Nothing outward. Mark was clearly a man used to getting his way.

Tight bands of tension gripped her stomach. She'd felt the power struggle several times already with Mark, and she'd only just met him. Why had her thoughts gone to Gerry? She hadn't typically viewed him as controlling during their sixteen-years together. Except once in a while, starting very early in their marriage.

"Honey, I know we just got married, but I'd really love to go ahead and start our family." Gerry reached next to him on the bed and stroked Eden's hand with his thumb.

She turned to him and realized he was not simply being amorous when she saw the glint of determination in his eyes. She swallowed. "Wouldn't it be nice to have some time alone together first, you know, as a couple? We'd have more freedom to do things together before the kids come along. Besides that, I really want to finish my degree. I only have a year to go."

"I know that's important to you. But think of it, it might take us a year or two to get pregnant. That sometimes happens. You could be in school during the time we're trying, so that'll give us both what we want."

She sighed but felt the pressure of his desires, of wanting to please him. "We have our whole lives ahead of us, Gerry. Why are you in a hurry for parenthood?"

"You're young, Eden, but I'm thirty. I don't want to be an old dad. I want to be able to play with my kids and be young enough to see them grow up."

"If I finish my degree, it's only a year. Why don't we start trying then?"

His jaw hardened. "Okay, whatever you want," he said in such a way that made her feel like the most selfish person on earth.

But Gerry hadn't given up since that same discussion arose regularly. Finally, he wore her down, and she discontinued birth control, though a swath of anger remained behind. Anger she was only now remembering. Had it never gone away?

She hadn't felt ready to be a mother and desperately wanted to finish her degree, praying that she wouldn't get pregnant for at least a year. The summer after their spring wedding, she got pregnant with the twins. By the time school started again in September, she'd be showing. And when the semester ended in December, she'd be too big to be comfortable at school. So, she dropped out. A year shy of getting her college diploma, a fervent desire since the age of fifteen. With a diploma, she'd reasoned back then, she could be fully independent, treated like an adult, no longer required to do what her parents wanted. But there she was, an adult, but more dependent than ever. Twenty-two and pregnant with twins. Marriage hadn't saved her. Her own dreams would go on the back burner for a long time.

The irony of it all, Gerry's argument for having a family early was to play with his kids and be involved in their lives before he was too old. But he rarely did, thanks to the endless demands of a popular restaurant. In truth, he'd been married to his work, and a father to it, while Eden and the kids lived in a parallel world, maintaining his home life like a well-oiled machine.

Over the years, when Eden saw the same look on Gerry's face that she saw on Mark's that night, she learned to back down to avoid conflict and because she quickly tired of the power struggle.

The same struggle she knew too well from her childhood.

Eden almost swerved out of her lane as the revelation hit her. Her dad always got his way, not always through verbal or emotional manipulation, but more often by his drunken state. Her mother's specialty was subtle control to maintain the balance of the family and be an effective enabler for her alcoholic husband. During those years, Eden and her brother Keith learned how to stay out of their father's way. How to placate. How to duck at the right moments. How to find activities, like school clubs, part-time jobs, and later, college, that could take them for long periods out of the house. Out of the battlefield.

Had she done the same thing throughout her marriage? Had she gone along and stayed quiet about her own desires, just to avoid the tension it caused to be herself, to express what she wanted?

When the twins were only four, Brent was born. With three toddlers to take care of and a mostly absent husband, Eden's own dreams had splintered and blown away. No mystery that she hardly knew what she wanted. But at that moment, it was crystal clear to her what she didn't want.

℈   ℈   ℈

"I feel almost ready to give up." Eden remembered sharing the same sentiment with Jordan only a week earlier.

49

She'd wedged her phone into the back pocket of her shorts. Earbuds allowed her to catch up with Marissa while dead heading her roses. The gentle morning sunshine warmed her bare shoulders, and a light breeze fluffed her hair.

"So soon?" Marissa had called that morning in response to Eden's request for a chat. "How many dates have you had?"

"Three. Three duds out of three. But I have to tell you, the last one, Mark, gave me a lightbulb moment."

"Really? How so?"

"That's what I wanted to talk to you about. He seemed like a good guy when we were exchanging messages, but as soon as we went out, I began seeing signs that he wanted to be in control." She recounted the evening to Marissa, including how it ended. "Then on the way home, it hit me that Gerry could be that way. He wasn't so blatant in wanting control, but he was subtly in charge of me and our family for our whole marriage." That's why she'd told Jordan she wanted an equal, a partner. At the time, she hadn't known where that thought had come from.

"After all those years with Gerry, you could recognize it easily in Mark. That's great insight, Eden. It's the last thing you want, so you'll be able to avoid it."

"Darned right, I don't want it." A fresh surge of unbidden rage filled her throat and for a moment, she couldn't speak. She squeezed her eyes shut as if to refresh her mental screen then took a breath. "For years, I never knew what was wrong in my relationships with men. They never felt right. A couple of years after Gerry died, I went on a date with a guy named Art. He was controlling and reminded me so much of Gerry and also my dad that I didn't date for years after that. Everyone's been bugging me lately, lovingly of course, about not having a relationship for so long. Now I know the reason."

"You just now realized that was the reason you didn't date?"

"It all became crystal clear when I went out with Mark. I'm tired of being treated like a thing. During my marriage, Gerry often treated me almost like one of the kids, not as an equal. And in my family growing up, I wasn't a real person who had distinct needs and wants. I was part of this sick family system where we all had our roles and duties."

Suddenly a scene from that awful last argument with her mother flashed into her mind, the night Eden had finally expressed her feelings with unfiltered honesty. She shut her eyes against the wave of guilt. Her mother hadn't understood but defended herself and implied that Eden was ungrateful. She'd died three months later. Eden swallowed, a pain like metal bands gripping her throat. She shook off the memory, realizing Marissa had spoken.

"You're having a lot of insight coming at you, Eden. That's so important in this phase as you're getting back out there, don't you think? God wants to protect you from getting into something similar, so he's giving you all this understanding."

"That's why I want to quit now. Before I get back into trouble and realize it five years later."

"Eden, not all men are like that. My Robert wasn't like that, and Jarrod isn't either. I think you're more equipped to recognize the difference between a man who's healthy and one who's controlling, don't you think?"

"I would hope so. My motivation for all this has gone downhill."

"That's because you're remembering all the bad things and ways you were treated when you felt helpless. You're an adult now and you have more insight. You'll recognize it like you did with Mark. And Art. The next guy could be completely different. I encourage you to keep going."

"I'll think it over, but I'm not at all sure." Eden disconnected. Maybe it just wasn't worth the risk of repeating past experiences. Were they simply inevitable, impossible to escape?

Chapter Five

Colin Taylor. A nice name. He had a nice face too. Friendly, open. Hazel eyes looked back at her from his main profile photo. Wavy dark brown hair extended just below his ears and a subtle cleft graced his chin. Eden scrolled through his many photos. On a ski slope. With two older kids at a beach. All three of them in front of the Eiffel Tower and another at the Roman Coliseum. Colin in hiking gear. Colin in a suit with no tie, the top buttons of his shirt open, projecting a relaxed vibe. So far, no dog. Not that she had anything against them.

She'd taken a two-week break from the dating site but forced herself to return, spurred by Marissa's exhortation to not give up just yet. While she stared at the screen, she stirred the flax and chia seeds into her yogurt, per the health article she'd recently read, tried a bite, then scrolled down to Colin's profile. She carefully pored through each line. Her eyes caught on one phrase in particular. *My relationship with Christ guides my life.*

Her heart pounded. *Don't get excited, Eden. Too early to tell.* He could be as controlling and self-oriented as the others she'd met, despite his claims of faith. She'd write him a note. Up to then, she hadn't reached out to anyone, only responded to a few of them. Either this guy had only recently joined the site, or the algorithm decided to show him to her then and not before. *Hello, Colin.* Her fingers hovered over the keys for a long moment. She'd keep it simple, mainly because her mind was scrubbed of anything intriguing to say. *I enjoyed reading your profile. Read mine and write back if you'd like to talk some more.*

By the time she finished typing those few words, her stomach had tightened as though a fist gripped inside. It usually wasn't hard for her to reach out to a stranger for any other reason. This was a different story.

He wouldn't respond immediately, since he was likely at work. At least, she hoped he worked. She only checked twice in the hour that followed. An hour after that, Colin had responded. *Hi Eden, I did read your profile and I liked yours too. I'm not very experienced with this online thing, so I guess I'll start by telling you a little bit about me, to add to what you've read.*

Colin sounded warm, unguarded. So far, she liked him. He'd written, *You already know the basics from my profile. I'm divorced, 51 years old, and I have 2 great kids, who I raised alone from their teen years. My daughter is a junior at IU and my son lives in Colorado and works in graphic and web design. I'm an attorney, but I work for myself, so I don't have to do eighty hours a week to climb the ladder.* (Smiley face.) *Not so interested in the ladder anyway. I won't say too much here since I hope to meet you in person soon. I look forward to hearing from you. Colin.*

Eden leaned back in her chair and smiled. She liked what she'd read. Finally, someone with potential and it hadn't taken seventy-five dates. And they already had something in common. She too had raised teenagers alone. She wouldn't assume anything yet. But she kept smiling as she went downstairs to start a load of laundry. She made a salad for lunch, watered her plants, then returned to her ground floor study to respond to Colin.

Didn't want to look too eager.

Hi, Colin. She took a long breath and closed her eyes. She pretended he was across a table from her, an affable smile on his face. Her heart slowed as she kept breathing, then opened her eyes and set her fingers on the keyboard. *Thanks for writing back to me. I'm 50 and I've been a widow for about 12 years. My kids were teens when my husband died in an accident.* Was that too much information for an online chat? *We owned a restaurant for many years, but I sold it nearly 2 years ago.* Did he wonder what she'd been doing ever since? She was unable to answer that question even for herself. *I agree, it's easier to chat in person. But I'm glad to hear more of your story.*

That was all she could think of to say. It was better to be brief anyway. After she pushed 'send', she gasped, and her hands flew to her cheeks. Had she just expedited a face-to-face meeting by her 'easier to chat in person' comment? Too late now.

ଔ   ଔ   ଔ

Colin had suggested they meet at a tapas restaurant. That impressed Eden since it differed from the predictable coffee date. Her previous dates, as dead-end as they'd seemed, had served as a training camp to make her less nervous for the next one.

It was early June, and temperatures rose to nearly eighty degrees. A gentle breeze, scented with pear blossoms, surrounded her as she waited for her date on the porch of the tapas restaurant. She wore white linen pants with a cobalt blue and long white print blouse, knotted on her left hip. The outfit was one of her favorites. Everyone said it highlighted her blue eyes. And, of course, she wore wedge heels.

A man approached from the parking lot. She recognized him as he neared. "Eden?" All her dates so far had addressed her with a question. Understandable. In that context, no man wanted to assume an identity, even with a photo as a reference.

"Hi, Colin. You look just like your photo." In fact, better. The same warmth beamed from his eyes as he seemed to find humor in her statement. He seemed just under six feet tall since he didn't tower over her as Gerry had.

Long dimples appeared in his jaws as he smiled. "Did you expect me to look different?"

Eden's face warmed. "Well, lots of people don't look at all like their photo. I mean, I haven't *seen* a lot, but those I've seen . . ." Great start. Just wonderful.

Colin opened the restaurant door for her. "I made a reservation for the terrace, so we shouldn't have to wait very long."

"Good idea. It's such nice weather." A true statement as well as a handy filler.

A hostess led them through the noisy but attractive restaurant to the terrace. Green and yellow tarps spread out overhead, lending a festive atmosphere. Candles flickered on the tables, though night hadn't yet fallen, casting inviting and intimate points of light across the darkened patio.

"It's nice that we could meet without two years of online chatting," he said.

She chuckled. "That could get tedious. And people like to save details for the in-person meeting, and not say everything in advance." She stopped. Another possible faux pas. What was with her? "I don't mean . . ." She took a breath.

"I know what you mean. You don't want people to find out about your prison record or your six previous marriages *too* soon." They laughed.

"Yeah, how'd you know?" His humor released her tension like air from a pierced balloon.

"Relax, I'm not interpreting all your words."

The warmth in his eyes reminded Eden of melted brown sugar. She liked the longer hair too. Made him look more like a professional surfer than an attorney. "Whew, thanks. I won't interpret yours, either."

He held the menu open at an angle so they both could read it. "We'll need to decide on a few of these small plates to share. What do you like to eat?"

For several minutes, they discussed options. Once when Colin looked down at his menu, Eden stole a glance at him. She had to do it carefully, though, so he wouldn't catch her. She liked his relaxed manner, his style of clothing, and the down-to-earth composure he exuded.

They finally settled on empanadas, garlic shrimp, goat cheese dip, lamb meatballs with yogurt, and arancini, which were fried risotto balls.

"I'll get the chance to try arancini in Italy this August," Eden said. "I'll see firsthand which Italian meals we eat here are authentic."

"A vacation?" Colin cocked his head to one side.

"That and a wedding. I have three close friends I met almost thirty years ago in college. We drifted apart for a while, but in the last three years we've started getting together twice a year for a girls' weekend. They've again become my closest friends. One of them is getting married in Florence this August."

"That's fantastic. Not only visiting Florence but keeping up with college friends. I wish I could say the same. Have you been to Florence before?"

Eden shook her head. "I always loved the idea of travel, but never had the chance to do much. I hope to catch up with that, now that I don't have kids at home anymore."

The server arrived and took their order.

"Tell me more about your daily life. Do you work, or did you?" Colin asked when the server had left.

Eden thought she'd cringe at that question, but he'd asked in such an inviting tone, she didn't mind. "Going back a little, my husband and I owned a restaurant, which I think I told you online. Godfrey Gourmet. People usually just call it Godfrey's."

"I know the place. I've eaten there a couple of times, once recently. The food was good, and I liked the atmosphere."

She felt gratified by his comment. "I'm glad you liked it. When my husband, Gerry, died, I had the three kids to raise, but the restaurant was our only source of income, so I took it over. I didn't have a choice, but I'd been around restaurants for years, so I tried to do what was instinctive. I sold it almost two years ago."

"Whatever you did was a success. I noticed they've kept the name and menu, so they thought it was a winning formula too."

She smiled. And now was the moment to come clean. "Since that time, I've done various things, involvement at my church in women's ministry, working on my house and yard. Trying different things to find my niche. I'm not sure yet what I'm supposed be when I grow up."

Colin nodded, an understanding twinkle in his eyes. "You'll know. God will show you when it's time. Sounds like you may have needed that break."

There it was again, that comforting validation of her activities over the last two years. About time she validated them herself.

"What about you?" she asked. "Tell me more about your life or whatever you want to tell me."

He held up a hand. "Hey, I have no secrets. Let's see, I'm a native of Indiana, but grew up west of Bloomington. I'd been married about sixteen years when my wife, Adele, decided she needed to find herself. So, she left me with the kids."

"You're kidding. She left, just like that?"

"She told me she'd felt restless for years, like she didn't know who she was and what might fulfill her. But she wanted the kids to be older, more independent, when she finally made her move. My son, Davis, was about seventeen and April was fourteen."

"Huh. Hardly the time to abandon the kids."

Colin's nod a tightened jaw showed agreement. "It was a shock, for me and for them. Our marriage wasn't perfect, a bit dull, and I worked a lot. Maybe that eventually created a tipping point for her. We had a pleasant life, or so I thought. Overnight, I was a single dad, trying to juggle a demanding job and the needs of two teenagers. That's when I decided to start my own practice, so I could call my own hours in case the kids needed me. No way was I going to let Adele's decision mess up their teen years. They still had one responsible parent, and that was me."

Eden blinked as her throat ached for him. For all Gerry's faults, he was a loving father. Not very involved, but he'd never have walked out. "I can't imagine how hard that must have been. But I'm impressed by how you responded. Judging from the photos online, it seems you three traveled and did a lot together. You must be close."

Colin's expression softened. "Yeah, we're tight. We talk on the phone randomly throughout the week. Over Christmas, I'm going to Colorado to see Davis and we'll ski together a few days."

She couldn't suppress a smile. It wasn't hard to picture him at the top of a snowy ski slope, poles in hand, goggles perched on his head. "I'm closer with my girls than my son," she said. "The girls are twins. They're twenty-six and share an apartment in Indianapolis. They come spend the weekend every month or so, but we talk and text during the week too. My son, Brent, lives in California. I hear from him less often, though we get along fine." Talking about their kids was an easy way to break the ice as well as get a glimpse of Colin's life. The first puzzle piece, among many others.

Their meals arrived on a steaming platter as a variety of mouth-watering smells, from pungent to wood-fired, flowed around the table. The server set several aromatic dishes in the center and gave them extra plates. Colin glanced at Eden. "I hope this meal meets with your approval, Ms. Restaurant Owner."

Eden laughed. "I just love food, that's all. Especially the small plates, where you have so much taste variety. I'm sure it'll be great."

Colin murmured a brief prayer for them, which made Eden happy, and they served themselves from each of the delicacies. During the meal she learned Colin enjoyed jazz and British mystery shows, as well as cooking. They shared stories and laughter about awkward online dating experiences, though neither she nor Colin had spent more than a couple months in that world. She told him about how Jordan signed her up.

"I was almost as reluctant as you were," he said. "But I've met some nice people."

Eden hadn't yet, until that evening. In fact, she'd been on the verge of giving up, but was glad she hadn't. Jordan had reminded her *it only takes one.*

"How did you come to faith, Eden?" Colin's question interrupted her thoughts, but she was thankful at the shift in topic of conversation.

She dabbed her mouth with her napkin and slipped her tongue over her teeth, just to be sure. "My dad was an alcoholic, so growing up was tough." Eden didn't see any reason to hide where she'd come from, since she'd overcome so much. "I was about thirteen, I think, when a friend from a class invited me to her church for a youth activity. I loved it and met a bunch of kids. That church kind of saved my life in one sense. I started spending more time there than at home. I met the Lord during that period. My new faith and friends kept me from going down the wrong path." She smiled at him as a wistful wave of gratitude stole over her. "It changed everything for me." She likely still had plenty of scars from her upbringing, but it could have been so much worse.

Colin nodded with understanding, and she thought she detected a film of tears glistening in his eyes. "I love those kinds of stories. Mine was simpler. I was raised in a Christian home but didn't get serious about my faith until college."

"Your profile was the only one I read that made a distinction between a relationship with God and involvement in church activities. The idea of a relationship with God doesn't occur to a lot of people, though I can't judge someone's heart."

"It's not a relationship in that case. It has to be cultivated, just like a human relationship."

"Yes, it does." All the lights were green, as far as Eden was concerned. Colin Taylor was not a disappointment, as the others had been. If he asked for another date, she knew what she'd respond. Not only a man of faith, but those gorgeous hazel eyes set off a flutter in her stomach.

After the meal, Colin patted his abdomen. "That was deserving of a repeat performance. Another day, of course."

Eden laughed. The sumptuous meal likely put a pound back on her hips, but it had been worth it.

"Here's a question for you." Colin wiped his mouth and took a long sip of water. "Now you're free from the restaurant and you said you're trying to find your niche. Is there anything you can think of that you've always wanted to do, but haven't done yet?"

Eden pursed her lips. "Hmm. There are probably quite a few. Sometimes it takes me a while to get around to things. Ah, the Florence trip is one on my list that's already on the schedule. After the wedding, my other girlfriends and I are going to rent a car and tour Tuscany. I'd like to catch up on some of the traveling I missed while I was raising kids and running the restaurant."

"Florence sounds fantastic. Anything that doesn't involve travel come to mind?"

Yes, there was something. Eden cringed. Oh, why had that just come into her thoughts? She didn't want to talk about it, but Colin was so open, so nonjudgmental, she could, couldn't she?

"There is something I've always wanted to do, but at this stage of life, I've pretty much dismissed it. It's a regret more than a goal, I guess you could say."

Colin's gaze was attentive.

Eden moistened her lips and swallowed. "I told you about the home I grew up in. I wasn't the type to run away or get in trouble, so I sought my escape through academics. That's how I was able to leave Indiana and attend college at U.N.C. in North Carolina. I had a partial scholarship. That's where I met the girlfriends I told you about." She blinked a few times and looked at her plate. "So, I'd escaped. It felt like heaven to be on my own, away from home. I dutifully kept in touch, but I wasn't there, and it didn't hurt me anymore. Then, during my junior year, my mom called me and told me Dad had taken a bad turn. He was bedridden and she cared for him at home." Eden met his eyes. "She wanted me to come home."

"But you hadn't finished your degree, right?"

"Right." Eden's voice emerged softly. "I thought I'd gotten away, finally had my own life, my own choices. But Mom reeled me in with guilt. You can imagine, I was devastated to leave the school I loved, my friends, and return to that dark situation." She paused as her throat tightened. Colin waited silently. "I went into a tailspin. I started messing up in my classes, losing sleep, losing weight." Her words came out in a rush. Colin was a stranger, almost, but she couldn't stop the flow of stale pain. "But I couldn't tell her no. She poured on the guilt. It was my father, didn't I care . . ."

She shifted her eyes to a colorful lamp swinging gently over the next table. "My older brother Keith had already left some time before and had his own family, so it was up to me to help my mom. I negotiated with her to let me finish my junior year. I said I'd come home for my senior year. I transferred to Ball State for my final year and moved back home. Since I'd lost my scholarship, I had to go to school part time and pay my way. That summer, I got a job waitressing, and that's how I met Gerry. He owned the restaurant where I worked. A month or two later, we started dating and by Christmas, we were engaged. I still had a semester or so to go, but he promised me I could finish after we got married. I got pregnant with the twins before I could even start the fall semester, so that was the end of that."

She paused for a long moment then met his eyes, which were full of compassion. "In answer to your question, I'd like to finish my degree." And finally close that open door which, despite her accomplishments at the restaurant, kept her feeling incomplete.

A tentative smile emerged on his lips. "Thanks for sharing that story with me, Eden. That sounds so hard, being pulled between family and your college dream."

"It was. I survived that year by working a lot. I helped a little at home with my dad, though he didn't really need much. That was why I was there, after all, but I got to working more and more. I took extra shifts trying to make enough money to escape. My mom didn't say anything. Maybe it was enough for her that I was there."

"What did you study?"

"Business. Lots of kids take business because they don't know what else to major in at first, but I'd always been interested in business."

"Did it ever cross your mind during those years after the kids were older to finish your coursework online?

She shook her head. "If it did, I never let the idea take root. I told myself it was too late, I didn't need a degree, since I was busy enough with the family. And I would have wanted to be on campus, to have the full interactive experience. I'd always loved that so much." Stale grief swelled in her stomach then faded like receding surf.

"What would stop you from doing that *now*? From finishing your degree?" His voice was soft.

Eden opened her mouth and closed it. Her gaze latched to his. "Go back to college? Now?"

"Yeah, sure. Now. Why not now?"

"Um, because I'm fifty years old, that's why."

"So? Lots of people return to school later in life for whatever reason."

"I don't know. I just considered it a lost goal. Told myself it didn't really matter, since I'd had a successful restaurant and people respected me, in the restaurant world, at least."

"Exactly why you don't need to worry about what people think. Age is irrelevant. What would stop you?"

Tension sprang up inside her. What *would* stop her? Her terror, that's what. Being a middle-aged undergrad traipsing across campus surrounded by eighteen-year-olds?

"You could register this week to meet the deadline so you can start in the fall."

"*This* fall? What about my trip to Italy?"

"When is that?"

"Mid-August. Most colleges start before that, don't they?"

"Depends on the school." He reached for his phone and within seconds a smile spread across his face. "Says here on the school calendar that classes don't start until the last week of August." Triumph glowed on his face as he thrust his phone toward her so she could see the dates. "You can do it, Eden. You can accomplish your lifelong dream. On campus, no less."

She felt the warmth of the evening evaporate. "Are you always this pushy?"

"I'm not being pushy. You said yourself this was a big dream of yours. It was the first thing you said when I asked you the question. I'm only encouraging you to fulfill your dream."

He was logical, but Eden still felt thrust into a corner. Colin, who'd been so warm and friendly, so low-stress and accepting, was pushing her, telling her what to do. Typical. Story of her life. Were there any men on earth who weren't controlling? Or too passive? Were there any who fell nicely in the middle, showing godly leadership, but infused with love and understanding?

"Like I said, you're being pushy, Colin."

Colin let out a sigh. He leaned back against the bench. "I'm sorry you feel that way. Though I suspect, if I were a woman, one of your college girlfriends challenging you to do what you've always wanted to do, you'd take it as a sign of friendship."

Eden stilled. He was right. But he was also putting pressure on her. "Maybe." Then she forced out a celebratory smile. "I *will* think about it. I promise. And I'll do it on my time schedule, no one else's."

He stared at her for a moment then the ghost of a smile pulled at his lips. "Point taken. I'm a friend who wants to see you accomplish a dream."

The server came with the bill and cleared off the plates. Colin waved away Eden's offer to share the cost. While he calculated the tip and pulled out his card, Eden tried to push down the panicked voices flowing through her mind. Was he just like the others? This man who'd had so much potential, who loved the Lord, who communicated well?

"Thank you for a nice evening, Colin." They stood by her car as dusk deepened in the sky and pricks of starlight shyly appeared.

"I enjoyed it too. Sorry if you think I came on strong. I'm enthused about your dream, is all. But you'll know the right thing."

"Yes. We'll stay in touch. Goodnight, Colin."

She drove toward home, but a tangle of emotions wrestled inside her. On one hand, they'd had a nearly perfect evening. Until she opened Pandora's box, her sealed repository of painful memories. She should have kept that private.

Had it been his manner or the idea of returning to college that had thrown her into a state of panic? If Julia or Sydney had made the same suggestion, would she have considered it or politely offered a reason to decline without thinking they were pushing her?

Why had the idea of returning to school, a topic she herself had volunteered, thrown up such a wall in her heart? This lifelong desire she'd abandoned. Colin's suggestion had been natural. Innocent. What was she afraid of?

She'd struggled all her life to have legitimacy, to no longer be treated like a child or a blond stereotype. Going back to college would give her a whole new stereotype, marginalized this time for being too old. Out of step, out of date. College life would be another world from what she'd known three decades ago. Her mind told her it was a stupid argument, but her heart dug in, saying *no way*.

Eden pulled into her driveway and sat for a moment in front of her brick home, knowing she had to come face to face with her resistance at some point. Had she sabotaged her evening with Colin? Or was he just like all the others but with a handsome face and Christian testimony?

Maybe she wasn't ready for all this. She should tell her friends and daughters she'd tried, and it hadn't worked for her. She'd wait to meet someone in a normal way.

Whatever normal was.

Chapter Six

Eden pressed the brakes as the car in front of her stalled then jerked into motion. She let out a breath. Not the day to be late since it was the launch of Vacation Bible School. And she was one of the leaders. Usually, she only helped with the older kids each summer, but when the director needed surgery, she persuaded Eden to join the leadership team. That filled many hours in early June, and for once, Eden was grateful since it distracted her from her questions and dating blunders.

Within minutes, she parked and hurried into the back of the brick church building next to the gym. The first person she saw was Vanessa, her friend and neighbor, who stood with a clipboard in one hand.

"Sorry I'm late." Eden flashed a half-smile.

Vanessa waved away her apology. "You're only two minutes late. Relax. Sonia's running late too. And we never start on time."

Some of the other leaders already sat around a table to go over last-minute check lists and pray together before the children arrived. Eden and Vanessa joined them.

An hour later, the meeting ended, and everyone stood. "Can you help me finish up the snacks?" Vanessa hitched her head toward the counter along the back wall. "We have a few minutes before the kids get here."

"Be glad to." Eden followed Vanessa, who'd been a friend and neighbor for almost two decades.

They worked side-by-side putting cookies onto small paper plates and crackers in plastic sandwich bags. "Are you guys taking a vacation this year?" Eden asked Vanessa.

"The usual. Beach in July, then to Grandma's in August. We do the same thing every year, but I always enjoy it. You have a big one coming, don't you? We haven't talked about it in a while."

"Florence, Italy." Eden couldn't stifle a grin. "I've never been out of the country before, so it's bigger for me than for most people, I guess. I'm going to the wedding of a dear girlfriend, then afterward, other friends and I will travel in Tuscany."

A wistful look of longing passed Vanessa's tanned face. "I'm jealous. Maybe Steve and I can do that on our thirtieth anniversary. Take pictures while you're there. I want to see them when you get back and pretend I was there."

"I'm excited about it, but at times my anticipation gets mixed together with my fall plans." She looked up from the snack bags and stared at Vanessa. "Oh, I forgot to tell you. I'm going back to college this fall."

Vanessa's jaw dropped open as if unhinged. "You're kidding! When did you decide this?"

Eden and Vanessa walked two mornings a week in the neighborhood, but she hadn't told her friend of her sudden decision. It was all too fresh, too dramatic in her own mind. She'd wanted to savor it before speaking about it. *And* be absolutely sure.

"Sorry I haven't told you yet. I decided only recently. I never finished college but only have a year to go. A friend of mine encouraged me to go ahead and do it, that it wasn't too late."

"That's fantastic. Of course, it's not too late. Will you do online class?"

Eden shook her head. "Everyone asks me that, but no, I want the interaction. I'm alone a lot these days, now that I don't go to the restaurant anymore. I want the campus experience. All of it."

Her date back in June with Colin Taylor may have ended poorly, but it scattered sparks in the core of her lethargy, sparks that smoldered into a flame. His words, *what would stop you,* had cycled through her mind repeatedly over the following days. Had her objections been valid? No, they were based on her excuses: too late for a missed opportunity, it's not that important, wouldn't it be weird to go back to campus. In the end, none of her excuses had a spine and they all fell down with honest scrutiny. So, she decided to enroll, though it took a weekend of wrestling with her thoughts and in prayer to finally release the struggle.

Once she'd opened her mind to the idea, she registered in time for the fall semester deadline. She was on target to finish her lifelong goal of a college degree in about one year. That would plant seeds for her bigger desire, to make her life count in a concrete way.

Following her season of academic life, she had few solid plans, but for the coming year, she was set. Her kids and girlfriends supported her wholeheartedly, likely relieved she finally had a target.

What else would she be doing? The absence of an answer wasn't a great reason to enroll in college, but it *did* contribute. Just a little.

"What will be your major?"

Vanessa's question jolted Eden out of her reverie. "Business. The general option will allow me to transfer most of my credits from ages ago."

"I'm proud of you, girl. You're such a go-getter."

Eden laughed. "Yeah, that's why it took me almost thirty years to do it."

Vanessa grabbed the cardboard box of sandwich bags and placed it under the counter. "To change the subject, I wanted to give you a heads up about a new older single man who started coming to church recently. His name is Rob, I think. He looks to be in his fifties. I'm looking out for you, you know."

Eden took a breath and forced out a smile. Well-meaning friends with the hearts of matchmakers abounded. "Thanks, Vanessa. Not sure I'll have time for a relationship with my trip and school coming up, but I appreciate the thought."

During the month of June, she'd thought many times of Colin. She'd mistakenly assumed he was controlling. When he told her his words would have been received if he'd been a woman, he'd peered into her soul with sharp insight. In her mind, men equaled control and she wanted no part of it. Colin had simply challenged her, but that simple act of friendship had hit her red button. He'd treated her as an equal, which she'd claimed to want, but she'd been unable to recognize it at the time.

Her insight had come too late. She wrote to him online a week after their date and apologized for her reaction. Despite her initial judgment, she'd told him his words had stimulated her to enroll in college. He'd responded warmly, glad about her news, and that he understood her reaction and didn't hold it against her. He hadn't initiated further, though she'd hoped he would. She didn't either, sure she'd offended him or maybe by that time, he'd found someone else. Within a few more friendly but unsubstantial messages, their correspondence dropped off.

She tried to convince herself it didn't matter. As a full time college student, she knew exactly how she'd be spending most of her evenings for the coming year.

ଔ   ଔ   ଔ

"Another one bites the dust." Sydney lifted her glass along with the sixty-five other wedding guests in the expansive garden behind the DeLuca villa in Florence. "Our Julia is married off now."

Sydney, Eden, and Marissa sat at a round table along with five other American guests following the ceremony and an elegant, drawn-out meal. The night air circled like a balmy caress. Laughter and conversation in two languages hung in the air as flickering lanterns and torches infused orbs of golden light through the approaching dusk.

"Not so appropriate for the happy couple, Sydney." Eden gave her friend a reproving look of fake chastisement then sighed happily. She'd eaten so well, she could barely move. She'd forgo the dancing that would take place on the flagstone terrace as soon as the cake was served. If she'd known Florence was so fabulous, she'd have come decades ago. Maybe she'd drop out of college for the second time and simply stay there.

She wanted to pinch herself to make sure she was truly in Italy, after months of planning and a crescendo of anticipation as the date approached. June through early August had flown by in a flurry of tasks and planning. In July, she'd taken another watercolor class, figuring she wouldn't have time for at least another year due to studies, and she participated in a women's Bible study and in women's ministry. That too would fall by the wayside at least to a degree as she took on collegiate life.

Occasionally during the summer months, the wounds from her childhood that had resurfaced during her dating experiences nibbled at her mind during reflective moments. She found that buried frustrations popped to the surface more frequently. Apparently, her friendly, optimistic *conscious* identity disguised a few dark corners she thought had already healed. Partly, though not fully. She considered joining a support group or going back to counseling but opted instead to check out some books from the local library on recovering from an alcoholic family. Even finding time for that was challenging, with trip preparations and home maintenance tasks which filled her daily to-do list.

Then finally, Florence. For so long, the trip had existed only in conversation and on paper. At last, reality. There she was in a stunning and timeless city of history and love witnessing the fruit of both.

The Italians among the wedding guests called, *bacio, bacio,* and the Americans quickly learned to join in. The commotion continued and glasses remained raised until Julia and Craig kissed.

This brought a celebratory shout, and the familiar ritual would be repeated about fifteen minutes later.

Eden turned to Marissa, seated beside her wearing a deep blue gauzy dress with slits up the sleeves. "Your turn next, girlfriend."

Marissa responded with a smile. "Probably next spring, I'd say. Though I can't top this for a setting."

"I'm sure you two will come up with something equally unforgettable." Sydney absently slid two fingers down the stem of her glass.

Jarrod and Tyler had been invited to Julia's wedding, but both had declined, saying work obligations wouldn't allow a trip to Florence. The women knew the real reason. The men had wanted to be sure Sydney, Marissa, and Eden enjoyed their trip together without men around. Eden was secretly relieved. It was their last chance to be together for a while, just them. A trip through Tuscany wouldn't be the same with spouses along. Selfish, probably, but she was being honest. And she needed to get over it soon, as her friends transitioned into married life. For sure, things would change.

No way would she let one negative thought enter her head. It was idyllic on that summer night in Italy, a moment she'd never forget. Her gaze roved over the guests. She'd met Julia's newly discovered relatives but forgot many of their names. Valentina, the famous cousin who'd planned the wedding, sat at a nearby table with her husband, Andre, and they looked at each other adoringly. Julia's blond cousin was as beautiful and friendly as Julia had described, and six months pregnant with her first child. She'd been Julia's maid of honor.

Julia's uncle Sergio had given her away in the outdoor ceremony on the terrace. Her Aunt Emilia had watched from the front row with misty eyes. Valentina's attractive sister, Isabella, was there with her husband, Giovanni, a distinguished looking older man, and next to them were Julia's Uncle Giuseppe and Aunt Paola.

On Craig's side, his kids, siblings with spouses, and some business contacts had made the trip. Americans and Italians . . . cousins with spouses, kids, and assorted siblings . . . the guests and their names tumbled into oblivion in Eden's mind. She assumed most of the other Americans who'd traveled there for the ceremony had had the same idea, to combine Julia and Craig's wedding with a tour through Italy.

Soon an army of servers cleared the large glass table and brought out an eight-layer wedding cake. Julia and Craig approached to cut it and take the first bite, their hands locked together, appearing to be lost in one another. After the ritual, the crowd again cried, *bacio, bacio.* Julia and Craig laughed, kissed again, and the servers dispatched platefuls of cake among the tables.

"What a night." Marissa's soft phrase echoed in Eden's heart, and she silently agreed.

℣   ℣   ℣

After Julia and Craig departed toward the Italian Lake district for their honeymoon amidst a shower of rice and well wishes, Eden, Sydney and Marissa remained in Florence for two additional days. They explored every narrow street, gelateria, and several museums, and took a city tour and several walks along the Arno River. The next step on the itinerary was picking up a rental car to head west to the town of Lucca.

As dusk settled over Lucca, an hour west of Florence, the women sat under an umbrella after a delicious Tuscan dinner in the shadow of the city's Renaissance walls.

"You athletic girls wore me out today." Marissa didn't look unhappy about it, though. On the contrary, a contented smile stretched across her face as she closed her eyes and tilted her head back toward the trees overhead. They'd spent the morning strolling cobbled streets and visiting Romanesque churches, markets, and shopping squares. In the afternoon, Sydney urged them to rent bikes to ride atop the tree-lined walls, an elevated circular park around the city.

Eden fiddled with her napkin and silently agreed. "So worth it, though. And we stopped so many times for photos, I don't know how we could be tired. My opinion? We're spent from the extravagant sensory overload."

"You got that right. What great views from the wall. I'm so glad we went up there. Wasn't it a great idea, ladies?" Sydney's widened eyes invited their agreement.

"Absolutely. Tomorrow, on to Pisa. Finally, we get to see if this tower really leans," Eden said. But really, could Pisa top Lucca?

"Just don't stand under it," Marissa warned.

Pisa was only a short drive southwest of Lucca. Next on the list was the town of Greve, where Julia had spent the day getting to know Craig for the first time two years earlier. "Not only is it a wonderful town, according to Julia, but we'll be commemorating the start of their love story." Oh, how Eden loved a good love story. One day maybe she'd have her own, but it didn't stop her from enjoying those of her friends.

"Maybe we could make a quick stop at the village of Barga," Marissa said. "It's on the way and looks really cute in my travel book."

"We can't do everything." Eden and Sydney pronounced their new mantra in unison, one which they'd had to say several times in planning the trip. They all erupted in laughter.

"Right, okay, we'll see how it goes." Marissa closed her travel guide.

"Okay, girls, let me practice my Italian for just a moment." Once Sydney had their attention, she licked her lips and took a breath. "*Vino Nobile de Montepulciano.* How's that?"

"Not very useful, unless you want to order wine. But it sounds beautiful, Sydney. You really have the accent down." Eden threw her crumpled napkin at Sydney. She'd treasure these moments of beauty, culture, and friendship in her heart when she was back in class wondering what she'd done going back to school.

"What? A shadow crossed your face, Eden. What are you thinking about?" This from Marissa, ever sensitive to nonverbal changes.

"Oh, you caught me letting my mind wander. Shame on me. I was just thinking for a second about my fall semester and how much of a shock it will be, though it's been easy to forget in the last few days. I do *not* want to think about it."

"But you're excited, aren't you? Not only the classes, but the ideas you have for a nonprofit, or for doing something else with your experience?" Sydney asked.

"Yes, of course. Nervous, excited, motivated. So much has happened in a short time, my mind is spinning. But I don't want my brain to go there when we have all *this* going on." She gestured toward the gurgling fountain and café tables around them.

"Don't worry, we'll help you push all that way into the future." Sydney's voice was firm. She pulled a crumpled list from her backpack. "First, Pisa with a possible side trip to Barga, Livorno, possible side trip to Volterra, Greve in Julia's honor, and Craig, of course. Siena, Arezzo, possible side trip to San Casciano, then finally Florence. Will that be sufficient to distract you from your upcoming college career?"

A gush of joy billowed inside Eden as she gently rebuked her wandering thoughts. "Quite sufficient."

Chapter Seven

Eden hoisted a canvas tote bag higher on her shoulder as she walked across the quad of her new setting, the college campus. The late August air carried a slight tinge of difference as it prepared to welcome fall. The landscape surrounding her—brick buildings in various architectural styles, winding paths between them, and crowds of students her son's age—reminded her of where she was, though rich and detailed memories of Tuscany still hovered in her mind.

"Come back to the present, Eden," she whispered. All around her, young adults clad in shorts, jeans, and t-shirts clustered together like bees in a hive or walked, laden with backpacks.

Like a bee herself, she buzzed inside with excitement and anxiety, despite her fading post-vacation glow. Her fixed gaze targeted her destination, a brick building across McKinley Avenue. As she approached the street, her eyes wandered to the stately bell tower visible all over campus. The sight of it anchored her in her new reality, but also filled her with a sense of respect for the institution of higher education, her current solemn responsibility. She'd take it seriously. Even six months ago, it would never have entered her mind to become a college student again, but here she was. Her first class, Project Management, and her new life would begin in ten minutes.

Eden entered the imposing brick building. The chill of air conditioning greeted her, along with a slightly musty smell and the garbled sounds of multiple student conversations echoing through the hallways. She followed the numbers on the doors until she found her classroom. Only a few students were already there, seated in metal chairs with wood grain tabletops. She slid into a row and sat down, scanning the room for anyone who looked about her age. There must be older students on a campus of seventeen thousand. The seats around her filled as young adults shuffled into the rows, chatting with one another, slinging their backpacks to the floor, and pulling out their phones and laptops. Eden spotted one older woman across the room and another in the front row. Maybe she'd befriend them during the semester, though they looked significantly older than she was.

Someone approached the front of the classroom. Her professor, Dr. Marcus Siler, who was also her advisor. They'd had an initial meeting the other week so she could choose her fall classes. Tall with slightly graying brown waves, he fit her mental picture of a college professor, albeit a somewhat handsome one, with wire-rimmed glasses and a look of cool detachment. He strode across the front of the room. "Good morning, everyone. I trust you've all enjoyed your summer. I'm Dr. Siler and this is Project Management. I assume most of you have taken lower-level management courses. If not, this course will be challenging. But I'm here if you need help. My office hours and location are on the orientation sheet that's coming around now." He nodded toward a grad assistant who passed out a stack of papers row by row. "On the sheet, you'll also see your online access information for finding the syllabus and all other materials for the class."

When he finished speaking, his gaze panned the room. It landed on Eden, and he nodded slightly, probably since they'd already met. Maybe he somehow sensed her awkwardness at being an older student, though the discomfort faded with every passing hour. In its place, her interest in the topic stirred and she grew impatient for the lecture to begin.

After an hour, Eden's hand cramped from writing. Most of the other students had laptops or tablets for taking notes. She'd be smart to bring one if she wanted to preserve her right hand. After another hour of class, she slid her notebook into her tote bag and stood, stretching out her back and arms. As she moved toward the doorway, she passed the older woman who'd sat in the front row. What was the best way to make her acquaintance? An old fashioned greeting?

"Hello." She smiled at the woman, but then didn't know what else to say. *Nice to meet another old student.* No, probably not.

The woman turned to her, startled. Her face looked older than she'd appeared to Eden from the back. Maybe she was retired. The woman smiled. "I think this will be an interesting class, don't you? Better than the intro PM class."

"Oh, I haven't taken that one, though I probably did an equivalent. I did most of my degree thirty years ago. Thought it was about time I finished." Eden let out an awkward chuckle.

The woman didn't respond, but an unfocused polite smile remained on her face. Eden mentally prepared another question to ask the woman, but she'd slipped away through the crowded hallway and Eden found herself alone.

She didn't try the same strategy in her second class of the day and was thankful to arrive safely home to a place of no expectations or discomfort. She'd survived her first day of college.

Eden emptied her tote bag of books and notebooks onto the dining room table and took a breath. Her evening occupation stared back from the table. She'd get through this. The classes had been interesting, and the reading and projects would be too, though there seemed to be a ton of it. Then she'd be finished. She'd mark off the objective she'd carried around for years, decades. She didn't need to make friends or feel a part of the social scene. She knew her objective, and she'd hunker down and accomplish it.

Three weeks went by, and Eden settled into a routine. Her days on campus filled her mind and her notebook, and eventually the tablet she bought. She went to class and left without talking to anyone, but most of the other students seemed to do the same. Out on the quad and in the entryways and hallways, students often clustered in conversation. That was when Eden felt the loneliest, the most isolated. And the *oldest.*

Dr. Siler was finishing his final point then, with a glance at the wall clock, dismissed the class. Eden had one more that afternoon, but for now, she'd enjoy the break. Noise filled the room as she closed her tablet and slipped it into her tote bag.

"Excuse me." Eden turned and saw a young woman who'd frequently sat in the row behind her, though they'd never spoken. Tight black ringlets surrounded her olive-skinned face and fell to her shoulders. She wore a multicolored embroidered vest over a tunic and jeans and a matching cloth headband.

"Did you happen to get Dr. Siler's last point?"

"Yes, sure." Eden fished her tablet out of her tote bag.

"Oh, I'm sorry, you've already closed your tablet."

"No problem. It won't take a second to find the notes." Eden opened the lid and the screen illuminated to the last page she'd typed. She read out the information to the young woman, who jotted it in a notebook.

"Thanks so much. I was busy typing his previous point and I missed it." A warm smile stretched across her pretty face. "You're Eden, right? We've been in class a few weeks and have never spoken. We all run in and out without even looking at each other. Are you new to the business department?"

"Yes, the department *and* the university. I haven't been a student for about thirty years. Can you tell?"

The young woman's face softened. "I think it's great that you're back in college. I'm sure there's a cool story behind that. My name is Mariella."

"Nice to meet you, Mariella." A cool story, maybe not, but part of her story in any case. And it didn't matter anymore. She was going to finish her degree.

"Are you a senior?" Mariella asked. "I assume you're not a freshman, since this isn't an intro class." The women strolled through the mostly empty class toward the door.

"I should be in an intro class. Most of my credits are from a different school. At the time, I transferred back here for my senior year but wasn't able to finish my degree. I'm about a year short. It should have only been a semester or so, but requirements have changed in the last thirty years."

"No lie, I'm sure that's true. Do you want to grab lunch?"

The young woman's suggestion touched a tender place inside Eden. She'd been prepared to spend her year alone as an older student misfit, but maybe that was about to change. "That would be nice. If you don't mind hanging out with someone your mom's age."

Mariella laughed. "No worries. My mom's pretty cool. I don't even notice her age, and I wasn't thinking that about you, either. I admire you, in fact. Was it hard to start college again after thirty years?"

"After I stopped waffling forever about the decision, it was kind of exciting. I'd always wanted to finish my degree. A friend of mine challenged me to finish, and I couldn't think of a reason not to." Mariella didn't need to know that Eden had pushed her friend away when he was only trying to help. A thread of guilt still hung inside when she thought about Colin.

They walked through the halls and out into the still pleasant mid-September day. The humidity of summer had passed, but the pinch of autumn chill hadn't yet arrived. "I brought a lunch, but I'll come with you if you want to buy something," Eden told her.

"I have one too. We can sit under those trees if you don't mind the benches."

"Not at all." Her first friend. *Thanks, Lord.*

They sat at a picnic table and Eden pulled out yogurt with chia seeds and a plastic container filled with salad.

"Are you specializing in any area of business?" Mariella looked up from tucking lettuce back into her sandwich.

"Not at this point. After thirty years, I figured general was a good option. That way, I don't have six more specialty courses added on, extending my one year to three." Seemed like good advice, following her brief meeting with Dr. Siler. "What about you?"

"My program is apparel design. I've been designing clothes since I was a pre-teen. They have a good program here for that. I'm sure this class will help me manage my own business one day."

"That's so interesting that you design clothes. Are you wearing your own designs?"

Mariella nodded. "I make most of my own clothes because I can't find anything that suits my personality." She laughed. "I guess I'm eccentric."

"No, you're artsy and creative. And absolutely beautiful too." Eden pointed to Mariella's embroidered vest. "Bohemian is really in. It might look goofy on me, but on you, it's fantastic."

Eden herself wore jeans, thinking that it would prevent her from standing out like someone's mom instead of a business student. And of course, she'd left her wedge heels in her closet and chosen thick-soled slip-on sneakers instead. In this context, her height might work in her favor, helping her to appear, at first glance, more youthful than she was. She looked back at Mariella's outfit. Maybe she could learn a thing or two from her new friend about fashion.

"Thank you. You're sweet," Mariella said. "And I think you'd look great in a bohemian style." Her smile fell, and a sigh slipped out. "I love being in school, but I kind of dread the day my diploma is handed to me."

Eden furrowed her brow. "Why? Aren't you eager to get out there and make a statement with your wonderful designs?"

The young woman frowned. "It's so *hard* to break in, as you can imagine. I can have great ideas, plenty of prototypes, but making a living is the tough part. I sometimes wonder how long it'll take me to be profitable and if I should minor in something else, so I have something to fall back on. I ask myself that question every day."

"Really? I never thought about that." Eden leaned her elbows on the wooden table. "I never had to, I guess. I was in college when I got engaged. That's why I didn't finish school. I had kids right away. When my husband passed away twelve years ago, we had a restaurant, and I took it over. I knew restaurant work pretty well and it was our only livelihood, so I dove in. I didn't have a choice, but he'd built it up and I just stepped in and made it a little better. I can't imagine having to start from scratch."

Mariella frowned. "Especially in a field like mine. Seems like artistic fields are the hardest. I don't know why it should be that way. If I invented some kind of app or tool I could patent, I'd probably be set. Though, I know that's hard too."

"You clearly have the talent. Have confidence in that, and everything else will fall into place, sooner or later." Eden spoke with certainty, fueled by the obvious beauty of Mariella's clothing, but doubt shadowed the young woman's eyes.

"I hope you're right. It's a tough world and there's a ton of competition, even if you *do* have talent."

Eden nodded, having no answer. Mariella was young to express such a sentiment, as if she felt the world was already against her. Eden herself never had to start from scratch or face obstacles or competition. But now she lived in *their* world, these young entrepreneurs starting out. Maybe there were burdens and barriers in that world and in the current day, which she knew nothing about.

Ꮳᏹ   Ꮳᏹ   Ꮳᏹ

Dr. Siler's door stood open. Eden knocked lightly but waited in the hall, where a rumble of voices came from students changing classes. She was a few minutes early for her appointment, a follow-up on the short meeting she'd had with him prior to the first day of class. She heard his voice as he talked to someone on the phone. He leaned forward over his desk, saw her hovering in the doorway, and gestured her to a seat beside him.

She entered his office and sat down, leaving her tote bag on her lap. Dr. Siler hung up and turned to her. The cool expression he maintained while teaching warmed almost to friendliness. "How has your first month of school gone, Eden?"

"Wonderful. It's exciting to be here. I'm learning so much already."

Dr. Siler smiled. "Sometimes older students have an eager, thirsty attitude compared to the twenty-year-olds. It's refreshing. You're in such a different place, having lived life, raised a family. They're young and, for some of them, going to college is merely the next logical step after high school. It's very different for you and that makes you a different kind of student."

"I appreciate that observation. And as you may already know, after my late husband died, and even before that, I got quite a bit of business experience in the restaurant world. That's one thing that makes everything sink in like I'm a thirsty sponge. I already know many of the questions. Maybe the younger students don't yet, though they'll still learn a lot." Returning to college hadn't been anything close to a logical next step for her, as it was for her younger counterparts. She'd been metaphorically dragged by her heels back to the campus. "And in my case, I'm completing something I've wanted to do for a long time. I didn't think I ever would."

"That has to be a good feeling. Well, by a year from Christmas, you'll have your diploma in hand."

Eden frowned. "I thought I'd be finished by next May."

"You'll be *almost* finished." Dr. Siler leaned back in his chair. He seemed far more relaxed in his office than he did in front of his class, where he was strictly business. "Unfortunately, there's a class that's required for your program, Management Economics, but it's only offered in the fall. You aren't ready to take it this fall, so you'll have to do it next year. But that's the only course you'll still need unless I've overlooked something." He scanned his computer screen and turned his attention back to her.

So, she wouldn't be able to graduate next May. Disappointment pooled inside her and she sighed. "Okay, it's just one class."

He seemed to sense her discouragement. "Since it *is* only the one class, you'll probably be allowed to walk next May during commencement. Many students do that, if they just have a summer course or one in the fall to complete."

"That's good news." She smiled and folded her hands over her tote bag. Despite his dispassionate appearance while teaching, he seemed to be a nice guy. She appreciated his comment about her eagerness to learn. Even though her ultimate goal was getting her college diploma, the material itself was fascinating, and she hoped it would lead her and prepare her for the next step in her life.

"Do you already have a business idea or product in mind for the future?" he asked.

Eden shook her head. "Not yet. Maybe a nonprofit, or a small business. It's too early to say. I'm hoping something will spark as I go through this year. I'm in the right place for that to happen."

He smiled. "Yes, you are. Well, just to let you know, our department has different activities on campus that help outside of class, like guest lecturers, student business clubs, and campus-sponsored mentoring programs. There's a lot of help available for students who have an idea of a company or a product. Then, outside the school there are a few partnerships to be aware of. One in particular is called Business Innovation Launchpad. Kind of a long name, but I think you get the idea they want to convey. They sponsor a contest for students who have a business idea or innovation. The winners can receive mentoring from industry professionals and a grant into the tens of thousands of dollars to launch their companies."

"That's wonderful. What a big help to students with the vision for a company or invention." She'd be sure to let Mariella know about this. "Innovation . . . What was the rest of it?" Eden pulled her notebook from her tote bag.

"Business Innovation Launchpad. Or just *Launchpad,* as we call it around here. Last spring, a team of students received twenty thousand dollars of venture capital to help fund their new company."

"That's good to know. The mentoring sounds like a valuable benefit too."

"Yes, it's indispensable. Many students have an interest in business, but no experience at all. So, that's extremely valuable if that's their situation. *You* could probably mentor other students, given your experience."

Eden finished writing the name and closed her notebook. "I've had all the ups and downs in the restaurant business, that's for sure." She didn't miss that life at all. "I'd really love to do something completely different. Just have to figure out what." She'd told Jordan she wanted her life to be part of a bigger story. To help people. Maybe that was her first clue in her new life chapter.

As Eden walked to the student parking lot following her appointment, the idea of the nonprofit returned to her mind. She'd have to think and pray about it, about a need that weighed on her, where she might make a difference. Other ideas would come with time. Only one month had passed. Things changed so quickly, she could find herself in an entirely different place in a year.

Chapter Eight

October transitioned from summer to early fall, with crisp early mornings and temperate afternoons. Eden's favorite time of year. Besides less humidity and anticipation of a new season, fall campus activities infused additional energy into the atmosphere. Eden hummed a praise chorus as she prepared her lunch for the day and assembled the contents of her tote bag.

She'd settled into her new routine, finding a daily rhythm of driving to campus, attending between one and three classes, and spending some afternoons at the library and evenings studying and doing class projects. Her plate and heart were full, leaving her dating disappointments and revelations about her past on a back burner. She'd returned her library books on emotional healing, figuring she had too much to read already. Her mind was so committed to her new life she hardly thought of food and had lost an additional three pounds without trying.

The phone rang. Her son Brent was calling, a rare and welcome event. "Hi, sweetie. It's great to hear from you."

"Hey, Mom. I started feeling guilty because I haven't called in a while. I got a new project at work and did a bunch of overtime. I guess I could have texted."

"I don't mind texts if you don't have time to call. They're always better than no news. I'm not trying to add to your guilt. I'm just glad you're conscientious of your old mom all by yourself without me bugging you."

Brent chuckled. "Yeah, I appreciate that. I get around to it, eventually. How's school going?"

They exchanged news on both sides for a few minutes while Eden savored the reconnection with her last-born child.

Brent said, "I wanted to let you know I'll be home for Thanksgiving," he said. "I'd like to bring Kelly."

"Oh, wonderful, on both counts. I can't wait to meet your love. You haven't said too much about her, but you've been together for over a year, so it's looking somewhat serious." And he was bringing her for Thanksgiving. Yes, this looked serious.

They chatted for a few more minutes, then ended their call. Eden's happy world had just gotten a little brighter. And all this brightness with no man in her life. Was that even necessary? She'd had fewer pangs of longing in the two months since returning to school. Maybe she could put off a romantic relationship for another year until she got settled, as long as she didn't wait so long, she'd be unable to attract anyone. A silly thought, but one which slithered into her mind once in a while when she saw a new wrinkle or noticed her mid-section thickening ever so gradually despite her weight loss.

Before putting away her phone, she saw a new email and clicked on it. Dr. Siler requested that she stop by his office between one and three that day if she was free. She didn't think it was time for a meeting with him. Tension gripped inside. Hopefully, she wasn't deficient in any assignments or otherwise in trouble. Maybe he had other resources or advice to give her. She'd enjoyed his class, and he seemed to appreciate her responses in group discussion.

Eden had quickly overcome her shyness at being the older student on campus. Most of that she credited to her new friends, Mariella, Tara, and Cheyenne, young women who were in several of her classes. In the early part of the semester, she'd tried to befriend the other older woman she'd spied the first day of Dr. Siler's class. Shelly. Eden had initiated lunch one day. Shelly was pleasant, but seemed more focused on her grandchildren, who she visited daily after classes, than the material she was learning. She'd admitted that part of the reason she was there was to fill her time as a retired widow. Though taking classes for that reason was legitimate, why was she in project management?

Her young friends, on the other hand, stimulated and challenged her with their vision and ideas in ways she couldn't have imagined. Tara had an idea for a multi-generational elder care system and Cheyenne, who was also a single mom of a toddler, targeted a more traditional route, employment in a management role at a large company. Eden wouldn't have predicted her new college friends would be Brent's age, or even younger. The age difference awareness she'd expected was only in her mind, except for the respect the young women seemed to have for her years of life and business experience. It humbled her, but also reminded of the experience she *did* have.

Eden knocked on Dr. Siler's door at two-thirty, remembering the last time she'd done the same and how much had happened since that time. "Eden, come in."

"Hi, Dr. Siler. You wanted to see me."

"Call me Marcus outside of class. You're not twenty, after all." She stilled. "I apologize, that sounded bad, when I meant it with respect. What I meant was we're contemporaries both in age and in professional experience, so I don't mind if you call me by my first name."

"Oh, okay." She wasn't sure she deserved all the recognition she was getting in this season of her life, from her young friends and now her professor. "I may have life experience, but I still have a ton to learn."

He gestured to the chair beside his massive wooden desk. "I just wanted to touch base with you and see how things are going."

Relief. "I'm glad I'm not in trouble for anything."

Dr. Siler chuckled. "Even if you were, I'm not able to put you in detention or anything. No, I know this is new for you and wanted to make sure you were finding the resources you needed."

"That's very kind, Dr. Um . . . Marcus. That feels a bit weird to me." They both laughed and their eyes locked for a moment, his behind round wire-rimmed glasses. A buzz of attraction began inside her. Her professor? Eden scolded herself. He'd been kind enough to step outside the bounds of his professor role dispensing wisdom on eager young minds and into that of a friend, almost. But she'd have to push anything else away, including seeds of attraction. Entirely inappropriate.

She broke the pause that seemed charged with electricity. "Yes, I'm finding a lot at the library, and I've checked into a couple of the campus business groups and clubs you mentioned to me the last time we met."

"Ah, that's good. Do you have any further thoughts about a business idea? Of course, there's no assignment or deadline associated with that, not unless you enroll in the Idea Incubator class next spring. That's where students come with a specific idea and get some mentoring and first steps."

"That sounds like a great class. I may enroll in that in hopes I'll have an idea by then. I think I mentioned a nonprofit to you before. I'd need to zero in on one of several issues I have a heart for, identify an injustice and obstacles for a particular demographic. I know that's general, but I expect it will get clearer with time."

"It's a good starting point. Good thought process. You seem to have a lot of heart, especially for the other young students."

Warmth spread through her at his comment. And surprise. He'd noticed the way she'd clicked with her young group of friends or possibly had seen her on campus with them.

"I guess I do have a heart for lots of things and I'll have to narrow that down at some point. Honestly, I thought as an older student, I'd be an outcast—" Eden paused to make air quotes. "But these lovely young women adopted me into their group of friends. I don't want to come off like a mom to them, but an older, more experienced friend. And I think they appreciate that."

"I'm sure they do. We need more heart in the business world. Sounds like you already have a mentoring influence on these young ladies. A nonprofit might be a great direction for you."

After his statement and Eden's nod of agreement a silence fell. That must be her cue it was the end of their meeting. She pulled her tote from the floor and stood. "Thank you for following up with me."

"Don't mention it." He paused then said, "Eden, would you like to meet sometime for coffee between classes?"

Surprise made her stop and blink a few times. He awaited her response, but she couldn't detect anything else on his face, though her heart pounded. "That would be nice."

"A nice, friendly break during an intense day of teaching." He pushed a folder a few inches on his desk, as though he too suddenly felt awkward. "Are you free on Wednesday at two? We can meet over at The Rabbit Hole, near the mall entrance."

"Yes, I think I'm free then. I'll look forward to it. Thanks, Dr. Siler. I mean Marcus." She left his office with a straight face, though her thoughts were anything but calm.

As she drove home, she replayed her conversation with her professor. Was he asking her out? No, surely not. He'd said himself that she was a contemporary. And his words *friendly break* were meant to reassure her of his platonic intentions. Maybe he was lonely for like-minded adults he could relate to, since he spent his days surrounded by twenty-year-olds. But what about his colleagues? Or others in his personal circle? And the Rabbit Hole wasn't near campus, so he'd chosen a place where students weren't likely to flock at that hour. She would *not* read too much into this. But there was that split second of chemistry she couldn't deny, and she suspected it went both ways.

CR CR CR

Wednesday afternoon, Eden parked in front of the Rabbit Hole, a brick building with a cute giant rabbit on one end of the roof near the door. Her nerves jangled inside her. "Just coffee, just coffee", she chanted to herself. What was she afraid of? Dr. Siler was being friendly, and wasn't that a good thing? Was that all it was? She'd learn more that day, sense his motivation, and wouldn't assume anything. If she did, she'd likely make a fool of herself.

She spotted him seated at a small round table near the counter. His face was buried in a magazine. Either he was not looking for her or hiding the fact he was. Eden forced herself to relax as she approached his table.

He looked up from his reading. All scholarly pretense fell away, replaced by a warm smile. "Hello, Eden. Can I get you something to drink?"

"Hot chocolate would be great. It's an old favorite in the fall."

"Would that be pumpkin spice chocolate, peppermint twist, or regular?" Humor laced his voice.

Eden laughed. "Regular chocolate is just fine. Thanks."

She glanced around the small tables and cozy seating area but didn't see anyone she recognized. Thankfully. What would she talk about with her professor? She couldn't imagine.

Marcus returned with the drinks and settled in across from her. "Have you taken in any of the fall sports events? Cardinals games?"

"Cardinals?"

"The school football team."

Eden laughed. "I guess I answered that question, didn't I? I'm not very sports minded and really have too much to do. Once I leave campus, I go right home and get to work."

"What do you do for fun or to relax?"

Eden sat and thought for a minute. "Would that be before going back to college or since?"

They laughed.

"Maybe I should rephrase that. What would you do for fun if you had any time to do it?"

"I did have a couple-year gap between selling my restaurant and starting back to school. During that time, I took a couple of painting classes. Watercolor. I enjoyed that a lot and was surprised that I wasn't terrible at it." She'd even had one of her landscapes framed and hung it in her upstairs hallway. "I worked a lot in my garden, which ended up being more of a need than a pleasure. I go to the gym sometimes, though less lately. Nothing very exciting, I'm afraid. I'm also active in my church."

Her last comment may very well weed him out as a potential date. He didn't respond, except with a smile, likely thinking she merely attended services, a perfectly acceptable civic and social activity. Though at the moment, attending Sunday worship was all she felt she had time for. She'd let both her women's Bible study group and hospitality fall by the wayside. "When I need to relax and I'm *not* a student, I read, though probably not the same thing you read."

He gave her a dry smile and tilted his head to one side. "I wouldn't jump to conclusions. I like a good thriller in the evenings."

"Ah, that would keep me awake. My novels keep me up also if I read them too late. I keep thinking about the characters like they're real people." She laughed. She probably laughed too often to mask her nerves and to appear relaxed.

A brief silence fell. Her discomfort deepened. "Can you tell me more about the organization you mentioned, the Launchpad one?" He might not appreciate her veering back into business topics, but she couldn't think of anything else to say. And she *was* curious about it.

His face brightened at her question. "Of course. It's a great resource for students who have a fully developed idea. What I mean by that is they've done market studies, have a realistic grasp of the capital needed, and basically have already done their business plan.

The Launchpad examines all these elements before accepting their application. Even if they aren't selected, they're given a review of their strengths and weaknesses, as well as a list of what they're missing. They still gain something, even if they don't win the award."

"How many are selected each year?"

"The organization recently changed its structure by offering smaller grants to more winners. They award prizes to five individuals or teams of students. Each team receives between fifteen and thirty thousand dollars of venture capital, depending on the idea and their needs. And the fund fluctuates, depending on corporate sponsorship, so that's a factor as well."

"That's wonderful. What a leg up that would be for a young entrepreneur. I'll be sure to mention it to my campus friends. One of them in particular has a clear vision of what she wants to do."

"You don't want to apply?"

Eden shook her head. "I don't think it's appropriate for me since I haven't invented anything and I'm leaning toward a nonprofit. That will need funding too, but I don't even have a specific idea yet. I'm glad to know about the Launchpad. It's a great idea. I'm planning to take the incubator class in the spring. Do they address nonprofits too?"

"I'm not sure, but I could ask Dr. Asher, who teaches that class, or you can ask him yourself. I believe there's a class you can take which walks you through nonprofits, how to start them as well as legal considerations. That would be a worthwhile class for you."

"Yes, absolutely. Thanks, Marcus."

Silence fell again. Eden focused on her hot chocolate, which had become tepid chocolate. She made sure not to get a chocolate mustache as she downed the last few gulps.

"Have you ever been to the Gray Heron Restaurant? I'd like to take you there sometime."

No mistake there. That was a date. She wiped her mouth. "Um, am I allowed to go out with you, Marcus?" She slipped in what she hoped was an engaging smile, so she didn't sound like a third grader.

"Allowed?" Though his eyes widened, his mouth tipped into a smile.

"I'm a student and you're a teacher."

"Are you a rule girl?" She saw a challenge in his eyes.

Eden cocked her head. "Not necessarily. It depends. I just don't want any trouble."

"No worries. It's not something either of us would advertise. It's no one's business but ours. That's all there is to know."

"Hmm. If you say so, though it sounds to me like you're guessing."

Marcus splayed his hands and shrugged. "I don't worry about things like that very much. If you're uncomfortable, that's fine, I understand." He looked as though it were completely equal to him whether she accepted his invitation or not.

Eden took a breath. "I'll think about it and let you know, okay?"

"Fair enough."

 G
 G
 G

The next day Eden had two classes, though fortunately, not with Dr. Siler. Marcus. Who'd asked her on a date. It was an understatement to say she had mixed feelings. On the one hand, they talked easily together, especially about business topics. Discussing business with him was interesting, especially given his knowledge and experience. He was attractive, she had to admit. And equally significant, she'd met him in a *normal* way, instead of online. However normal it could be to date one's college professor. On the other hand, it was doubtful he was a believer.

Her decision about her date with Marcus hovered in the back of her mind all day, but it would have to wait. She was meeting Mariella, Tara, and Cheyenne between classes at the campus coffee shop to connect and blow off steam. It had become a weekly Tuesday routine she looked forward to. Often, they managed to squeeze in another meeting or two later in the week.

The four of them settled at a square table in the noisy coffee shop. The comforting aroma of ground coffee hung in the air. Daily, Eden felt thankful to be included in their group, the last thing she'd expected when she'd become an older college student.

"I wanted to ask if any of you have heard of the Business Innovation Launchpad," Eden said once their hot drinks were in front of them. "Dr. Siler told me about it. You can submit an idea in a contest and if you win, they give you money to launch your business. They also provide mentoring."

"Yes, I've heard of it," Mariella said. "I've heard mixed reviews about it."

"Really? Like what?" Eden leaned forward.

"I have too." Cheyenne took a sip of her tea, then swirled the teabag a few times. "Anyone can apply, but I've heard most of the winners are guys."

Eden frowned. "Maybe most of those who apply are guys, so it's a simple matter of ratio." She met their eyes in turn. "It's just probability, don't you think?"

At her statement, Cheyenne shrugged and flipped her straight, auburn hair over one shoulder. "That's just what I've heard. That wouldn't necessarily stop me from applying if I had an invention."

"I haven't heard of the Launchpad," Tara said. "Sounds like a good idea, in theory. But not if it's fixed in advance."

"I don't know that it is. I've just heard things," Mariella said. "Like, several times from different people."

Eden had no answer. Could it just be sour grapes from those who hadn't won and started rumors about the fairness of the contest? "I'm guessing from what I've seen in the department that business students are about two-thirds guys and one-third women. Wouldn't you say?" She scanned their faces, waiting for a response. "Maybe it's simply statistics. More students are guys, more applicants are guys, so more winners are too."

"Wouldn't surprise me, though, if things were skewed toward guys," Cheyenne said as she fingered her phone. "It's always been like that. And women sometimes have other challenges too." She gave them a half-smile. "Like a little guy at home." A troubled look passed over her face. She averted her eyes again to her phone.

Blond Tara, who'd been asked several times if she were Eden's daughter, frowned. "True, that's a hard thing too." She turned to Eden. "And if you're right about the numbers, women are still thirty percent and growing."

"And to be reckoned with," Mariella said emphatically. "But I don't trust the Launchpad. I'd rather go with an on-campus organization that has history with the school."

Cheyenne stood abruptly. "Sorry, guys, just got word my babysitter has an emergency, so that means *I* now have one. A childcare emergency."

Eden, Tara, and Mariella looked up at her. "Oh, sorry. See you soon?" Mariella said.

Cheyenne gave them all a tight smile. "Sure thing." She was out the door in a matter of seconds.

"Poor girl. She's been having childcare issues for the last couple of weeks. With her *third* babysitter this fall. She tries so hard." Tara's voice trailed off as she drew her gaze back from the front door.

Eden frowned. "That's a shame. I hope she can find someone reliable and get that worry off her plate. Has she tried daycare?"

"Too expensive," Mariella said. "Although private babysitters are too. This one was a friend of her mother's." She let out a sigh. "Anyway, what were we talking about?"

Yet another heavy issue for young women trying to move forward in their lives. Cheyenne was young to have such a lot to juggle. Eden turned her darkened thoughts back to their conversation. "Do you think, in general, women are discriminated against in business?"

Both women nodded vigorously. "Absolutely." Mariella's voice rang out. "And it's nearly impossible to prove, because they can always say a guy was the better applicant or had the better idea."

"Women always have to work twice as hard for the same recognition," Tara said, frowning into her half mug of chai. "And it's especially hard to get a foot in the door at the start."

Eden sighed. "I guess I thought things had changed in recent years."

"They have, but not enough. The status quo wants us to be happy with that little bit of improvement without demanding full equality," Tara said.

"Is there a way to get data on applicants and past winners of Launchpad contests?" Eden ventured. She took a deep sip of her chocolate, which had cooled off.

"They have a website and there might be a link to past winners. Otherwise, maybe in the business library they have some information." Mariella seemed the most knowledgeable and the most suspicious of the Launchpad.

"I could always ask Dr. Siler about that," Eden said. He was her reference. He would know. She could ask him during their dinner if she went with him. Maybe she should since he'd help her in her research.

Still, where had the rumor come from? Was there any basis to it?

It would be nearly impossible to prove.

Chapter Nine

"You look very nice, Eden." Marcus's eyes swept down her midnight blue dress when he met her at the door of the Gray Heron Restaurant Saturday evening. She'd insisted on meeting him there rather than allowing him to pick her up. And she still wasn't certain she should be there. She'd argued with herself for a day or so, swinging between the desire to know him better and an inner warning they weren't on the same page in several ways. Finally, she said to herself, *Why not*, fully aware that it wasn't always a valid or safe question.

"Thank you. Have you been waiting long?"

"No, I got here a few minutes ago."

He looked more handsome in the intimate lighting, wearing a stylish gray jacket and a crisp dress shirt. A subtle fragrance of cologne wafted toward her. A low and dangerous hum began inside.

"I have a table for us but wanted to make sure you found it. It's tucked back in the next room, but worth the effort. You'll see." He turned and led the way.

Soft music, muted conversations, and the clink of glasses and silverware hung in the air as she followed him. Cloth-covered tables glowed with candlelight. Beyond a short, carpeted hall was another dining area. Eden stood still at the sight. Before her, a wall-to-wall picture window displayed a silvery lake, its surface glowing with paths of orange and blue under the setting sun.

"I might not have found this by myself," Eden said, once she'd recovered from the stunning sight. "What a view."

They settled into a table which he'd apparently reserved. Her eyes kept straying to the lake, already a shade darker as the sun set.

"I'm glad you like it. It's one of my favorite restaurants, though I haven't been here for at least a year."

Maybe that was the last time he'd gone on a date when he wanted to impress someone, though Eden seriously doubted that. He likely led an active social life, and she was his latest interest. Next month, it could be someone else. She kept wanting to ask, *why me?* Had he ever invited one of his younger students here?

Soon, a waiter arrived at their table. "Welcome to the Gray Heron. My name is Justin." He spread a large hard-back menu for each of them and took their drink orders. After spending a few minutes reading over the extravagant food descriptions, they ordered dinner while Eden tried to relax.

"Did you teach or work anywhere else before coming to Indiana?" she asked.

Marcus took some time explaining the professional path that led him to his current position. He'd worked in several companies in high level management roles before deciding to complete his doctorate. "I found myself in a teaching role so many times while I worked in the corporate setting, and I loved that. I received frequent praise for my ability to make things clear to new hires and employees learning new skill areas, so when the day came that I needed a new challenge, I thought about teaching. I continued working while I got my doctorate, which took a few years. I was married at the time with one child, so life was intense. But having the degree was a necessity for teaching. Even if I hadn't liked the academic world, the degree and knowledge I received would have served me well if I'd returned to corporate life, or if I ever do in the future."

He continued explaining the various steps of his career while making a passing comment about a second ex-wife and a stepchild, now grown. Otherwise, he divulged little about his personal life and values. While Eden found his extended resume interesting and one-sided, she was also grateful for the focus of conversation that led up to the moment the food arrived.

"I think even a former restaurant owner like yourself will approve of the cuisine here." Marcus nodded toward Eden and smiled. People often said things like that to her, once they knew she'd owned a restaurant.

She leaned over her plate and breathed in. "Right now, I'm absorbing these aromas. I'm sure the taste will exceed them."

And they did. Even if her evening with him was a bust, she'd have had one of the best meals of her life.

Eventually, he asked her about herself. She shared a few things about her years in restaurant work, but then talked mostly about her children, since she wasn't sure what else to tell him. "Brent works in California in finance, so he got the business gene from me, I guess. Jordan has some too. She's in marketing and Claire is an ER nurse. I get along well with all of them and I'm especially close to my girls."

Though Marcus nodded politely, he didn't ask further questions. Eden wondered if she should say something about her faith but struggled for words to broach the subject. Regular church attendance alone wouldn't incite any fascination in this worldly academic seated across from her. At times, her spiritual life didn't even stimulate *her*. Yet, the walk of faith had its ups, downs, and deep joys, which he'd never understand.

A playful smile pulled at his lips. "So, tell me something about yourself that most people don't know. It's kind of a game, but a fun one."

"Hmm. I'll have to think about that one. Do you want to go first?"

"Sure. I have one, but don't tell anyone." He chuckled. "My legal first name isn't Marcus. It's Eugene. I didn't much care for that name, and apparently my parents didn't either since they called me Marcus all my life."

"Was Eugene a family name?"

"Yes, my dad's brother was called Eugene, and he died, unfortunately, when he was just a child. I'm sure that made an impact on my dad. He was kind enough to come up with a better-fitting middle name for me. *Marcus* is a good fit for me, better than Gene or Eugene." He dabbed a cloth napkin on his mouth. "Have you thought of something yet?"

"Hmm. Feels like my life is an open book. Ah, here's one. When I was little, I had a make-believe friend who was really strong and protected me." She'd forgotten about her strong imaginary friend who gave her courage she didn't have when her father was drunk and on a rampage.

Marcus smiled. "Did your make-believe friend have a name?"

"Yes, I think so, but I forgot what it was." Seemed so long ago, those fearful nights huddled in her room invoking the presence of an imaginary force. Later, when she learned about God's love for her, she'd been overjoyed to have a *real* protector, wise and powerful as well, though she knew she didn't always rely on him often enough.

While they ate dessert, the conversation circled back to business as Marcus described a few of the courses she'd be taking in the spring. Business might be the only thing they had in common.

Eden licked her fork. Where had she been able to fit dessert after the sumptuous meal? "I find the idea of the Launchpad so interesting. Is there a way I can learn more about past winners and what became of their ideas?"

"Yes, there is. It's encouraging to see all they've done. You can find some of their stories in the online archives of the college website, though most of the material there pertains to university sponsored groups. Several articles about the Launchpad have even been published in business magazines. I'll send you some links by email tomorrow or Monday."

"Great, thanks. I think that could be a big encouragement to students if they see how others have gone before them and made their ideas into a business." Additional research could also answer the question that had been nagging at her since her conversation with her friends at the campus coffee shop. Did the Launchpad discriminate against women entrepreneurs?

The evening ended in a bland but pleasant tone. Eden's stomach was uncomfortably full, but it had been worth it. To her relief, Marcus didn't try to kiss her goodnight or show any affection when he walked her to her car.

As she drove home, questions tumbled through her mind. Was Marcus a kindred spirit? Aside from their mutual interest in business, that was easy to answer. No, he wasn't. She'd wondered if he might be an equal in terms of their shared business orientation, but that wasn't enough, and she knew it. Had she been unconsciously motivated by a desire to be treated like an adult, and a social invitation from her teacher filled the need? Eden frowned. Maybe a little bit.

A question that cried out even louder. Why had she been so adamant about meeting a Christian online when she willingly went out with a man she'd been sure was not? What was the true nature of her walk of faith? She had to admit, once in a while she caught herself almost holding God at arm's length instead of basking in the loving truths she claimed to fully believe. Yes, she had those moments too. Bottom line, she wanted to share her spiritual side with whatever man entered her life. Not just any man would fill what God wanted for her and what she wanted for herself.

Sometimes her outwardly faithful habits clashed with a cool heart of doubt. Where had that come from? A faded memory slipped into her mind, herself as a college junior arguing with her mother on the phone while tears streamed down her face. Her mother's plea for her to return home dug up the tender young roots of Eden's new life in North Carolina, tossing them to the wind. And at the same time, a voice inside her told her God wasn't for her. He loved her, of course, but he wasn't *for* her. He didn't care about her happiness or her best interest, as long as she was useful to her alcoholic father. Her father had controlled her life for too many years. She'd believed too quickly that she'd finally found freedom from his control.

Lord, is it true I've believed you aren't for me all these years because I lost my happy life back when I was in college? Have I been bitter against you all these years without knowing it? Was I convinced you weren't on my side because people tried to control and persuade me to do what they wanted? Her throat tightened and her eyes stung. She blinked and narrowed her eyes on the darkened road. More tears followed. She swiped them away and slowed the car as oncoming lights became blurry.

Tears of regret and loss. And something else that almost took her breath away. Anger. She was *angry* at God for not being for her. Was that fair? Was anger behind the periodic moments of tepid faith?

True, in the last few months she'd encountered hidden anger toward memories involving her parents and Gerry, like a lion let out of its cage. She still wasn't sure what to do with it all. But God too? Yes.

But what about her children? If she hadn't returned to Indiana, she wouldn't have met Gerry and she wouldn't have Jordan, Claire, and Brent. She'd loved Gerry, and they'd been reasonably happy together. Yet, the moment of returning to Indiana from North Carolina as a college student had been so wrenching, she thought she'd never recover. She did, but a twisted, unwholesome root of bitterness and resignation had grown into place. Was that root still there, unchallenged?

❧   ❧   ❧

Eden's uncomfortable thoughts stayed with her through the next morning as she prepared to go to church. There, she might have more insight into her current state. *Where am I now, Lord? Am I a hypocrite, giving you activities but not my heart? How is it I'm not healed when it all happened so long ago?*

Pastor Ryan began a new series that morning on God's character, beginning with his holiness. Eden listened attentively during the message and took notes but doubted it would help her resolve her feelings. The question was, did she *still* doubt that God was for her, that he was in her corner? *Show me, Lord. Am I still mad at you and doubt you're for me?*

Following the service, Eden greeted several acquaintances in the church lobby, then hurried home. The topic of God's holiness wedged her even further from him since she felt anything but holy. A large slice of it emerged from her evening with Dr. Siler. She had no business going on a date with him, not because he was her professor, but because he wasn't partner material. First, spiritually. Not long ago, she'd said to her daughters over dinner that she wanted a partner, an equal. Marcus wasn't either one, and she'd known it, yet had gone out with him, anyway. He'd likely always look down on her professionally, or else she'd assume he was. And the question that had grazed her mind the previous evening as she drove home, had it stroked her ego to be asked out by her professor, who was a respected academic as well as attractive?

Once she was home, Eden went to the kitchen and slumped onto the stool, leaning her elbows on the island. A faith partner first. Then a partner showing mutual respect. Non-negotiable. She'd lived too many years with Gerry treating her as the one who kept the home fires going, keeping her in the dark while he made important decisions involving the business, managed people, and kept their family supplied with food and housing. In retrospect, their lives had had little intersection apart from the kids. She'd made it possible for him to excel in his own passion. Now she wanted more. She wanted a partner, and she wanted her own passion. And equal who would applaud and encourage *her* passion.

Her mind went to Colin, and she smiled. A sad smile since she'd ruined her chance with him. He'd challenged her because he respected her. She hadn't recognized it at the time because of her stubbornness, her blind spot, born of previous experiences. She wouldn't do that in her next relationship if there was a next time. She'd face her blindness with courage. Beginning with Marcus.

After making a lunch of heated leftovers, Eden took her plate to her office and turned on her computer. That morning, while she was at church, Marcus had sent her the links he'd promised. She'd start there.

An hour passed. Eden had found the winners of the Launchpad awards for the previous five years. Over that period, there had been twenty winners, made up of both individuals and teams. About seventy percent had been male. That statistic was useless, because she had no way of knowing how many of each gender had applied. Maybe eighty percent of the applicants had been male, but only seventy percent of the male applicants had won. She shook her head. No way to know.

She chewed on the end of her pen. What *did* she know? She could start there. She knew it was difficult for young people, especially young women, to get started as an entrepreneur. Young women often had obstacles many men didn't have, small children, parental needs, or an unsupportive home culture, as she'd had, one that didn't foster a daughter's unique passion and potential.

The possible obstacles in the Launchpad were nameless, formless, and unmeasurable. Could be simple favoritism or heartless discrimination. Or maybe the best ideas had won, period. Impossible to prove in the realm of ideas. Again, she should start with what she knew. Focus on the needs of women standing on the threshold of a new business, instead of trying to ferret out foul play in the Launchpad. Was there a way she could help *these* women, like Mariella, whose passion for their ideas burned bright in their eyes?

Next, she would research existing organizations for female entrepreneurs. Another hour passed and Eden found several strong nonprofits for women already involved in business. That encouraged her, but little existed locally for women just finishing their degrees or starting out with their ideas. Once they'd been shoved from the cocoon of university life, as Mariella had expressed, they faced a cold, uncaring world in which they were already disadvantaged by their gender.

She glanced toward the window. Late afternoon shadows streaked the sky preparing for dusk. Her research and intuition told her that things had improved for women in the last few decades, but not enough. Was there anything she could do to help them in those critical first years?

The next day after class, Eden headed to Dr. Siler's office before she lost her nerve. She knew she could take the easy route and wait until he asked her out again, then decline. But it might take another week or more, if he even approached her again, and her emotions jumped around too much for her to wait. No, she'd act on her conviction and face the consequences.

Her quiet knock on his door brought a glance, then a smile from where he spoke on the phone. He gestured her into his office. She sat quietly, waiting for the call to end.

"Eden, I wasn't expecting you. Is everything okay?"

"Yes, of course. I enjoyed our dinner very much." She swallowed. "I just wanted to tell you that even though I enjoyed it and appreciate your friendship and your insights, I don't think we should see each other socially. I'm . . . I'm not sure we're that compatible."

She couldn't read his face. He stared at her for a silent moment. "It hasn't been long, Eden. How can you know?"

"I just sense it, that's all. For one thing, my personal Christian faith is important to me. Am I right in thinking you might be nonreligious?"

He shrugged. "I, uh. Yes, that's accurate. I was raised nominally Catholic but haven't practiced much since grade school. So, yes, that would be a difference. And if you say it's important to you . . ."

"Yes, it is. I've had ups and downs over the years myself, but I'd say it's a very important element in my life."

Marcus linked his fingers over his stomach. "Aside from that, maybe we don't sharpen each other."

Eden stiffened then forced a chuckle. "I know *I'm* not sharpening *you.*"

A smile played around his lips. "I was referring to like-mindedness in a variety of areas. Actually, you do sharpen me. That's why I wanted to get to know you, Eden. I find you courageous and determined, and I like that. Your mind is sharp too, despite being out of school for so many years. I think you have natural instincts in business. You probably don't even need to be here."

Her mouth dropped open, then she closed it. "Thank you for saying that, Marcus. I'm touched that you think so." She gave him a crooked smile. "I'd like to stay friends if that's okay. Please know that it isn't you, it's just not the right fit."

"Yes, of course. I understand. We might not have enough things in common aside from our love of business. Thanks, Eden. This won't reflect on your grade." They both laughed. The pounding of her heart eased. "And hopefully I'll continue to sharpen you in class."

"No doubt about that, Dr. Siler."

Eden strolled to her next class, lighter and more peaceful. He'd taken it well, and she'd been surprised and touched by his comment. Maybe she didn't need to be in school pursuing that piece of paper that had eluded her so many years ago. Maybe her real reason to be there was completely different.

Chapter Ten

Orange, brown, and yellow leaves swirled through the air like confetti, carpeting Eden's back porch and landing on the covered patio furniture. In two weeks would be Thanksgiving and Brent's visit. Eden hadn't seen him since the previous Christmas. She had a hollow feeling that his visits would become more infrequent as the years went by. She looked forward to meeting Kelly and seeing how her and Brent's relationship progressed in months to come.

Normally, she'd have planned the Thanksgiving menu by this time. Her recent round of midterms had thrown her orderly life into a tornado. With a smidgen of focus, she could pull together a reasonable Thanksgiving feast at least a few days before her children arrived. She might even have to order a pie instead of making one. Or ask Claire, who loved to bake when she wasn't resetting broken bones or staunching hemorrhaging gunshot wounds.

Eden glanced at her bedroom clock as she attached her second earring in front of the mirror. Only five minutes before she had to leave for church. In the last two weeks of Pastor Ryan's series on God's attributes, he'd spoken about God's wisdom and his omnipresence. It disturbed Eden to notice how distant she still felt after hearing the pastor's impassioned words, as if a layer of doubt still coated her heart. Was God's wisdom working on *her* behalf? Had his wisdom led her back to Indiana all those years ago instead of allowing her to stay in North Carolina?

It wasn't as though she'd lived since then in the shadow of that trauma. But her recent epiphany revealed she'd unconsciously developed a chip on her shoulder that hadn't completely vanished with time. To combat her apparent grudge against God, she spent more time than usual in prayer, drilling into the resistance that had formed so long ago. *Show me, Lord. I want to believe you're for me. I want to find your joy again. I want it to reach my heart and not just my head.*

The pastor had announced the previous week that the next topic would be God's sovereignty. Eden was tempted to skip church that day, sure that the topic would heighten and harden the walls that surrounded her. But dutifully, ever dutifully, she went. And sang praise songs and listened. And took a few notes. *He controls the course of world events; he removes kings and sets up other kings.* She'd written the verse from Daniel on the back of her program. *In his heart, a man plans his course, but the Lord determines his steps.* This from Proverbs. Was he equally involved in *her* small life? And was it always good?

The service ended with a melodic chorus and final prayer. A hollowness rang inside, despite the upcoming holiday. The prospect of returning to an empty house deepened her heaviness. Maybe instead, she'd take herself to lunch and start her Christmas shopping.

"Eden?" An unfamiliar male voice called close behind her.

She turned and her eyes widened. Colin Taylor stood in the row behind her, an impish smile on his face. "Colin, what are you doing here?" The same dark wavy hair streaked with hints of gray, same angular clean-cut jaw with a cleft chin, the same hazel eyes warming her with a direct gaze. She'd recognize him anywhere, even after five months. Especially because he'd inhabited some of her random thoughts recently. "I mean, it's nice to see you."

His smile widened. "Likewise. I didn't know you attended here. I've been coming to this church for a couple months, but normally attend the early service. That's why we haven't seen each other. How have you been?" His voice sobered and his face looked almost apologetic, probably because he'd faded out of her life with no explanation.

"Good, um, really busy. I just finished midterms, so you can imagine." Her heart thudded inside her chest. Why was she reacting like a pre-teen with a crush?

"How did your first round of midterms go after years of not being a student?"

"Fine, I think. I'm glad they're over, or almost. I have one more this week, but it's not a big one. Then I'll be on break for the holidays."

"Bet you're looking forward to that."

"*So* much. I can't wait. My son and his girlfriend are coming in from California, so I'll have all three of my children home at once. That's getting to be a rare event. How have you been?"

"I've been well. Would you be interested in catching up over lunch? I promise I won't pressure you."

She laughed, heat creeping into her face. "I've already excused myself for misjudging you. We'll start over, okay?" The words were out of her mouth before she realized how he might interpret them, but that was okay. He could take it as an invitation, and that would be fine.

"Yes, we will." His gaze caught hers with a twinkle.

"I'd enjoy catching up over lunch. I'll behave myself to make up for last summer."

They exchanged a smile and threaded their way through the humming crowd filling the aisle. Eden was relieved that they could joke about the tension of their first date.

"Are you in the mood for Thai or would you prefer something else?" Colin turned to her. "I believe I chose the last time."

"Thai is perfect. The one up on the corner?" They stood together near the double door as people filed past.

"That's the one. I'll meet you in the entrance."

She never thought she'd see Colin Taylor again. Her lonely day had taken a surprising turn. Sovereignty of God? She wasn't sure but was glad in any case. A smile teased her lips as she drove the short distance.

Colin waited for her inside The Thai Pad Restaurant. A hostess led them through the dining room, decorated in yellow and mauve. Eden breathed in the delicate scent of basil and coconut.

They slid into a booth. "Eden, I'm sure you thought I blew you off last summer after our one dinner together."

She stared back at him and swallowed. He got right to the point, but she liked that. Fewer chances for misunderstandings. "I assumed that despite my apology, I'd offended you deeply."

Colin shook his head. "No, not at all. At first, I thought you might be closed or stubborn, I'll be honest. At the time, I didn't understand your reaction, but I appreciated your apology and your self-awareness. It's a good sign when someone recognizes their own mistakes. Shortly after that, I had a huge client that needed a lot of attention, then I met someone else, and we dated for a few months. That's why I didn't reach out to you again. But I'm glad to see you today."

She gave him a rueful smile. So, he *had* been put off by her knee-jerk reaction. And he'd met someone else as well, but apparently was no longer involved with her. "I owe you an explanation. I told you about my alcoholic dad. For years, I felt like my life was controlled by the ups and downs of his alcoholism, which I always viewed as his choice rather than an illness. That's why it always made me so angry. Then when I got married, over time, I saw occasional controlling behaviors in my husband. A lot of my reactions were subconscious or forgotten. But just a week before meeting you, I had a date with someone who triggered all those feelings, and I went on the defensive."

Colin nodded as she spoke, a smile playing around his mouth. "So, it spilled over on me. It happens."

An Asian waitress placed glasses of cold water and menus on the table. "You were perfectly appropriate," Eden said. "In fact, as you're aware, *you* influenced me to return to college. Just for the record, challenging people to become their best selves is definitely okay in my book."

"Glad to hear it. And it helps to know that bit of your background. You figured I was just one more to add to the controlling men list. Control benefits the controller, but a challenge benefits the one being challenged. Theoretically."

Her hand closed around the cool glass of water. "Well said, though it's still possible to pressure someone when you're strongly convinced it's in *their* best interest. If my friend is doing something harmful or not doing something helpful, I can challenge her to change her behavior. What she does or doesn't do, though, is up to her. If I keep trying to push her to see things my way or take my advice, then it becomes controlling. I'm sure I've done that to my children over the years."

"I probably have too. When it comes to people we care about, it can be a fine line between pressure and suggestion, one that's hard to distinguish unless we're self-aware. Or else the Holy Spirit gives us a kick."

She laughed. "Yes, I've been kicked plenty of times lately for different things."

The waitress returned to their table, order pad in hand. Colin looked up at her. "Three more minutes? We've been catching up."

Like old friends. A swell of warmth invaded Eden's chest. "We'd better decide now and catch up after." Their eyes met and locked for a moment. A tingle started deep inside her, though it felt cleaner, more solid than what she'd felt for Marcus.

"I like the Moo Ping," Colin said. "And you want the Pad Thai. Since we both like both, would you like to split them?"

"Great idea."

"You know how I'm spending my Thanksgiving," Eden said after they'd ordered. "What about you? Any plans with the kids?"

"I have a younger sister, Gaelin, who lives outside Chicago. My daughter April and I are driving there for the long weekend. I think I told you my son, Davis, lives in Colorado. I'll go see him over Christmas. I'm flying out the day after so I can spend Christmas day here with April and my mother. Davis and I will hang out, ski a few days, and I'll be back January third."

"Christmas in Colorado. How nice." A cozy cabin in a snowy forest filled Eden's mental vision. "Maybe you'll have snow."

"On the slopes, especially. I'd like to see some flurries while I'm there, as long as I don't get stuck in a blizzard."

Eden laughed. "Don't pray too hard for those flurries."

"It snows often, but at the lower elevations, it doesn't always stick around. I love it out there, really. Feels so free to be near the mountains."

Eden smiled at him. "You're lucky. Davis gives you a reason to visit regularly. And it sounds like you both enjoy some of the same things. But I thought Denver was a mile high. Do you call that lower elevation?"

"I'm comparing five thousand feet to *fourteen* thousand." Colin chuckled. "Although most of the ski areas aren't that high, some get close. The one we like best is at thirteen thousand, which is one of the highest ski resorts in the country."

Eden struggled to imagine enjoying being so high in the air on a snowy incline. As she marveled at his statement, the waitress arrived with a tray of steaming plates. "Moo Ping . . ." She placed a plate of skewered meat with rice on the table in front of Colin. "And Pad Thai." Then the noodles and two extra plates.

Colin reached for her hand. "Pray?"

Eden nodded and slipped her hand into his while he murmured a brief prayer, including gratitude they'd run into each other again.

They released hands, though his thumb lingered, leaving a pulse of electricity behind.

"This looks and smells fabulous."

"What did you think of the sermon this morning?" he asked. When she hesitated, he pinned her with a questioning gaze, though humor danced there too. "Don't tell me you were napping."

She wiped her mouth. "With such a topic? Hardly. Honestly, I struggle a little with the idea of God's sovereignty. Lately I've realized I'm kind of fearful of it, like I don't have choices, or like everything's predetermined. As I shared with you before, during my childhood, I often felt powerless. My parents made decisions that affected me in some bad ways, and lately those memories have started popping to the surface more than they used to. But from God's perspective, I'm sure his sovereignty has to be a good thing."

"Especially if you believe in his goodness." Colin pulled a piece of meat from the skewer and popped it in his mouth. "If you do, then it's a comfort."

"I *did* consider it a comfort when I first became a believer at the age of ten. In the midst of the chaos of my home life, I had security and hope. But life happened, and it didn't always seem like someone benevolent was in control. I'm not saying I had a terrible life, but I never felt like it was really mine. I've always felt like I was at the service of other people, and my wants didn't matter." And that included Gerry.

"It makes me sad to hear that." Colin's face was serious. "But it's understandable you'd feel that way growing up in an alcoholic home."

Eden swallowed and blinked as the ache of old wounds radiated in her throat. "Maybe that means I haven't fully embraced God's goodness." She heard her voice come out small, like a child's, as she stated what she'd only just realized. "Is Pastor Ryan planning to talk about that too?"

"Next week. That'll dovetail with sovereignty, you'll see. You'd better be there." He picked up his fork again and pointed it in her direction, along with a mischievous grin. "I'll quiz you afterward."

"A quiz? Oh, no." She put her hands over her eyes for a second. "You have no mercy. I just finished midterms." At least he was assuming they'd see each other again, at the very least, in church. Maybe God's sovereignty had led Colin to attend the late service that day. "I'll work on it, though. I *am* curious about something. You told me what you went through with your ex-wife. Did you still feel comfort from God's sovereignty back then?"

"Absolutely. That's the only way I got through it. My ex-wife, Adele, came to me out of the blue and said she was moving out. I think there was another man because she found one awfully quick. My world was upside down from one day to the next. The knowledge that God is good and was overseeing things was a huge comfort to me, because I knew it would eventually be okay. He thought I was up to the challenge and promised to walk with me through it."

Eden dropped her gaze to the table, regret frothing up inside, alongside a wave of longing for the kind of faith he had. "I wish I'd done that. I didn't consider that there might be something good in the way things were turning out. It just wasn't what I wanted."

"Did something good come out of it?"

She lifted her eyes to his. "Yes, of course. My children." She couldn't stop a smile from rising to her face. "How can I regret when I have them? And I developed a lot of determination. Not sure if that was always good when it was misdirected. I was determined to escape home and probably got married too young. I don't regret my marriage, but I'd have done it later if I'd been in a better place." She sighed and leaned against the vinyl of the booth. "Everything's so clear when you look back."

"Have you ever asked yourself why you didn't just tell your mother no, you weren't going back?"

"Many times. I've often wondered why I was so weak I had to cave in. And what my life might have been like if I'd done that." Maybe she'd have fallen out permanently with her family then instead of later. Maybe she'd be living in North Carolina instead of Indiana.

"Do you blame yourself too, or only God?" His voice and his gaze were soft. No way could she accuse him of being pushy just then. Rather, his question x-rayed her heart, though in a gently prodding, caring way.

"You're messing with my head." Eden squinted at him. "No, that's a valid question. I do both. I should really blame myself, but it's easier to blame God."

"At least you're honest. The cool thing about God's sovereignty and goodness is that even when you're the one who makes the wrong choice, he can make it okay. Not that there aren't consequences, but he can still rearrange the pieces."

"Like a safety net to save his children from themselves. Or others." She couldn't block her smile. "I see a little better why you say it's comforting." She did. And something new and warm pushed inside her like spring flowers pushing through hardened soil.

Their conversation lightened as Colin described some of his hobbies and the tempo of his daily life. "Since I work for myself, I can create a rhythm, but there are still intensely busy periods. I try to run a few times a week and do some weights to stay fit, but for enjoyment I kayak on one of the nearby rivers, or I golf with some buddies. I like local jazz concerts when I can find them. When I'm in Colorado during warm months, my son and I hike a lot. At times, I dream of moving out there when I retire."

She wiped her mouth and pushed her plate aside. "I enjoy my hobbies, but for the last two years it feels like that's all I did. Most people surround work with hobbies. I know I shouldn't feel bad about it." She remembered Sydney's statement that her life was just fine, if she was content with it. "I needed a break and ended up doing a variety of things. I went to the gym. I took some watercolor classes." The activities blended in a blur without seeming very significant. "Somehow, I stayed busy, and the time went by. Now I miss all that free time. I really enjoyed learning to paint."

"What do you like to paint?"

She shrugged. No one ever asked about her painting. "I like landscapes and flowers. I prefer subjects that are part of life. A town on a hillside, a bridge, things like that. In fact, as soon as my last exam was done, I pulled out a photo of the Ponte Vecchio I'd taken on my trip to Florence and started sketching out a painting I want to do."

"That's an excellent way to start your fall break. And it'll keep your vacation memories alive every time you look at it."

"Yes, I was thinking the same thing. Watercolor isn't easy, so I didn't keep my early attempts. I *did* put a couple in frames and hung them up in my house."

"You must have a talent in art, among other things," he said. "I'd love to see them sometime."

Eden had never thought about whether she was talented as a watercolor artist. "I enjoy it and find it relaxing, but I haven't done it since summer. I should carve out time somewhere." That seemed an impossible challenge in that season of her life, except during school breaks.

"There's always next summer."

They both smiled. As his soft gaze met hers, the electric current ramped up a few volts.

Chapter Eleven

The oven timer squawked into the quiet morning, which was about to become noisier with the onset of Thanksgiving. From where she worked in the kitchen, Eden could hear the twins murmuring on the staircase as they descended. Claire had made a pumpkin pie to contribute to Thanksgiving dinner and Eden had found time that morning to make another one.

She slipped on an oven mitt and pulled a coconut custard pie from the oven, its sweet, nutty aroma swirling around her. Despite her heavy schedule that fall, Eden couldn't bear to relinquish any of the holiday preparations she'd done for three decades. An orange and green wreath of silk flowers and plastic gourds hung from the front door. Along the mantle over the fireplace in the living room, a leafy autumn garland flickered with tiny white lights. Red and orange candles clustered on end tables and in the center of the coffee table.

The dining room table, her crowning decorative creation, exploded with earthy colors. Plates, tablecloth, napkins, placemats, and a centerpiece all coordinated in oranges, yellows, and reds. Eden had told herself the kids were used to these seasonal touches, and she didn't want to deprive them just because she was a busy college student now. But truthfully, she also craved the creative outlet and longed for the fall holidays as a welcome change to her intense academic concentration of the three previous months.

"Morning, Mom. Boy, does it smell good in here." Jordan wore sweats and slippers, and her eyes were still crinkled with sleep behind her glasses. Claire followed close behind her into the kitchen. Eden gave each of them a tight hug. "It's your favorite. Coconut cream," she said to Jordan.

"I wait all year for your coconut pie, Mom." Jordan's high ponytail swung as several shorter layers escaped and dangled around her face. She pulled a mug from the cupboard shelf and filled it with coffee.

"And *my* pie will become your new favorite." Claire gave them a confident grin.

"Except that you tried a new recipe this year, I noticed. The advantage of us sharing an apartment. I know most of your secrets. So, you're experimenting on us, Claire. On Thanksgiving Day, no less."

"No worries." Claire waved the air absently. "I used an excellent source. Anyway, how many ways can you wreck a pumpkin pie?" She opened the fridge and scanned the crammed shelves.

"Are Brent and Kelly up yet?" Eden asked. "They seemed pretty beat last night when you all came in from the airport."

Their flight from Los Angeles had been delayed. Claire and Jordan had waited at the airport an extra hour to pick them up before driving to Wadesboro. Shortly after arriving, they'd both claimed fatigue and went up to their respective bedrooms.

Kelly was an attractive but reserved young woman. Her petite frame and luminous green eyes framed with a dark long bob gave her a childlike appearance, though despite her fatigue, she'd seemed vigilant and tense. During their brief acquaintance the previous evening, she didn't say much, deferring to Brent on several occasions. She was likely intimidated to meet those who might become her new family. It wouldn't cross Eden's mind to be anything but welcoming and warm to her visitor, whether she became a daughter-in-law or not. The countdown had begun. Eden had four days to convince Kelly that she would fulfill no negative mother-in-law stereotypes.

"I think Kelly might be up now. The bathroom door in the main hall was closed. Brent's door is still closed. Remember how long he used to sleep on weekends and holidays? Maybe when he's on vacation, he reverts to the old pattern." Jordan went to the stove and took a deep breath from the cooling pie. "Mmm. Can't wait to try this."

"He was legendary in high school, remember, Mom?" Claire settled onto one stool along the kitchen island.

"I do remember." Eden perched on a stool next to Claire, savoring her daughters' presence in her home. "But as soon as he got to college, he became almost regimented in discipline."

"Like Dad. Wonder where *those* genes came from." Claire laughed. "I had to learn the hard way in nursing school."

Eden's phone buzzed from where it perched on the window ledge. She rose to look at it and couldn't stifle a broad smile. Colin. *Happy Thanksgiving, Eden. Bet it smells good at your house.* She nodded to the phone as a whiff of coconut enveloped her. *April and I left yesterday, and we got to my sister's around five. Hope your kids arrived safely. Enjoy the day!*

"Who's that, Mom? Or is it private? Your face is all pink. And you're smiling ear to ear." Jordan sidled up to Eden and tried to peer at her phone.

Eden pulled it away. "It is? My face is pink?" She knew she couldn't hide a thing from Jordan and Claire.

"Lemme see." In an instant, Claire was beside her sister. "Who is it, Mom? Do you have a new *friend*?" Her eyebrows wiggled up and down.

No sense in trying to keep Colin a secret. Even if, at that point, they were only friends. Eden sighed and rolled her eyes. "If you must know, yes, I have a new friend. It's not a boyfriend, but he *is* a friend."

"Who'll become a boyfriend, is my guess by the look on your face." Jordan's voice was triumphant.

"Yippee! Mom has a friend," crowed Claire.

"Stop, you two. You're embarrassing me."

They both stood in silence, still pressing around her. "So?" Jordan's eyes were wide with expectancy.

Eden moved away from them and returned to her stool.

"She's sitting down."

"Must be serious."

"Spill it, Mom. What's his name?"

"Hey, what's going on here?" Brent's voice sounded in the doorway. He wore sweats too, and his hair spiked at random angles.

Eden turned and gave a weak smile to her son. It always struck her how much he resembled Gerry, tall and wiry with wavy dark hair and intense brown eyes. There was the same set of his jaw, with serious intensity, analyzing the situation before him.

"Good morning, sweetie. Your sisters are harassing me, as usual. Do you want some coffee? There's a fresh pot I just made. Cream is in the fridge."

"Where cream usually is. You're stalling, Mom," Jordan said. She looked up at her brother. "Mom has a new friend, and she's about to tell us about him. You came just in time."

Brent joined them at the kitchen island, an expectant look on his sleepy face and an empty coffee cup in one hand.

Eden let out a growl. "Okay, I'll bring you all up to date, then you must leave me alone about him. His name is Colin. I met him on an online date last June. For whatever reason, we didn't continue meeting, but I ran into him in church a couple weeks ago. We had lunch and kind of picked up where we'd left off." She could see Jordan and Claire about to speak. "We're just friends at this point. Nothing but friends."

"Are you sure? Don't you even like him a little?" Claire set her elbows on the island counter.

"Yes, I like him. But I don't know him that well yet." There, that was a fully honest answer, minus the fragile hope that still dangled inside her.

"Have you seen him again since the lunch?" Jordan asked.

Eden shook her head. They'd tried. "It was less than two weeks from Thanksgiving. Between his work and my school project, we couldn't find time."

"Huh. Doesn't sound serious if you can't even find time for a coffee date." Jordan reached for her cup and took a sip, as if she'd just remembered it. "But it might be serious soon."

"His name is?" Brent finally spoke.

"Colin." Claire and Jordan said at the same time.

"What does he do?" Brent asked.

"He's an attorney. He works in real estate. He also has a few rental properties around town." Eden would give them the demographic details so Colin wouldn't become the center of their conversation for the next three days. "He's fifty-one and divorced. His wife deserted him some years ago. He has two kids, a son who lives in Colorado and a daughter who's a junior at I.U. He and his daughter are spending Thanksgiving with his sister near Chicago." She stopped and her eyes panned their faces. "Any more questions?"

"Are you going to see him again?" This from Claire.

"Of course. I mean, I think so. After the holiday, I would think." They'd made no specific plans, but had exchanged text messages several times since their lunch together. "He started attending the same church I do, so I'm sure I'll at least see him there."

"If he's smart, he'll snag you before someone else does." Jordan laughed and leaned forward across the granite island to swat Eden on the arm.

"Ha. Someone else like who?" Eden reached for her own coffee cup.

"Yeah, the professor is old news," Claire said. Of course, she and Jordan were up to date on Dr. Siler.

"The professor?" Brent's brow furrowed.

"Mom went out with one of her teachers a couple of times. She's more radical than any of us thought." Jordan laughed.

Brent's eyebrows shot up. "Really? You're allowed to do that?"

Eden chuckled and waved at the air. "I asked him the same question, and he didn't seem concerned. I guess my age makes me immune to teacher-student protocol. But he wasn't my type, nor a believer." Secretly, she thought her decision must have pleased God, since she ran into Colin just weeks later.

Brent frowned. "Maybe this Colin guy will be more suitable. Are you meeting people in your classes? There must be other older students on campus."

"Yes, there are a few, but surprisingly, my closest new friends are all in their twenties," Eden said. "Isn't that funny? I met one young woman, and she introduced me to her friends. It's nice that they accept me even though I could be their mother."

"That's kind of weird, isn't it, Mom? Are they, like, my age or younger?" Brent cocked his head, the troubled expression still on his face. "You ought to hang out with people your own age."

Eden shot him an indignant expression. "Who said my friends have to be my age? In fact, my current age and prior business experience are a help to these women, since they're young and are still finding their footing."

"So, you're like a mother hen for them," Claire said. "I think it's cool."

"I'm trying hard *not* to be a mother hen. That's not what they want at their age. I'm more of a helpful friend, a sounding board, and maybe an indirect mentor." Then Eden chuckled. "I should only be a mother hen to *you* three chicks."

Brent found his smile. "Who're you calling a chick?"

"Good morning, everyone." Kelly entered the kitchen and offered a shy smile. She was fully and neatly dressed, a burgundy cable knit sweater setting off her dark hair. Brent's grin spread wider.

"Good morning, Kelly." Eden turned to the doorway and spoke in a bright tone. She went to Kelly and gave her a hug. Kelly responded stiffly at first then relaxed into Eden's embrace. "I hope you slept well," Eden told her. "Coffee's on the counter, if you're a coffee-drinker." At least Brent's interrogation had been interrupted. It struck her that he must be a rule guy. Where'd that come from? Maybe Gerry and her both, though she was gradually breaking out. The thought brought a flash of humor laced with rebellion.

Eden stole a moment to respond to Colin before they all got involved in meal preparation. *Hi! I'm glad you got safely to your sister's house. I hope you all enjoy the holiday. My three are here as well as my son's girlfriend. Happy Thanksgiving!* She didn't need to add that he was the topic of her daughters' interrogation. He might think she was rushing things, and she certainly didn't want that. So, it was a boring and speedy text, but at least she'd responded to him.

As the morning progressed, Eden enlisted her houseguests, including Kelly, in helping with the meal preparation. As Eden had predicted, having a task seemed to put Kelly more at ease. She took part in the conversation as they prepared the meal and seemed to enjoy their banter. At the same time, she worked with diligence, trimming green beans, and preparing the sweet potatoes. Traces of dry humor slipped out occasionally while they worked.

Brent peeked over Kelly's shoulder. "Cut those in half and more on a slant, Kelly. That's the way we've always done it."

Eden frowned, glanced at him, and back to Kelly. "It's okay, Kelly, you're doing a great job. It doesn't have to be the way it always was. Where's the creativity in that?" She kept her voice light, although a surprising bolt of frustration shot up inside her.

The exchange hovered over her like the smell of burnt toast while irritation simmered inside. *Calm down, Eden.* Gerry used to correct and criticize her cooking, since he was the restaurant owner and thought he had the right to do it. She understood years later that this habit caused her insecurity as a cook, which she mostly overcame after his death, though it took several years. For him, there was a correct way to do everything and not much room for variation. Was her son becoming her late husband?

"Kelly, when will you finish your architecture program? You were telling me a little last night, but you both were so tired I didn't want to ask." Eden smiled across the island at the younger woman.

A timid, but authentic smile stretched across Kelly's face. "Next spring, I should be finished. I'm still technically an undergrad, even though this is my fifth year. That's normal for architecture."

"I've heard it's a tough program. Lots of late nights finishing projects," Claire said.

"It is." Brent spoke up. "She works like crazy." He glanced at Kelly. "Don't you? It's hard to get together at certain times when projects are due."

Eden's emotional tempest had only started to calm when the veiled accusation in Brent's voice stirred it up again. She saw Kelly flinch and found herself silently saying, *no, no!* "It's not as though Kelly *chooses* to be extra busy so you can't get together." She directed her statement at Brent, whose eyes widened at the uncharacteristic edge in her tone. "I'm sure you remember what it was like being a student and having deadlines."

Brent stared at her and blinked. His face was impassive. "I wonder if her career will end up being as intense as the education has been."

Kelly shrugged. "Shouldn't be, though I guess there will be intense periods, like with any job, including yours." She avoided Brent's eyes and then spoke to Eden. "The intensity of my program isn't constant. It's cyclical. Deadlines and stuff. I'm sure a job'll be the same. But it's okay because I love it."

"That's what counts," Eden said. "You're doing what makes your heart sing. You'll have ups and downs in any profession but doing what you love is a must." Her gaze wandered to Brent, who'd fallen silent.

Kelly shot him a tight glance. "Brent sometimes worries about how it would work if we had a family. He's more traditional than I am, I guess. I'd be willing to stay home for a few years, of course, for the kids. But I wouldn't want to give up my career altogether."

"We both agree that family is important," he said, as if reminding her.

"We'll see how it works out," Kelly finished with a half-smile, possibly to circumvent a volatile topic.

Eden suspected the two of them had discussed this before and it was a sore spot. And waiting to see how it worked out was a bad idea. "There's no right or wrong way, but it's important to agree in advance what you'd want to do when the time comes." They must have already discussed marriage and found they weren't on the same page when it came to her career. She sensed storm clouds about to gather around the young couple.

"What kind of architecture do you want to do? Residential?" Jordan asked, her question diverting the sudden tension in the room.

"I really like commercial, with an emphasis on combining offices with sustainable green spaces. An office complex should be a peaceful place to go, whether one is an employee or a client, not a block with mirrored windows and nothing more."

"Oh, I agree with that. I can picture it now. A pond and picnic tables for the employees to go at lunch, shade trees. A couple of ducks wandering around. All the stuff I don't have in *my* workplace." Jordan smirked.

They discussed Kelly's ideas and projects for a few more minutes, but Eden noticed her son stayed silent. Clearly, he loved Kelly but didn't appear to celebrate her ambitions for her career, nor her talent. There it was again, the concept of partnership and equality. Eden didn't know how it had become a theme for her, but there it was.

She longed to discuss this with Brent while he was there, knowing it would be a while before she had another chance. Silently, she prayed for an opportunity during his visit and that he'd have a receptive heart.

The turkey was due out of the oven in about ten minutes, so Eden snatched her phone and went to the living room to send Thanksgiving greetings to Marissa, Sydney, and Julia. She could easily guess who each woman was with and what she was doing at that moment. In a previous email and a couple of phone calls, she'd brought them up to date with Marcus, Colin, and midterms, but wanted them to know she was thinking of them that day.

As she turned to leave the living room, Claire appeared beside her. "You okay, Mom?"

"Yes, why?" She wedged her phone into her back pocket.

"I thought you and Brent were going to have it out. It got kind of tense in there."

"I'm sorry you sensed that. I was trying so hard to hide my frustration with your brother." She pressed her lips together, weighing her words. "I don't want to make a scene over Thanksgiving, but I don't like some of the views he's expressing. I didn't realize he was like that. Traditional in a rigid way."

"Kind of like someone else we know, right?"

Eden nodded. Her daughter had eyes in her head and a good memory. "Yeah. I guess that's where he got it from." She gave Claire a tight, fast hug. "I'm glad it's not just me being a pain."

"No, it's not you. I saw it. Made me mad too. He can be so dense sometimes. His way or the highway. Maybe Kelly can get through to him and they can talk about it."

"I hope so." How likely was Kelly to speak up for herself? She seemed rather timid, but she might be more confident when they were in California, far from prospective in-laws.

During the Thanksgiving meal, any agitation from the previous exchange fled away, at least on the surface. Each course progressed with banter, usually spurred by the twins, as well as other topics of conversation and appreciation for the food. With satisfied stomachs, they all played board games in the living room until the sun went down.

On Saturday afternoon, Eden was putting away some laundry and saw that Brent was in his room. She put his things on the bed, then turned to where he was crouched, rearranging his suitcase. "Brent, can I talk to you for just a minute?"

"Sure, Mom." He straightened and went to stand beside her, nearly a foot taller. "What's up?"

She glanced at the door and reached to shut it slightly in case Kelly heard them talking. "I wanted first to tell you I'm glad you brought Kelly for the holiday. I really like her. She's sweet and smart."

Brent smiled. "I'm glad you like her. It means a lot to me that you two seemed to hit it off so well. Mom, I think she's the one for me."

"That's wonderful. But—"

Brent waited and stared at her. "But what?"

Eden moistened her lips. "I felt like you were a bit harsh with her Thursday. You know, while we were preparing the food."

Her son's brow knit together, a familiar expression she'd seen all his life when he was perplexed or disagreed. "You did? I don't remember being harsh, as you call it."

"To me it seemed that you want Kelly to do things your way. She has her own ways of doing things, and part of love is being flexible with each other, validating each other. Let me put it another way. Can you validate *her* as much as she validates you?"

"I don't understand."

"Look, both of you have talents and dreams and interests that are separate. And personalities too. They're different, but you can share them together." She caught his gaze and held it. "I hope you show interest in what interests *her*. Just because you're considering her as your future wife and the mother of your children doesn't mean those are the only assets she has."

"What?" Brent's voice exploded like a pop gun.

Eden flinched. Tempted to back down to keep the peace, the simmering anger pushed her on. "You heard me. She's not only in your life to give you a smoothly running family while you go do your thing. It's a partnership." She'd just echoed a description of her own marriage, which only spurred her to continue.

"I know that. I'm not looking for a brood mare, *Mother*."

His acid tone felt like a slap. "I didn't say that. I'm talking about having a balance in your relationship. Her ways *and* your ways. Her dreams and yours, blending together. I know you love her, but Kelly doesn't exist to complement *you*. Lord willing, you'll complement *each other* and celebrate each other."

Brent's features tightened as he appeared to weigh her words. The familiar scrunch appeared between his brows. "You think I think it's all about me?" A defensive edge had crept into his voice.

"I'm only warning you about things *I've* learned over the years. And I want your relationship to be on good footing." Insistence coated her words. She had to make him understand. "I sensed tension the other day, so I think you need to work on this before marriage. Make sure your relationship is for and about *both* of you. The only reason I tell you these things is I want your relationship to succeed. It's vital that neither of you feels it's only about the other one."

Brent blinked twice. His jaw clenched. "Are you talking about whether she works or not when we have a family?"

"No, I'm not. That's between you two, if you get married and once you have children. I'm not only talking about her profession. I'm talking about her uniqueness. She's different from you, and I hope you'll support that uniqueness and allow it to shine. And she'll do the same for you, and it'll be wonderful." She searched his face for understanding. Brent's eyes had strayed from hers. "Brent, sweetie, I learned this much too late. Let's sit a minute."

She drew him to the bed, and they sat down. Her heart pounded as she pressed down the thread of anger still hanging. How could he not hear what she was saying? Was he bound to repeat the patterns of his father, regardless of what she expressed? Yet, she knew if she cut loose all the rage welling up inside her, he'd never hear her. Maybe even never speak to her again.

"I'm going to tell you something that in no way disrespects your father. He was a traditional man. We had a pretty good marriage, but there were times when I felt like he wasn't tuned into who I really was inside. He was all about you kids and his business, but I wasn't included in the mix as a person of my own. Neither of us really thought about it back then, so I'm not saying I was unhappy. I've seen the importance of this in retrospect. If you and Kelly get married, I wouldn't want her to ever feel that way, like her main purpose was to keep your life and household running smoothly. Loving someone doesn't mean just loving what they do for you. It means loving who they *are* and considering as important the things that are important to them. Do you understand what I'm saying?"

"Yeah, Mom." He squinted, but his face remained taut. "I never even noticed the stuff you're saying about Dad. I didn't know you felt that way."

"Of course, you didn't. You were a child. And then your father was killed when you were pretty young. I'm not really talking about how I felt then, but I realize now how important it is in a marriage to have a partnership. In the good sense, of course. I don't mean a business arrangement. Along with love and commitment, partners are *both* important in the relationship and they share what's important to them, even if it's different. You'd be surprised how many relationships aren't like that, tilted toward one person more than the other. Not always the man, either. And I want you two to have the best foundation possible."

Brent nodded, though his face was shuttered, cool. "I get it. Don't be selfish. Message received." They stood, and before she could speak again, he fled from the room. Her message hadn't gotten through. She'd controlled her tone and suppressed her anger, reined in her urgent need to make him understand. She'd parsed her words, begged for divine wisdom. But he hadn't understood.

Eden sighed. He'd likely only learn only from experience. Or else repeat the Godrey family cycle.

Chapter Twelve

Sunday afternoon, amidst hugs and held-back tears, Eden's weekend guests drove away. She stood on the porch and pulled her thick cardigan tighter around her shoulders as a chilly gust whipped up, matching the melancholy inside. She stayed outside until the taillights disappeared around the corner. Jordan and Claire would drop Brent and Kelly off at the airport, then return to their apartment in Indianapolis. Life would return to normal. The house would regain its empty post-holiday stillness.

The pall of quiet wouldn't last too long since classes would resume Tuesday. Tomorrow, she'd finish up her Christmas shopping, though the thought left her cold. She didn't enjoy being alone in the mall's bustle, but would anchor her thoughts on Christmas, only a few weeks away. Holidays would return.

For the present, she'd catch up on laundry, dishes, the clutter of four extra people in the house. The festive décor still dangled from the front door and in each room in a spent, lonesome way. After a moment of paralysis, Eden went to the kitchen and opened the dishwasher to empty it. Getting busy would help.

An hour and a half later, she checked her phone to see if Jordan had confirmed the safe delivery of Brent and Kelly to the airport, and the departure of their flight. She had, and they were on their way.

Eden had no idea if, with time, Brent would take to heart the motherly input she'd given him the previous day. She might have seemed pushy to him, but truthfully, she'd held back a roaring tidal wave. She'd been subdued, considering what she was feeling. He wasn't used to her talking to him like that. Speaking of it in advance seemed better than waiting until an issue arose, even though her son wasn't the most open or teachable of her children. He was his father's son, after all.

Throughout the remainder of the visit, he'd acted almost normal, though she detected a film of distance in his interactions with her, as well as a bit more consideration toward Kelly. Hopefully, that behavior wasn't only for Eden's benefit, but would continue once they left Indiana.

Just then, a text from Colin popped up on her phone, bringing warmth to her face. *I'm not used to sitting in a car for five hours! I had to swing by IU to drop April off, which added time. Just got home and I'm ready to go for a run. How was your holiday? Can we catch up by phone later?*

Yes. Absolutely.

Eden texted back. *Glad you made it home safely. My kids left a couple of hours ago. I'm home this evening, so available for a phone call whenever you get settled.* They hadn't talked on the phone before, though he'd sent a handful of text greetings since their Thai lunch. Maybe that was a new step.

Will call around six, if that's okay.

Great. I'll be here. She'd occupy her hands until then and hopefully her mind would follow along. Once the first phone call was completed, she'd surely be less nervous. She'd been relaxed at lunch with Colin that day, but for the moment, she felt like an adolescent getting her first phone call from a boy. She laughed out loud and shook her head. "Get a grip, Eden."

While the phone was still in her hand, she noticed text messages from her girlfriends. The messages had come in at different times over the weekend. She took an eager moment to scan each one. Marissa had spent the holiday with Jarrod and his daughter Bethany. Marissa's son, Sean, had driven up from Atlanta. It was the first time all four of them had been together, which was significant. Even more so, Marissa was now officially engaged. Eden smiled. She'd mark off one more.

Julia had responded Friday. *Happy Belated Thanksgiving, Eden! I just spent the holiday with about twenty of Craig's relatives. I'd met some of them at the wedding. We had another mini wedding reception for those who hadn't been able to come to Florence. Crazy time, but lots of fun. hope you had a wonderful holiday with all 3 of your kids and future daughter-in-law!*

Well, not yet. A thread of discomfort accompanied the question that hovered about Brent and Kelly's future, mixed with gladness for Julia. An only child to a single mother, she'd recently accumulated many family members on both sides of the ocean.

Sydney's text was humorous, of course, describing her first Thanksgiving with her new husband, his son, and her daughter. Eden smiled, then put down the phone. Back to work.

By the time the phone rang, Eden had stripped the beds, done laundry, and vacuumed and dusted the house. She'd have done that anyway, but it was a good outlet for her distraction. She'd tackle the decorations tomorrow. "Hi Colin. Welcome home. Were you able to unwind by going for a run?"

"Yeah, it felt great after being cooped up in the car. And of course, after eating way too much all weekend. When did this go from being a holiday of gratitude to a holiday of gluttony?" He laughed. "Need me a few more runs to make up for that."

Eden slipped onto the kitchen stool. "Glad you have that outlet." She should get back to the gym too. Most of her exercise routines had developed holes since her return to student life, though her daily walks across campus counted for something. Eden relaxed as they each recounted surface details of their holidays, glad for banality during their first phone conversation.

"Do you start classes again tomorrow?" he asked.

"Classes do start, but I don't have class on Mondays, thank goodness. I've enjoyed the longer weekends since it was such an adjustment for me getting thrown into college life again."

"Sounds like smart scheduling on your part."

A brief silence ensued, and Eden wondered if he'd ask her out.

"I'm off from class tomorrow but still need to do my last bit of Christmas shopping," she said. "Would you care to join me, or is shopping to be avoided at all costs?" She clapped a hand over her mouth. She'd asked him to go *shopping*. What was she thinking?

Colin laughed. "Eden, is that a male stereotype you're putting on me? I'd be happy to accompany you. I can take tomorrow afternoon off since it's not a heavily scheduled day following the holiday. I have a couple things to get too. And I enjoy the lights and everything during the holidays."

The following day, Eden stood inside the main entrance of the local mall, which was wedged between two department stores. She didn't know what had gotten into her, being the one to initiate with Colin. And shopping, of all things. He might have been on the verge of suggesting something, but she'd jumped in. He hadn't seemed to mind.

After another five minutes, she spied him dodging shoppers as he hurried toward the entrance. He slipped inside. "I'm sorry I'm late. There was a traffic tie-up out near the interstate. I should have texted you." His face was flushed, darkening his hazel eyes.

"No problem." Eden flexed her fingers inside her coat pockets, whether to warm them up or from nerves, she wasn't sure. "I was absorbing the energy of this place. I like to get all my shopping done in the first week or so of December to avoid the last-minute panic shoppers."

They turned to the hallway leading into the mall and joined the flow of shoppers carrying colorful bags and wearing puffy winter coats. "Totally agree on that one," he said. "In fact, I do most of my shopping online. Once in a while, though, I like to visit stores to see merchandise in person and also to keep one foot in the physical world of actual stores and real people."

"Good point. It's good to remember there *are* real people out there you can see without a screen." Eden scanned the festive scene. Twinkling garlands embellished with large red bows draped bannisters and handrails as far as she could see. The scent of cinnamon and toasted sugar wafted toward them from a nearby shop selling sweets. "I think of how things were when I was a child. My mom always took me with her grocery shopping, Christmas shopping, every kind of shopping. It never occurred to anyone that one day we wouldn't go to stores as much but do everything from home."

"Do you think we're becoming a nation of hermits, with ordering online, ordering takeout, and working from home?" They'd stopped in front of the massive triangular evergreen that stretched up to the second floor of the mall. Tiny white lights glowed from a pathway of sparkling red and white ornaments and ribbon festooned branches. Familiar holiday tunes floated through the air.

"No, not yet" she said. "You can't get this energy or visual enjoyment at home on the computer. And this place gets crowded every December, at least." She sighed, enjoying the ambiance of the mall and being with Colin. "I hope we don't get to the point of never leaving our homes for any reason. That would be sad." Eden's gaze panned the throngs of shoppers moving like colonies of ants through the cavernous levels of the mall, upstairs, downstairs, and vertically on escalators. "I'm not really a big shopper, despite how I was raised. I venture into the stores when I need something specific. I make my list and usually shop alone, so I can stay focused. I dash in, I dash out."

Colin dipped his head toward her. "I feel honored, then. Thanks for inviting me today."

Eden felt heat rise to her cheeks. "Christmas shopping is different from other kinds of shopping. It's a holiday outing, and certainly more fun with a friend."

His eyes latched onto hers as he smiled back. "So, what's on your list today?"

She blinked. "Yes, my list." She fished a swatch of paper from her pocket. "I've gotten a lot of it already. I still need a bottle of perfume for Jordan and something for my brother, Keith."

"I do remember you mentioned having a brother. He's older, right?" They moved away from the Christmas tree and started down an aisle flanked by shops.

"He's nine years older than I am, so it was like we were both only children. He lives in Salt Lake." She hadn't seen her brother in almost two years, but dutifully sent gifts for him and his daughter, Thea, each Christmas. He'd left home when she was ten, abandoning her to their dysfunctional family. He was almost a stranger to her, but she ought to reach out more often. Non dutifully. "What about you? What do you need?"

"I'm fortunate that I still have my mother, who's eighty-one and still pretty spry. April and I will spend part of the day with her. I'll pick her up at her retirement residence and she'll come over for a few hours. I've gotten her gifts, but still need a couple things for my son, Davis. A winter scarf and some jumper cables."

"That's so touching," Eden said, and they both laughed.

"Last year I got him a tool set, but I had it shipped."

"Good idea. The alarms would have surely gone off in the airport." They passed a department store. "Oh, I need to pop in here and get Jordan's perfume."

"I'll come with you." He saw her expression of surprise. "I don't mind, Eden. Really. Let's get some perfume." Humor laced his words.

They walked into the brightly lit store, and Eden made a beeline for the perfume counter. "This won't take long." So far, he was being very patient, but she didn't want to push it. Gerry had always been anything *but* patient on the rare occasions he agreed to accompany her to the mall.

An hour later, they'd finished with their lists. Eden relaxed, glad her rumblings of nerves had disappeared during the light conversation and banter. Colin was fun and relaxing company. She bought gifts for her brother and niece and a couple more impulse buys for the twins.

"Looks like we're done shopping," Colin said. "Would you like to get something to drink in that coffee shop, or do you need to get home?" He nodded toward a warmly lit restaurant with clusters of small tables and a pastry counter along the front.

Nothing awaited her at home but preparation for class the next day. An empty, quiet house? Or prolonging her moments with Colin? No brainer.

Soon Colin and Eden were settled at a small table in the corner of the busy restaurant. Her fingers encircled the steaming mug of chocolate on the table. "Remind me when you're going to Colorado. The day after Christmas?"

"Yes. I fly out early. Davis and I can celebrate the following day then do some skiing."

"Sounds like a great Christmas plan." Eden took a sip of the hot beverage and allowed it to warm her throat. "I've never been skiing."

"Never? I think you'd like it. Not sure, but you strike me as subconsciously adventurous." Colin's eyes danced with challenge.

Eden laughed aloud. "Me, adventurous? Not many people would accuse me of that. Why do you think I've lived in the same house for almost thirty years and never left Indiana? Stability has always equaled security for me. Some call it a rut. Even *I* think of it as a rut. Though I suspect I'm changing a little bit. Maybe being around college students has pushed me outside my own box."

Colin lifted a soaked tea bag from his cup and set it on a napkin. "Lots of people don't do well with change. Maybe you feel that way because of your childhood."

"You're right about that. Life was crazy. I felt like I had to create my own order by creating a rut and being unwilling to move." Not her best quality, but there it was.

"That's why I said *subconsciously* adventurous. There are a few examples I know about. You left home and went to North Carolina where you didn't know anyone. You took over your husband's restaurant after he passed away. And now you're a college student. You don't give yourself enough credit."

"Thanks for that. Maybe I don't. But I *do* think my box is getting bigger."

Colin grinned back as their eyes met. The vibration inside her radiated warmth. Suddenly feeling awkward, she looked down at the chocolate froth on the edge of her ceramic cup.

Colin broke the silence. "You told me your son and his girlfriend came for Thanksgiving. How did that go? Think she'll make a good daughter-in-law?"

Oh boy, *that* topic. She straightened against her seat. "I liked her. Her name is Kelly. She's studying architecture. But—" Eden paused. Did she want to get into that with Colin? Somehow, he made it easy to trust him with deeper issues.

"But?"

She sighed. "I observed some behaviors in my son, Brent, that bothered me. He didn't put Kelly down but didn't really validate her either. I almost got the feeling . . . well, like he thought his work was more important than hers." She shouldn't have brought this up. She didn't want to paint Brent in a negative light for Colin.

"Is she the type to stick up for herself?"

"I don't know. She seemed timid, but it might have been the context. She might want to please him and end up sacrificing herself. I think in a couple, the man and woman validate each other, respect one another's passion and work. And of course, they overlap on many things too. I know my marriage wasn't like that because we were more traditional. And I was young. And back then, that was more of an expectation, I guess. But now I know the difference, and I'm so afraid we created a mini-Gerry. Not that Gerry was a bad guy. I've already told you some about my marriage."

"Yes, you shared a little bit. So, what else happened?"

"On Saturday I spoke to Brent about what I observed. I don't think he understood. We didn't argue, but it wasn't peaceful either. I don't want conflict with my kids, but I just had to say something."

"Maybe he understood more as he thought about it."

"I hope I wasn't too pushy with him. My girls were always more open to suggestion than Brent. I don't know how self-aware he is. If I know him, it'll take some kind of painful experience before he sees it, and I wanted to spare him that."

"Sounds like you did what you could. You hate inequality, and you call it as you see it."

Eden pursed her lips. "Yes, that's a fair statement. If I didn't know it before I sure do now. I've been thinking about inequality lately. Among the women I know on campus, I think it's harder for them to get launched in their professional lives, compared to men. I'd like to help them somehow. There's this organization that's not part of the college but offers a sort of contest to students who have an idea for a business. My school friends think it favors male students. I don't know if that's true or not, but it got me thinking that it would be good if something similar existed just for women."

"Maybe there's an organization like that where you can volunteer."

"I looked online already and didn't see much for women just starting in their businesses, though there were a couple of great ones for women who are already established. I may have told you I'm thinking of one day doing a nonprofit, but I wasn't sure what my focus would be. I've been wondering what I had a heart for, where I could be of help. Then I've been running into these young women who need help and I wonder if *that* might be my focus. My professional experience is unrelated, though. All I'd have to offer is about ten years of running a restaurant."

"Oh, that's *all*?" He grabbed her hand and gave it a squeeze.

He released her hand. "Ten years running a restaurant is significant and can benefit women in a variety of industries."

Eden shrugged, her hand still tingling from his squeeze. "I guess you're right. Maybe I have something to offer these women. But the idea of starting a nonprofit seems overwhelming. I like the idea of finding one where I can volunteer first." But she'd tried that and hadn't found one. Maybe she'd do another research session online.

"It's obvious to me you want to help these women and others. They're your target."

"I think they are. Of course, I don't know diddly about running a nonprofit, though I have volunteered in a few over the years. Running one, starting one, then running it, is entirely different than just volunteering. It's intimidating." But even as she spoke, Eden felt something stirring inside, as if pushing to be set free.

"How would you describe the main objective of your nonprofit, if these women were your target?" Colin drained his cup of tea and leaned forward, as if he were in his element helping her define her ideas. "Assuming that one day you'd start one of your own." His added comment was likely a response to the terror that must show on her face.

Eden pushed aside her empty cup. "Okay, we're just brainstorming here. I'm not ready to do this yet. For one reason, I need to finish my degree. Then I'll be able to see more clearly what I want to do or what I'm even able to do. My spring courses will give more ideas."

Along with the stirring inside was an even bigger wave of panic. She pushed it down. After all, they were just talking. Conversing, brainstorming like friends. She wouldn't start or do anything until she felt ready. "Education will be an important component. Seminars on the basics of getting started in a business. And like the organization I mentioned, there could be a sort of forum for female students and start-up entrepreneurs to present their ideas. There would be funds available somehow to provide seed money to them to get started. There wouldn't be a contest, though. Anyone who had a viable idea could get some funding, though it would be on a first-come basis. Since, I assume, the funds wouldn't be limitless." What was she thinking? Funds would be non-existent. But she was only brainstorming. No harm in dreaming big, right? "Of course, they'd have to have a mostly developed idea and have written some version of a business plan. They'd have had to do their research and market study to see what potential customers exist and if there's a need for their service or product."

"Sound like you're already light years ahead. Did you come up with all that just now?"

"No, I thought a lot about what women would need without linking it to the nonprofit idea. But it's logical they should go together." And she'd borrowed a few ideas from the Launchpad.

"And what if a well-meaning applicant had a decent idea but hadn't done those things? What if they weren't ready?"

"Then there'd be mentoring. We'd find out if there were specific barriers and how to get rid of them. Might be just lack of knowledge, simple fear of getting started, or something external."

"You said 'we'. You're already envisioning a staff."

Eden's eyes widened. "Yes, I guess I am. See what we started?" She laughed.

"You mean what *you* started. These are your ideas and I get to come along for the ride. You've thought through a lot already. From my perspective, your ideas are sound. You'd have to raise funds, of course. Unless you plan to fund it yourself."

"Ah, I don't think so. I could contribute, but I couldn't do it all myself."

Colin linked his fingers on the tabletop. "Once you have your nonprofit status and some experience, maybe some successful case studies, people and companies will donate. Would you want to give yourself a salary? Do you plan to work full time or part time in the nonprofit?"

She made a sound in her throat. "I hadn't thought about all that. There's so much to consider, so you see why I'm not at all ready." She pondered his question for a moment. "It seems legit that I'd want a salary too. It would be nice to continue eating and paying bills." They laughed. "So, I guess that's a yes. I would need a salary."

"Well, there are certainly provisions for that in a nonprofit."

"Hmm. I guess I have a lot of research to do on this, don't I?"

"You do, but it'll be exciting. I'm here for you if you need any help or just need a cheerleader."

"Thank you. That means a lot." Eden held his gaze for a moment. She reached for her empty mug and lifted it. "Here's to the idea. The seed has sprouted a little more today. You can say you were there."

Colin laughed. "Yes, and what a historic moment it is." He clinked his empty mug against hers. His voice dropped. "I haven't had this much fun in a while, Eden."

"Have I made a shopper out of you?" Her gaze held his as warmth pooled inside her.

He smiled, not breaking their eye contact. "Not quite. But a good friend, certainly."

That was a start. An excellent start.

Chapter Thirteen

Eden was the first one to arrive at the coffee shop near the first floor of the university library. She sipped on a mug of hot chocolate, but a chill remained deep inside after a trek across campus on the coldest day of the semester. Glancing at the door, she saw Tara's bulky aqua jacket before noticing her blond hair under a gray ski hat. Tara dropped her backpack to the floor and slid wearily into the chair facing Eden.

"Last one. Gosh, it's cold today."

Eden smiled at her. "Your last final? Congratulations. You deserve a hot chocolate."

"Cold beer is more like it. Or something harder. I'm exhausted. I was up half the night, but it's over. How about you?"

"I took my last final this morning. I only had three, but also two enormous projects. I still have one to finish up so I can turn it in by tomorrow noon." A project for Dr. Siler, who'd remained coolly cordial since Eden's decision to break off with him. Which was absolutely fine with her.

Tara approached the counter to order a drink. Despite Brent's negative opinion of Eden befriending women her kids' ages, she was grateful to have this supportive group. Instead of only meeting weekly, they'd begun meeting two or three times a week between classes, depending on their schedules. And the support went both ways. Eden received as much encouragement as she gave to her younger friends.

Mariella entered the café and joined the corner table that had become their standard meeting spot. "Hi, Mariella." Eden moved her chair to give her friend more room. "Are you finished with finals?" Final exams and winter break had been a frequent topic of discussion for the last two weeks, as they checked in with each other and cheered each other on.

"One more." Mariella sighed. "By tomorrow this time, winter break officially starts. I'm toying with different options for celebration."

Tara returned with her drink and slipped into the chair where her coat hung. "Hey," she said to Mariella.

They settled into catching up on news, though they stayed loosely up to date on each other's lives, especially in the academic realm. Winter break was nearly there, blending excited anticipation with final exam pressures. Eden was thankful to have over a week before the twins arrived to ramp up her decorations and get a head start on food preparation. She hadn't even decided what she'd make. Her finals and projects had filled most of her out-of-class time. At least her gift shopping was done. The memory of her day at the mall with Colin brought a private smile to her lips.

"Has anyone heard from Cheyenne? I thought she'd be here today." Eden felt a pinch of concern since Cheyenne hadn't come to their last meeting either. She should have phoned her. "Is she still having childcare problems?"

Mariella nodded. Her expression was grim. "She was able to finish her finals but won't be coming back next semester." This brought a groan from Eden and Tara. "She called me a couple of days ago to tell me her babysitter dumped her without warning. Her mom was a backup for a while, but she got a job. Poor Cheyenne."

"She was so looking forward to finishing school and getting a decent job to support Josiah. And get her own apartment." Tara frowned and sipped her drink. "She doesn't know when she'll be able to re-enroll. Maybe next fall if she's lucky. The job she has sucks everything out of her, and that's after classes and all the rest."

Eden shook her head as sadness welled up inside her. "That's such a shame. I'll give her a call and let her know she's not forgotten." Maybe there was something she could do for Cheyenne. But what? Just encouraging the young single mother would be a start. Hard to imagine having a small child, a job, and a full course load at the same time. Even without kids at home and no need to work, Eden often felt like she was juggling sixty plates at once.

As Eden drove toward Wadesboro, her mind kept going to Cheyenne, picturing her eager face and wide green eyes as she came from a class that intrigued and motivated her. Instead of being married to her toddler's father, as she'd expected, she found herself alone with no idea where he'd fled. No sign of the dad meant no child support, and though she lived with her mother, she struggled to provide for her son's needs and help her mother with expenses.

Eden sighed, unable to imagine the stress of that life. At a stoplight, she groped in her purse for her phone and quickly tapped in Cheyenne's number. She hit voicemail. "Hey, Cheyenne, it's Eden. Mariella told us you had to take a break next semester. I'm sorry to hear that, but I'm confident you'll be back soon. Please give me a call when you can. Also, is there anything I can do to help? I'd really like to if you wouldn't mind. Let me know." The words *Merry Christmas* almost came out, but she knew that just then it was the wrong thing to say to Cheyenne. She didn't know if her friend would respond or not, or if she'd be too proud to accept any help. One thing Eden could do is phone the church the next day to see if they might have any leads on childcare for Cheyenne.

Her mind went to her conversation with Colin in the mall café two weeks earlier. They'd brainstormed about her possible dream nonprofit, but her thoughts had only grazed the idea a few times since then, because of the consuming burden of finals. Maybe there should be a provision in the nonprofit for childcare. Maybe even a place young single moms could live . . .

Despite her sadness for Cheyenne, Eden laughed aloud. She was dreaming big. Bordering on impossible, more like it. Now her ideas were taking colossal proportions. Housing? *Come back to earth, Eden.* Even if she did one day create a nonprofit, she'd have to narrow her focus, especially in the early days. If her vision was too broad, she'd fail before she began. No, she'd start with one simple objective, then add elements if and when the basic framework became solid.

Eden pressed the garage door remote with gloved fingers and pulled into the driveway, surprised she was already home. Her thoughts had been far away as she'd unconsciously followed the familiar route. She had to admit, it was as though she'd already committed herself to do the nonprofit. She had a target population now, the women whose situations had grabbed her heart and compelled her to want to help them. Was she ready? Of course not, but the embers increased in temperature with every research session and every conversation. And every needy women she encountered.

Eden turned off the ignition and got out of the car. *Lord, are you confirming that you want me to do this? If so, when is the right time? How will I fund it? where will I start? Is that what I'm meant for in the next chapter of my life?*

The question prayers continued as she went into the house and unpacked her tote bag. Finally, she stopped in the middle of her kitchen and took a breath. She'd get through the holidays and continue praying. Not for the next five years, but for the next few months. She'd know in the right time.

Colin came into her mind. She loved discussing her ideas with him, but mostly she'd love to see him again. Since their shopping day, she'd seen him twice, once for a holiday play at the local theatre and once for lunch. They texted each other a few times as well. It was all friendly and consistent. And unromantic. Was he just a friend, or was he interested in her? By his behavior, she didn't really know, except sometimes she thought she saw a flicker in his eyes that said he found her attractive. And she *was* interested in him. She, Eden Godfrey, after twelve years as a widow, was interested in a specific man. The years had convinced her she'd never meet a man she fit with or enjoyed being with enough to spend her future. In fact, she liked Colin more than she wanted to admit. She felt more . . . complete with him. She was never impatient or bored with him, either. But liking him might lead to loving him. And loving made her vulnerable to being controlled. An unbidden chill darted down her spine.

Did he like her in the same way? If he thought of her only as a friend, they wouldn't be seeing each other regularly, talking on the phone, texting. Wasn't that a sign? Or was she too out of practice to read the expressions on his face, his light touch on her arm, the attentive way he listened to her: It would likely take her another twelve years to meet anyone she liked as well as Colin.

Eden drew her phone from her purse pocket. She'd touch base. That's all. *Hi Colin, I just finished my last final and had to tell someone. What a relief! I'll finish my last project and turn it in tomorrow.*

A few minutes later, her phone pinged. *Congratulations! I'm proud of you, your first semester completed. I wish I could see you this week, but I'm trying to finish up with all the emergency stuff with clients before my trip. I'm sure we can do lunch or dinner before I leave if you're available. Then we'll celebrate.*

Friendly, but no sparkle. But he *did* say he wanted to see her. That was something, wasn't it? *That would be nice. I'd enjoy seeing you before you leave for Colorado. After I turn in my project tomorrow, I'll be available, so just let me know.* Was that too eager?

Let's have lunch next Wednesday if you're free.

Shoot, she had a dentist appointment. *Does Thursday work?*

I'll make it work. Looking forward to seeing you then.

Another week and two days. He didn't seem very eager, but he'd told her he had a lot of work to finish before leaving. For the moment, considering Dr. Siler's deadline the following day, so did she.

ය   ය   ය

Eleven-thirty Wednesday morning, Eden emailed her final project to Dr. Siler. Her first college semester in over twenty-five years was officially complete. The spring term wouldn't start for over two weeks. Her relief was palpable, and her mind scrolled through at least a dozen activities she wanted to do during that time.

The previous weekend, she'd assembled the artificial Christmas tree and placed it in the usual spot in front of the living room bay window. She'd even put strings of colored lights on it, but that's as far as she got with academic demands pressing down on her like a steamroller. She had allocated the first portion of her winter break to catching up on Christmas preparations.

By late afternoon, she'd made menus for the holidays, gone grocery shopping, and brought the remaining decorations down from the attic. She prepared a cup of hot tea and settled into an armchair, surveying the results of her efforts. A pine garland bearing tiny white lights snaked along the ivory-colored brick mantle while thick red candles adorned the hearth. The living room décor was finished. The dining table could wait until just before the twins arrived.

Eden took a sip of tea and let the comforting warmth slip down her throat. The evening stretched before her with no assignments to complete, no exams to study for, no chapters to read. After four months of academic intensity, free time was a foreign concept, but she'd figure it out quickly.

Up to the time she sold the restaurant, she spent many hours per day there. Especially at holidays, her schedule was crammed full. There were always multitudes of reservations for large parties, extended families, local businesses, friends reuniting. Seemed everyone in town wanted to reserve a holiday meal at Godfrey's.

They'd be booked solid for three weeks prior to Christmas. Eden herself had superintended the holiday decorations and was always proud of the glittering result, a wonderland of Christmas spirit. She loved Christmas, but also thought it was a great opportunity to increase business by drawing people with exceptional decorations.

Had the new owners continued that tradition? The previous year she'd stopped by and was gratified to see they'd maintained her holiday standards. That's what she'd do that evening. Despite the fridge full of groceries, she'd visit her old restaurant and say hello to anyone she knew who was still there.

Two hours later, Eden pulled the heavy door of Godfrey's as its familiarity washed over her in a wave.

"Hi, Mrs. Godfrey." The blond, pony-tailed hostess greeted her from behind a wooden table. "It's so nice to see you again. You're here for dinner?"

"Hi, Chelsea. Yes, I thought it would be fun to drop by and see everyone." Though in reality, there were only a few people Eden remembered from that chapter of her life when she spent twelve hours per day at the restaurant. Chelsea escorted Eden to a corner table near the window. Being the former owner must be her ticket to slipping into a prime table without a reservation.

Eden opened the menu and saw some changes, new specials, and most of the same popular specialties for which customers returned regularly. Soft Christmas music accented the room, and white lights twinkled on the bar and around each window.

As she watched tables fill up, a wave of wistful emptiness swept over her, along with countless memories. The years in that very room, first with Gerry at the helm, then afterward, when it fell squarely in her lap and became her full-time job. Looking back, it amazed her that she'd handled it alone, made it better, juggled its demands and those of three teenagers. In the early days, while she did all that *and* grieved her husband, she cried out daily for God's strength to get her through the next twenty-four hours. And he had. Repeatedly and for decades.

She'd fallen into a routine, especially as the kids got older, and found herself enjoying it. But she didn't miss that life. No, it was the season for a new challenge. Maybe the challenge was the idea taking root in her heart. She'd know the *if* and *when* of the nonprofit in good time. The perfect time. That thought brought a wave of peace nudging away her restlessness.

After a delicious meal, Eden dabbed her mouth. Fortunately, the food quality was still high. She'd bring Colin here one day. That is, if the relationship continued. Which wasn't at all guaranteed.

"Would you like coffee or dessert?" A voice pierced her thoughts. Caroline, her server, who didn't know her from the past.

Eden looked up and smiled. "No, thanks. It was wonderful. Can you do me a favor? I see Celine over there at table seven. Can you say hello to her from Eden?"

Caroline nodded, unsurprised that Eden knew the table number. "Sure thing. I'll let her know."

"Thanks. And Skye over at table two. She just started her shift."

After a puzzled look, Caroline smiled. "Yes, of course."

Caroline did as Eden requested. Across the room, Skye waved a quick hello in her direction and Celine came to her table, her dark-framed, elf-like face lit with pleasure. "It's so good to see you, Eden. Might have even been last Christmas when you came in." Celine and Skye had worked at Godfrey's for several years and had been Eden's favorite employees.

"I guess that's true. Lots going on. But I wanted to say hello and I hope you're doing well."

"I'll have a few minutes' break as soon as I check out table six, so I'll stop by and bring Skye. She's been in the kitchen all afternoon, so she'll be ready for a break too."

By the time Eden paid her bill, Skye and Celine returned and slipped into the chairs across from her. They began chattering all at once, asking for news. The two young women showed surprise when Eden told them she'd gone back to college.

"That's so courageous, Eden." Skye propped her chin on her fists. "Was it hard after so many years?"

Eden laughed. "Hard isn't the word, but you know . . . I feel fulfilled. It was a long-term dream. I'd never finished even though I only had a semester or so to go. Life just happened. I married Gerry, had the twins."

"So, now you're closing that loop." Celine's pixie haircut made her look younger than she likely was.

"How is Katie?" Eden asked her. "She must be about four by now."

Celine grinned. "She's a mess. So inquisitive and smart. And growing up fast." A shadow crossed her face. "It's hard raising a child alone, though. And I just got out of a bad relationship."

"Oh, Johnny." Skye rolled her eyes. "What a psycho. We heard a lot about him and everyone here was telling her to leave him."

Celine shrugged, though sadness lingered in her expression. "I finally did. We lived with him for almost a year, and I escaped with my life, just about." A chuckle devoid of humor slipped from her throat.

Eden scrunched her brows. "That's terrible. Katie's dad was abusive too, wasn't he?"

Celine looked down at the table and nodded. "Yup. I sure know how to pick 'em."

Eden couldn't find words. Her young friend's needs were bigger than encouragements could fill, or anything else Eden might offer. "I'm sorry, Celine. You deserve much better. I remember you had a desire to one day start a daycare. Is that still on the radar for you?"

A frown pulled at Celine's face. "Who knows? I'm back at my mom's now until I can get more housing. She's okay with that, but I'd like to be on my own again. Maybe after the holidays."

Eden turned to Skye. "Are you still attending community college?"

Skye raised blue eyes to Eden's. "I'm still in school but had to cut back so I could work more. You might remember when you still owned the restaurant that I was living at home and had to lock my bedroom door every night because my stepdad was prowling around."

"I remember," Eden said. "Your stepdad, the scumbag. You used to keep a baseball bat beside your bed." Skye had frequently come to work with stories of her stepfather trying to touch her inappropriately. "Is that still going on?"

"I finally had enough," Skye said. "I told my mom what he was doing. What he'd been doing for a couple years now. She didn't believe me, of course, and accused *me* of coming on to *him*. Can you believe it? So, I left and went to a girlfriend's house, but I finally got a place on my own. It's cheap and not in a good part of town, but at least I'm left alone." Her voice softened. "Haven't talked to my mom since then."

Eden swallowed, groping for words of comfort. Seemed lately, the hopeless stories of young women surrounded her. "I'm glad you found a place. Sounds like you girls have had a tough year." She turned to Celine. "I know being at your mom's feels like going backward but being safe is the most important for you and Katie. You have a lot in your favor. I believe you'll accomplish your dreams someday. It may take a little while, but you'll do it. I . . . I hope you'll both let me know if you ever need anything. I know we don't see each other often, but I'm still your friend and care very much about both of you." She held their surprised gazes until they both nodded.

"Thanks, Eden." Skye smiled shyly.

"Yes, thank you. You're sweet."

Would they or Cheyenne take her up on her offer? She understood how hard that was, despite the need, despite her sincerity. With a nonprofit, it might be easier for them to ask for help.

Celine glanced at her watch. "Break's up, hate to say. Old Frank'll be barking at us in a minute if we don't get back to work." She turned to Skye, who'd already slid out her chair.

They all stood up and hugged. "Keep in touch with me, okay?" Eden told them. "You have my number. Don't wait until I come to the restaurant a year from now." She took on fake sternness. "I mean it. I'm rooting for you both. And Merry Christmas." They might not respond to her offer, but it was Christmas, a perfect opportunity for her to come back the following day with a gift card for each of them.

Another drive home with her mind filled with the plights of young women. Had she crossed their paths for a reason? *Lord, what do you want me to do? Should I offer housing to Cheyenne and Celine? Or focus on what I'm doing so I can help more women later? I can't help everyone. I hope you'll show me what I can do and when.*

When? That was the question. Should she answer the urgency all around her, and risk getting distracted from the very idea that could help more women with a wider array of needs? She'd do what she could, to the extent that they'd let her.

Chapter Fourteen

Eden wound her scarf closer against her neck and bowed her head against the icy wind as she crossed the crowded restaurant parking lot. She pushed the door to the Indian restaurant and slipped inside as a gust of cold air whooshed around her. Once inside, the sweet-spicy scent of coconut and curry greeted her. She looked up and her eyes met Colin's as he came toward her. The sight of him brought an unreasonable tingle of contentment.

"I managed to get here first," he said. "I was feeling guilty you had to wait the last time or two."

The wind had mussed his dark wavy hair, making him even handsomer and slightly rakish. He gave her a hug and lingered a moment longer than usual. She savored his arms around her, closing her eyes.

"You smell good," he murmured into her ear as he pulled away. "New perfume?"

"You're thinking I stole Jordan's Christmas perfume, eh?" They laughed together. "Thank you. I know smells of Indian cuisine will drown it soon enough."

Eden enjoyed their lighthearted banter by text, email, and in person, but she was thankful their conversations often went deeper. They settled into a booth and caught up on the week's events while the menus sat untouched in front of them. "I have just a few more closings tomorrow and Friday, then I can turn my thoughts to Christmas and my trip out west," he said. "My clients know not to bother me for at least a full week."

"I'm sure you're looking forward to seeing Davis and being able to ski," she said.

"Absolutely. Whenever I'm in Colorado, I feel a sense of freedom. Maybe it's because I'm on vacation when I'm there, but the wide-open spaces and mountains not so far in the distance inspire me. I try to go every year in winter, and often in summer too."

"I've never been. It's a good thing Davis gives you a reason to go so often."

"Yeah, I should thank him for that." Colin's lazy smile conveyed a contentment and peace she envied.

The Indian waiter came a second time. "I promise we'll be ready in two minutes." He held up two fingers and leaned toward Eden. "We'd better decide and talk afterward. They may boot us out."

"Tell me more about what you'll be doing in Colorado," she prompted after they'd ordered. She didn't want them to end up talking too much about her interests and concerns, just because he was such a good listener.

"I won't arrive until early afternoon, so we'll probably go out for dinner. There's this taco place we both love, and we end up eating way too much. The next day, we'll have a somewhat traditional Christmas dinner, for which I'll be the primary cook."

Eden grinned. "You said the same thing about your sister at Thanksgiving. Everyone in your family benefits from your cooking skills."

"As *you* will once I get back in January. I haven't cooked for you yet, but it's top of my list."

"Looking forward to that."

He pushed up the sleeves of his dark plum sweater, which set off his hazel eyes. "Depending on the weather, we'll ski the next day or so. We won't ski every day, but I like to get some good runs in while I'm there. There are small towns around him we can explore and hang out, and we'll spend a day in Denver. It may even be warm enough to hike a time or two."

"Sounds cold to me. I guess I'm not that sturdy when it comes to cold weather."

The waiter returned with steaming, aromatic meals on a large platter and two tall glasses of lassi, an Indian yogurt drink. When he left, Colin reached across the table and took Eden's hand. While he prayed for their meal and their upcoming holidays, she was conscious of his warm hand clasping hers. She couldn't stop herself from wondering if it meant more to him than a mealtime prayer habit. In any case, his hand felt wonderful.

"I think we both have a taste for the exotic. Tapas, Thai, now Indian." Colin took a bite of Tandoori. "Mmm. Want to taste? I forgot to suggest we split."

"No need. I want my Chicken Korma to myself. But we can swap a taste." Eden tasted the morsel he'd slipped onto her plate.

"What have you been up to since finishing your finals and projects?" His warm gaze landed on hers as he gave her his attention.

"Last Friday was my first full day of Christmas break, so I went to my old restaurant for dinner. I wanted to see people I used to know and the Christmas decorations. I used to deck the place out every Christmas."

"I remember the décor of Godfrey's. I went there several times while you still owned it, never dreaming I'd meet you one day. We were probably there at the same time, more than once. What was it like for you to go back?"

"I hadn't visited in almost a year and I got a sudden urge to go. It was nice. While I was there, I saw my two favorite employees, young women who've waitressed there for years. Their stories were so sad, Colin. It's like every young woman I meet has a story of struggle in her life." She recounted Celine and Skye's situations as well as Cheyenne's need to drop out of school because of childcare. "These are women with dreams for their futures, but because they have no support around them, they struggle. Some don't make it.

They just give up, like Cheyenne. I don't think she's given up for good, but she's hit a roadblock. At the very least, she needs someone to come alongside and tell her to keep going, that it'll be okay."

A soft smile emerged on Colin's face. He reached again for her hand and squeezed it. "I love that about you, Eden. Your heart is so huge for other people."

As he held her hand for a long moment, his eyes held hers. Heat rose in her neck and a flutter began inside. "Thank you for saying that. I want to help them, but of course, I can't help everyone."

"I was about to tell you the same thing." Colin released her hand and took a sip of lassi. "The needs will always be there everywhere you go, regardless of where. Good preparation in advance will make you more effective later, so I encourage you not to rush it. For now, you can decide on some criteria, needs that you think are most critical as well as what gifts you can bring to the table. And of course, I mean for the organization, not Eden by herself."

"Yes, of course the nonprofit will provide the structure." Eden took a heavy breath and leaned back against the vinyl bench. "It's a big thing, but I'm taking a nonprofits class in the spring that'll be a huge help."

"You're still in school, so for now, just think about it, pray about it, and research. You found the cause you needed. Each time you encounter it, that need is reinforced in your mind."

Over the holidays, she could take time to mull over needs and narrow them down. She'd have undistracted hours to consider various ideas. Then, after her graduation next year, she'd be more equipped to dive in. She'd have more information, more resources. And less terror.

Eden's thoughts whirled in her head, though she was still conscious of Colin's nearness, his steady gaze on her face. "You're right, I shouldn't be in a hurry."

"I'm here for you, Eden. Sounding board, whatever you need." He took her hand again. "And a good friend."

She smiled back at him, but her spirit sagged. Good friend? A friend was a great thing, but was that all Colin saw for them?

"You've been a great friend helping me with all this. But I don't always want to be talking about *my* plans and ideas. Tell me more about *your* life and dreams." She didn't want to fall into the very thing she'd warned Brent about. Sharing vision and dreams was important for a couple. If that's what they were.

Colin shrugged. "The present is pretty mundane. I hate to say, I'm a bit bored practicing the kind of law I do. I've done it for a long time. I enjoy the real estate aspect, you know, vetting prospective renters, arranging for repairs, things like that. But my practice is getting repetitive for me. Especially after all these years. I may have told you I considered changing fields back when the kids were teens, but it was right about then when Adele left, so I couldn't make a move."

Eden nodded. "So, you stayed in the same field, but now there are no kids, no compelling reason to keep doing the same thing. Except that maybe you still might need to make a living."

They laughed. "Yes, that's important. At my age, I don't know if I'm ready to retrain in something. I'd more likely transition to the real estate investor side of things. Like you with the nonprofit, I'm mulling things over, but not ready to make a move yet."

"You'll know." Eden was sure of her words for Colin, though not as sure when she applied them to herself. "Unless you have the same weakness I sometimes do, which is waiting too long to do anything." Like selling the restaurant. Like finishing her degree.

He smiled, but something shadowed his eyes. "No, that's not my weakness. Once I decide on something, I rarely have trouble following through. I have other weaknesses, though, which I'm sure you'll get to know in time. I may have told you about my older brother, Stan, who was always a life-of-the-party type of guy, very loud and funny. I knew I could never compete or outshine him, so as a kid I tried not to make too many waves. I didn't always speak up in the family about what I wanted or was thinking."

"You might not be loud, though you *are* sometimes pretty funny. You have lots of abilities that likely *do* outshine him." That much was obvious to Eden, though the question popped into her mind with a rumble of discomfort. Was he avoiding saying what he was thinking? "Seems like your family wouldn't know who you really were, if you spent years like that."

Though it was bound to have been a source of pain, Colin's face seemed peaceful.

"For a long time, they didn't, but I came out of my shell as an adult. Sometimes I think they'd like to put me back into it."

They laughed. "Makes me wonder . . ." she began carefully. "I hope you won't do that with me. I want you to feel comfortable enough to say what you want to say."

"I *am* comfortable with you, Eden. Can't you tell?" The relaxed jaws and smile didn't seem forced. Maybe he was telling her the truth.

"You seem comfortable, but I haven't known you that long."

He leaned forward and grabbed her hand for the third time that day. "It's been a weakness in the past, but I have little trouble stating what I need and think. I try not to be obnoxious about it, though. Promise."

Calm flowed back to her with his reassuring touch and grin. Would there be any unwelcome surprises she'd find out later?

By the time Eden drove home, gunmetal gray clouds had scuttled in, layering the sky. Her thoughts grumbled and grew heavy, like the impending afternoon storm. The weight of her concerns for young women competed with new concerns about Colin. Every time she saw him, her attraction to him deepened, but it seemed to him it was a friendship. Was that one of things he hadn't yet told her?

He didn't seem reserved, but by his own admission, he'd struggled with it in the past. It wasn't a negative thing, but she felt uneasy, as if she didn't know where she stood with him romantically and otherwise, despite the lively conversation and similar values. Despite the occasional lingering touch, or spark of warmth in his eyes when he saw her. Despite his desire to support and help her with her project, evidence of equality and partnership. When would she ever find *that* again?

Eden frowned and shook her head as she closed the front door behind her, slid the door chain in place, and hung up her coat and scarf. She refused to let that discussion wrap her in knots. She had her studies, the holidays, her ideas for the nonprofit, plenty to occupy her mind. Plenty to distract her from the shards of disappointment that stung inside. The certainty that things were not as glowing as they appeared.

For the next two weeks, her life would brim and overflow with tasks. Christmas was around the corner. Pushing dark thoughts away, she'd start with that.

ڇ   ڇ   ڇ

Candlelight flickered on the dining room table, casting shifting streams of light across the tablecloth. Eden's centerpiece, a gilded bowl filled with fabric poinsettias, and gold-colored beads sat as a festive reminder of another Christmas day. The rest of the table resembled a war zone, with dirty plates, small dessert dishes, and half-eaten side dishes.

"That was great, Mom. But I'm done," moaned Jordan. She pointed to the turkey carcass at the end of the table. "Like that turkey. I'm absolutely stuffed."

"No one forced you to eat seconds." Claire raised her eyebrows at her sister. Jordan threw a wadded napkin across the table. Claire leaned just in time, and it missed her head. "That turkey has seen better days."

"I only pig out at Thanksgiving and Christmas. And it was worth it. Especially the key lime pie. Delightfully untraditional."

"I thought you'd be tired of pecan and pumpkin," Eden said to Jordan. Maybe I'm becoming less predictable, eh?"

"What surprises will our mother reveal in days to come?" Claire said in a spooky voice. "Don't do anything too shocking, Mom. We're used to the way you are."

"No worries. I'm expanding my horizons, but I'm still your ma." She twirled the napkin absently and wondered what Colin was doing. Likely preparing for his flight the following day. He'd called that morning to wish her a Merry Christmas before leaving to go to his mother's retirement residence. The memory brought a smile to her lips, despite her doubts about his level of openness. She doused the smile to avoid interrogation from the twins.

"Bet you're glad to be out of school," Claire said.

"Very. As much as I enjoyed the semester, I need a break."

"What'll you do when we leave? You'll be alone for over a week since Colin is gonna be out west." Jordan tapped a droplet of wax pooling on the candle.

"I have some research to do." She may as well tell them. "Not for school, though. I'm considering starting a nonprofit one day, maybe after I graduate."

"Really? About what?" Claire asked as both girls' faces perked to attention.

"Well, in the last few months, I've met young women who have business ideas, but they have obstacles in their lives." Eden spoke slowly, her mind sifting through each aspect she'd seen repeatedly over the last several months. "Obstacles like lack of funds for a startup, or lack of clarity about their ideas. Sometimes they just need moral support so they can believe in themselves." Claire and Jordan listened in keen interest.

"Sounds great, Mom. How could you help them?" Claire asked.

"I've been brainstorming that question. I could raise money to help women with start-up costs for a business or invention. I could pull in experts in the community to give guidance through mentoring and workshops. And maybe find a way to connect them with community resources for things like childcare and housing. Those are just some of my ideas."

Eden felt exposed, as though voicing her vision committed her to following through. Her gaze roved back and forth between Claire and Jordan.

The twins stared back at her with wide grins and sparkling eyes. "That's awesome," Jordan said. "Does anything like that already exist? You could learn from them, or partner with them if you didn't want to do it by yourself."

"That's a good idea. I've looked online and there are organizations that help people starting up, but they aren't just for women. I want to focus on women because, in the business world, they have more challenges, like the ones I mentioned. I found a couple of associations for women established in business, but not many for those starting out." Eden's mind went to Mariella, who dreaded leaving the cocoon of college to enter the competitive world of the beginner entrepreneur.

"Seems like you've researched a lot already. I think it's fantastic." Claire's eyes held a spark as she spoke.

"I want to spend some time learning the legal aspects and how to start and run a nonprofit, to see what I'd be getting into. The idea interests me but frightens me too." Eden reached for her water glass, relieved that her idea was no longer a secret from her daughters. "Ever since I sold the restaurant, I've been looking for something to do that would help people and use my life experiences.

I'm wondering if this might be it." She shrugged. "Then again, with more research, I might discover that this *isn't* it."

"I can help you with marketing once you get it going," Jordan said. "At least I'd be helping you and the women instead of making money for someone else."

"I hadn't thought of that, but I'd sure need your savvy with marketing. I know zero about that." Eden added with a smile, "Thanks, honey."

"When would you start the organization?" Claire asked.

Eden tilted her head. "If I do it, I'd probably start sometime after I graduate."

"That's a long time from now, Mom. You should start sooner before life happens and takes you away from your dreams." Jordan stared at Eden.

A thread of discomfort dangled inside. "What if I'm afraid?" Her gaze panned the twins' faces. "I'm being honest. I want to go slowly because it's a huge thing. It's like creating a company, only the rules and objectives are different. If I do it later, I'll be more equipped. I'm taking a class in the spring on running a nonprofit. That'll help."

"For sure it will. Keep us posted. We're on board with you, Mom."

Surprising tears sprang into Eden's eyes. She reached out to them and grabbed their hands. "That means a lot, girls. I'm thrilled to have your support." Aside from the birth of Jesus, that was her best Christmas gift.

Two days after Christmas, the twins hugged Eden at the door and drove back to Indianapolis. Unlike the last time they visited, sadness didn't overwhelm her when they left. She had a mission. Research.

Hours later, Eden turned off her computer, exhausted, and massaged her shoulders and neck with her fingertips. She'd only planned to spend an hour doing research online, just to get her feet wet and discover the first steps of starting a nonprofit. As fascinating as it was overwhelming, she found herself sucked down numerous rabbit holes, all of them useful.

When her grumbling stomach finally drove her downstairs to scope for turkey and dressing leftovers, her mind was spinning. This would take months. Was she up for it? From her online study, it seemed her first step was a needs assessment. That would require additional hours of research. She'd met a few women with needs, but how many more were out there? How many of them had barriers that her organization could help remove? That would require talking to people in the community, researching statistics, and cross-referencing with other similar nonprofits. Step one.

Eden sighed and chewed absently on salad greens and a cold slab of turkey dressing. Her enthusiasm had flagged when she saw what it would take to begin. What had she been thinking? That it would be a matter of completing a form and voilà, all done? She'd also have to write up a mission statement, find a board of directors, write up by-laws . . . *Then* she'd be able to file her application with state government to create the organization. Even if she were ready to plunge in, she couldn't bypass the multitude of preliminary steps. Once the new semester began, how would she find the time? Despite Jordan's urging, Eden couldn't create the nonprofit just yet.

But she could take baby steps. At each new juncture, she'd determine if she had enough green lights to continue. It would be a long process, and at any moment, she could be redirected.

Her phone pinged. A text from Colin. Just the thing to lift her dismay. A smile crept across her lips even before she read his message. *Good morning, Eden. I got safely to Colorado yesterday, and it's been great to catch up with Davis. He has a cute little house in Longmont. We'll celebrate Christmas today and make dinner together. He never forgets that I like to cook and takes full advantage! His girlfriend and another couple of his buddies will join us. Then tomorrow, the slopes. How was your Christmas?*

Eden grinned. Colin's text was wordier than usual, though he was by no means shy, despite what he'd said the other day. *Hi Colin, All that sounds wonderful. Merry belated Christmas! We had a lovely time together. I told my girls about the nonprofit idea, and they're excited for me. I started researching what's involved and I'm already overwhelmed!* She attached an emoji with a frazzled expression.

He wrote, *That's fantastic. Sounds like things are moving ahead. Can't wait to talk more with you about it when I get back. We'll do a belated New Year's Eve, since belated seems to be my rhythm this year. Hope your week is productive. Be sure to do something fun too. I'll be in touch.*

Hmm. Belated New Year's. That had promise. Sounded like she was still in his mind and on his schedule.

While she still held the phone in her hand, it rang. Marissa. "Merry Christmas, Marissa." She couldn't suppress a smile hearing the voice of her closest friend. "I hope your holiday was wonderful."

"Yes, it was really nice." The warm familiarity of Marissa's voice, laced with a genteel southern accent, dispensed a layer of calm. "Sean didn't come this year since he'd just been here for Thanksgiving. He went to Portugal with some friends. Jarrod's daughter, Bethany, and her new boyfriend, Luke, were here. I like Bethany. It took her about a year to fully warm up to me because of losing her mother. That's one reason Jarrod and I waited so long to get engaged. Bethany's sweet and very accepting now of her new stepmother-to-be."

"Does it feel weird calling yourself a stepmother? Of course, it was bound to happen sooner or later, if not with Jarrod, with some other lucky man." Eden hooked her feet on the bottom rail of the bar stool.

Marissa chuckled. "At our age, there are usually grown children to consider, so I'm glad it's working out for us. And I'm getting used to the stepmother idea. It's just a label. I see myself more as an older friend for Bethany. How are things with Colin?"

Eden hesitated. "So far so good, I guess, though he hasn't declared himself yet."

"Really? You've been dating for over a month, haven't you?"

"If you call it that. We text and call each other and sometimes go out for a meal. It feels like we're good friends, but I'm not sure what else."

"Sounds to me like you're dating."

"We went to lunch a week before Christmas. He's with his son now in Colorado. He texted me and said when he gets back, he wants to get together for a belated New Year's."

"I'd say that's a good sign. Give it time, Eden, though if it's bothering you, you could always ask him what he's thinking, couldn't you?"

Eden drew in a sharp breath. "I'd rather let things coast along and see what happens. But I do like him." And she preferred that he take the lead on defining their relationship.

"How *much* do you like him?" Marissa prodded.

Eden bit her lip. "A lot, I admit it. The fact that he doesn't say anything clear about his feelings confuses me. Once in a while, he makes a reference to being my friend." And he'd admitted he doesn't always say what's in his heart. How she hated being in the dark when she'd spent most of her life seeking certainty.

Could she really be that out of practice in reading men?

"You're wondering if he's sending a message when he calls you a friend? And yet, he keeps asking you out. I might be confused by that too, but he'll probably bring it up. Then if he doesn't, you can ask him why he uses that word."

Marissa had a point. Colin told her he was comfortable with her. He seemed to enjoy their time together and kept inviting her.

"Sometimes I think I'm too old for this, Marissa. I like certainty." No, she *needed* certainty.

"I understand, but certainty is overrated. You don't grow if you cling to certainty. But you started over in school, didn't you? To me, that's a huge example of your openness to uncertainty and adventure."

"I hope I'm getting less fearful and more open." And quicker to make a decision and move forward.

"But it's never too late to start over in any realm. Romantic, business, spiritual. You name it."

A wave of conviction flowed over Eden as she thought about her forgotten spiritual commitment. "All fresh starts seem really hard."

"No one would argue with you that fresh starts are hard, least of all me. But I can also assure you that once you start, they can really be worth the initial discomfort. I'm proof of that. I had questions like, was I only meant for one person, or could it ever work with someone *else*? It was a walk of faith every moment. Walking, by definition, occurs one step at a time."

One step at a time? That may require her to *not* press Colin to define their relationship simply to make her feel more secure. Was her need to know where she stood normal, or was it a stale remnant from her childhood? Another way to control her own life?

Letting go of her need to know his feelings might push out her walls of safety, forcing her to trust God in a deeper way. For her romantic future, her business future, her whole life in its next chapter. It would take a lot more faith than she had, but that faith could grow a little with every terrifying step.

Three days later, Eden had physical and computer files filled with information about starting a nonprofit. She'd written a list of potential board members, researched needs online, and sketched a preliminary vision. On her list were phone calls to local homeless shelters, job training programs, and the local community college.

They'd give her some data about struggles women faced as they tried to create a new life. Her objectives weren't clear enough, but her foundation was taking shape. That done, she planned to spend her afternoon reviving her Ponte Vecchio painting that had gone by the wayside between Thanksgiving and Christmas.

Her phone buzzed on her desk. She hadn't heard from Colin since the day the twins left. Could be him or one of the twins. She looked at the screen and was surprised to see Mariella's name pop up. Her friend had only texted her once over the holidays to wish her a Merry Christmas. *Sorry to bother you. I have some information I think you'd be interested in hearing. Can you talk on the phone sometime today?*

Eden frowned. That was odd. The timing and the request. She tapped Mariella's number. "Hi Mariella, I hope you had a good Christmas."

"Hi, Eden. Yes, it was great. I hope yours was." Her voice sounded agitated.

Eden's stomach tensed. "Is everything okay?"

"There's nothing wrong, it's just that I've learned something that's strange and troubling about the Launchpad, that organization you told us about."

"Oh?" Eden held the phone closer to her ear.

"Yesterday I spoke to an old friend named Joanne who applied for the Launchpad maybe three years ago. She had this great idea for an educational toy. Her brother helped her develop it and she presented it to the Launchpad. She didn't win but kept working on her idea. Then, a few months ago, she saw her toy on the website of a big toy company. It had to have been stolen by someone on the Launchpad because only her brother knew how it worked. It broke her heart because she was in the process of launching it herself. She'd even saved money for the patent fees."

"That's terrible, Mariella. Could it be that someone else just happened to have the same good idea?" Eden stood and went to sit in her recliner.

"It's possible, but unlikely. The idea was unique, according to Joanne. I guess most people think that of their creations, but she had technical data to back up her statement."

"I see. It's fishy." Eden's stomach tightened.

"Oh, it gets fishier than that. She told me about two other people she knows who had the same thing happen to them. One was a guy, so apparently it doesn't just happen to women. They'd applied at the Launchpad about five or so years ago with a great idea. They weren't chosen, but later saw their idea produced by a big company. They both had products they'd invented. A kitchen tool and I don't know what the other one was."

"And they didn't have patents, either." It wasn't even a question. Eden knew the answer.

"No, not when they applied to the Launchpad. People hope they'll win and get financial support to do the steps of getting a patent and developing the product."

"That's logical. I'm pretty sure no one who takes part in the Launchpad has a patent in advance. It probably wouldn't occur to them."

"Exactly."

Something in the crisp certainty of Mariella's voice caused a chill to ripple down Eden's spine. "Wait. What? Do you think—"

"Yes, someone is stealing their ideas then selling them to companies. It must be someone inside the Launchpad who turns the person down, then takes their idea to a company likely to buy it."

"If that's true, Mariella . . . I don't know what to say. That's awful. I was upset at the idea that guys might get preference over the women applicants, but this is far worse. If it's true, that is."

"The evidence is accumulating."

"But how could it ever be proven? Anyone could say they had the same idea. There's the tricky thing about inventions. Someone else is bound to come up with the same one. Or say they did."

"That's right. There must be some way to protect people and their hard work. Not everyone can pay for a patent before applying to the Launchpad."

"No, but we can warn them away from the Launchpad."

"How would we do that with no proof?"

Eden let out a long breath. "No idea." None at all.

After they disconnected, Eden chewed absently on the end of her pen, sifting through the shocking news Mariella had dropped. Helplessness fell onto her shoulders like a bronze weight. What she'd told Mariella was true. Discrimination against women was one thing, but theft of ideas for both unsuspecting men and women was quite another. It was criminal.

What could she do? Not one thing, though she did have *one* idea. And it might be their only chance to expose the Launchpad.

Chapter Fifteen

Eden stood on the steps of an attractive brick ranch house surrounded by mature but bare winter trees that stretched spindly branches into the dusky sky. The colonial blue door bore a pine wreath with red berries scattered through its needles. She reached for the brass knocker and rapped twice. The door opened and a smiling Colin filled the doorway. It felt like months since she'd last seen him, but it was only just over a week.

He swept her into the foyer and enfolded her in a warm hug. "Happy New Year, Eden. It's so good to see you."

As he held her for a moment, a whiff of his manly cologne blended with the tang of seafood in the air. When he released her, his hazel eyes latched onto hers. "Thanks for coming over. It occurred to me I hadn't cooked for you yet."

"Well, thanks for inviting me. It was no trouble at all for me to come."

He laughed and drew her away from the door.

She reached into her canvas tote and pulled out a bottle of Riesling wine. "Will this go with the seafood? I chilled it."

"Absolutely. Good choice." He took the bottle from her. She shrugged out of her coat and handed it to him. She'd worn a soft pink sweater tunic over light gray pants, accented by a string of freshwater pearls.

"You look nice, as always. So, this is where I live. Living room, kitchen." He held out his hands as they passed through the living room. A tan couch and blue armchairs complemented the artwork and large area rug for an attractive but manly style. Once they were in the kitchen, he gestured her to the stool. "Have a seat. Can I get you some wine or sparkling water?"

Eden perched on the square wooden stool in front of a large granite island similar to the one in her kitchen. Over it hung three brushed nickel lamps that cast circles of light onto the gray and black granite. The kitchen was bright and functional, with long counters and an eat-in area. "Water would be great. I'll have wine with our meal. Can I do anything to help?"

"No, enjoy your drink and relax. I'll benefit from your company while I finish up." He poured sparkling water from a chilled bottle into a glass and set it in front of her.

"Smells great. Shrimp?" Eden took a sip, and it tingled in her throat as she swallowed.

"And scallops. I'm sauteing them here, but in warmer weather I like to do kabobs on the grill."

"I'm sure they'll be fabulous." Her eyes wandered to the opposite counter where spinach salad fixings sat near a teak bowl.

"Thanks for your faith in my cooking skills when I haven't yet made you a thing." He lifted the glass lid of a pot on the stove and gave it a stir. "That's the sign of a true friend."

Eden's smile froze. There it was again, that reference to friendship, every time she thought they were moving toward definition. Patience, Marissa had suggested. Eden would know in time how Colin felt about her, she was certain. One way or the other. For now, she should simply enjoy the man's company and his cooking and not dissect his statement.

Colin had called her two days earlier while he waited for his flight from Denver on January third, suggesting that he cook for her instead of taking her to a restaurant. That was a step in the right direction, as he opened his home and personal space to her. Or so she'd thought. But his hug had expressed that he'd missed her, cared for her. *Don't analyze, Eden.* And dinner communicated something, didn't it?

While he finished preparing, he told her about his trip to Colorado, described his son's friends, and some of their experiences on the ski slopes. "Since you aren't a skier, you may not know we have a few slopes here in Indiana." Colin spooned a mixture of zucchini, onions, and carrots into a ceramic serving bowl and handed it across the island to her. "Can you put that on the table for me?"

She returned from the dining table, which filled one side of the rectangular living room, and waited for her next task. Colin was searing the scallops in a cast iron pan. Sauteed shrimp sat steaming on a nearby plate.

Eden cocked her head. "Though I'm not a skier, I have a sixth sense that Colorado has *much* better skiing than Indiana. Am I right?"

"You must be clairvoyant." Colin smirked. "Considering it's a flat, corn-growing state, Indiana does an admirable job with its ski resorts. But there's still no comparison with the Rockies. Since Davis moved out there, I don't even ski here anymore. But it would be fun to take you one day so you can try it." He went to the fridge and pulled out a butter dish. "I hope you like wild rice." He placed a dollop of butter into a bowl of multicolored grains and handed it to Eden.

"I'd like that. Skiing *and* wild rice." Skiing had never appealed to her before, but she'd gladly try it if Colin could show her the ropes and catch her when she was about to eat snow.

Soon after, they sat at the dining table next to a tall picture window overlooking a flagstone patio and darkened backyard. Candles flickered fingers of warm light across the tablecloth. Aromas and vapor from the warm seafood ribboned upward from the platter.

Their conversation moved easily as she enjoyed Colin's cooking and his animated facial expression painted in candlelight. She hadn't wanted to bring up the information Mariella had told her too soon in the evening, but soon a silence prompted her to speak. "I got some disturbing news the other day."

He set aside his napkin, folded his hands, and gave her his full attention.

Eden recounted what Mariella had told her about the three students who suspected they'd had their ideas stolen. "If it had been just one student, I'd be more likely to think it was a coincidence. After all, we know that more than one person can come up with the same idea. But it's happened several times and the common denominator is the Launchpad."

Colin nodded slowly. "I can see how you might conclude foul play. It *is* suspicious when there are so many in a short period, but it would be nearly impossible to prove anything. At any point, people could say the competitors had the same idea but acted on it sooner. That happens all the time."

Eden sighed and her shoulders sagged. "Yes, I know. All along I've had a gut instinct there was something unfair happening. Seems like it must happen to guys and the girls alike. It's deeper than I thought if that's what is going on. It's actually a crime instead of mere discrimination, which is bad enough." She met his eyes. "It's intellectual property theft. The only way to prove anything like that is with a patent or a copyright. Of course, there's nothing like that in this case. Just a handful of trusting students wanting help for their vision."

"If I were a patent lawyer instead of a real estate lawyer, I'd be able to help with some of the patent information. Lawyers don't necessarily speed the process, though. You've got the patent office to deal with and they have their timetable, usually two years."

Eden gasped. "So long! And it costs a lot too, doesn't it?"

"Depends, but sometimes a few thousand dollars. By the time the average college graduate saves that kind of money, the idea could easily be discovered by someone else."

"Another reason it's so hard to detect and prosecute, if there's theft happening." When Colin tilted the wine bottle to offer a refill, Eden extended her glass. "Just a bit."

"Right. I have a dessert coming, so leave some room."

Despite the grim conversation, Eden smiled. "You've outdone yourself, Colin. Everything was delicious."

"That from a former restaurant owner is a high compliment. Thank you." He lifted his glass. "May the New Year bring you joy, a diploma, a resolution to the Launchpad mystery, and many fun times with the man in front of you."

Eden laughed. "I will certainly drink to that. All of it." Their eyes met over their raised glasses just before they clinked. She took a sip to distract herself from the butterflies flapping their wings inside her.

Colin stood. "If you're full, we can have dessert a little later."

"That's a good idea. I'll appreciate it more later. Now, I'm still savoring the scallops and shrimp."

He stood to gather the plates. She filled her hands with serving dishes and followed him to the kitchen. He took the bowls from her and set them on the counter.

"I'll help you do the dishes." Eden stood by the island, awaiting instructions.

"Absolutely not," he said over one shoulder as he ran some water into the sink. "You won't do dishes, nor will I. I don't want to waste our time together doing dishes. I'll soak them and take care of it later."

"Okay, understood. You're the chef." As a child, she'd been taught to offer, but was always relieved when the host or hostess declined. Doing dishes felt too much like eating at home.

With his back to her, Colin rinsed and stacked the dishes in the sink and zipped around the kitchen, putting food into the fridge. As she watched him, she couldn't deny her simmering attraction to him. True, he was a man who cooked and did it well, which had always been attractive to her. Yet something else was building, a need for clarity. He hadn't left her without clues. Hadn't he made overtures throughout the evening, communicated without words? But words would be so reassuring. Her persistent curiosity got the better of her. "Colin?"

He turned to her with an open smile, wiping his hands on a dish towel.

Eden's heart pounded. "I was wondering . . ." She swallowed, then immediately cursed herself. She couldn't do it. She had to wait, even though she'd already begun. No, it was Colin's place to define their relationship. Call her old fashioned, but she preferred it that way. She wouldn't be controlled by her need to know. Gradually, it was becoming clearer to her through his gaze, his gestures, and his suggestions to teach her to ski, to spend more time with her in the New Year.

"Wondering what?" Colin turned and must have seen something in her face. He stared at her for a long moment, which seemed an eternity, as he waited for her response.

"Never mind." Her fingers flapped at the air. "It's just me thinking aloud." Hopefully, that would satisfy him, and he'd let it go. But a slow smile spread across his face. He walked toward her and didn't stop until they were almost touching chest to chest, though her shoulders fell well below his. She lifted her head to look at him.

His head shadowed hers and she felt his breath on her cheeks. Colin held her gaze. "I like you a lot, Eden."

"How did you know that was what I wondered?" she asked quietly.

"Just guessed." He reached with one hand to trace a gentle line down her cheek with his finger. She shivered at his touch. "Apparently, I haven't done a good job showing you how much." His eyes roved over her face, to her lips, back to her eyes. He tipped her chin up, lowered his lips to hers, and kissed her.

He drew her tightly into his arms and pressed into her lips, taking his time, gently exploring. Eden relaxed into him, tasting him, lost in him. She slipped her arms around his waist, where they fit perfectly.

After several moments suspended in time, Colin drew his head back, though his forehead still touched hers. "I hope that makes it clearer how I feel about you, Eden." His voice was low, husky. "In fact, I'm crazy about you."

Eden caught her breath as words escaped her. Her unspoken question had been answered. A smile crept to her lips and in response, she stood on tiptoe and kissed him again.

The creamy tang of cheesecake lingered on Eden's tongue as she and Colin sat together on the living room couch. She set her dessert plate on the coffee table and relaxed against his arm. He slipped it around her shoulders, and she nestled close, savoring the warm feel of him.

"That was delicious," she said. "If I still owned my restaurant, I'd have to convince you to provide a regular supply of cheesecakes." A moment went by. "Can I ask you something?"

"Sure, anything. But I don't know if you can top your last unspoken question." His voice was as warm as his eyes as he looked down at her. As a couple, they were defined and everything felt different in a small space of time, as though an invisible barrier had fallen.

"Why did you keep making pointed references to friendship? I thought you were sending me a message."

Colin stared at her and nodded with understanding. "From my perspective," he said slowly, as if carefully choosing his words, "calling a woman a friend isn't a blow-off statement. I'm not saying friends is all we'll ever be, though now I see why you'd take it that way. Friendship means mutual respect and enjoyment of another person. If you can add romantic attraction to that, then you have a keeper. And you, Eden," he leaned forward and brushed her lips with a light kiss, "are a keeper."

Her mind cradled his words. *A keeper.* She found her smile. "I understand what you're saying. But you *did* throw me off. Why did it take you so long to—to kiss me or even tell me how you felt?"

His face grew serious. "I remember how sensitive you were to being pushed around and controlled."

"I knew it." Eden frowned. "I scared you off."

He laughed aloud. "It takes much more than that to scare me off. After I saw you in church that day, I realized we had a chance to start over. But I wanted to go slowly, so you didn't feel hemmed in and end up running away. I wanted to avoid that, so I took my time."

The opposite of what she'd feared. "That could have backfired, you know." It almost had, but she wouldn't dwell on that. She was too conscious of his fingers rubbing her shoulder.

"You've had some hard experiences with men in the past, even your husband. The last thing I was going to do was act like I owned you. It's not what you want, but it's not even who I am."

"I like the sound of that." She smiled up at him. "Equals. I haven't always been treated like an equal." An equal and maybe a partner. As she snuggled into his arms, a curtain of well-being fell over her from head to toe. "I have one more question."

"Mmm?" he murmured against her hair just before kissing her temple.

"How would you like to be on my board of directors?"

He met her eyes with a wide grin. "Sure thing."

"So now I have two. I've begun."

"Yes, you have. And *we've* begun." He gently leaned her back against the couch and pulled her close to kiss her again

CR CR CR

Eden hovered outside Dr. Siler's door as she waited for the young woman ahead of her to finish her conversation with him. Noisy students passed her in the hallway as academic life resumed a normal pace.

In retrospect, the winter break she'd feared would be too long was anything but. She'd relished the extra time she could dedicate undistracted focus to developing her mission statement and objectives for the nonprofit. Well, as undistracted as she *could* be with thoughts of Colin simmering in her mind, playfully pulling her attention away from her task. He'd just sent her a tiny humorous video in a text message and the ball of warmth inside continued radiating for several minutes.

Marissa, of course, had been thrilled at the turn of events with Colin when Eden phoned her during a round of post-holiday calls to her girlfriends. *Sounds like it's your turn, Eden* she'd said. Yes, it felt like maybe it *was* finally her turn, after years of seeing her friends pair up and find genuine love. Her relationship with Colin was new, so she didn't yet know if it was the real thing, but it sure felt like it might be. She no longer felt like the aimless widow. She was still a widow, but no longer alone and certainly no longer without purpose.

Although Colin's work picked up speed after the holiday, she heard from him either by phone or text each day. They'd gone to dinner and a movie on the last day of her winter break.

Eden sighed. The relaxed vacation rhythm had finished for a few more months. Her new semester had begun that morning at ten-fifteen. She'd already transitioned back to academic life following a twenty-plus year hiatus. After a three-week winter break, she could do it again.

Once the student left Dr. Siler's office and slid past her, she peeked around the corner. When her professor saw her, a wide smile crossed his face, and he gestured to her. "Happy New Year, Eden." He motioned her toward the chair. "Have a seat. How was your holiday?" His face was ruddy or suntanned, making him even more handsome, though Colin's face was the one that kept floating into her conscious thoughts, creating a giddy well of pleasure inside.

"It was fantastic." She smiled at him and placed her canvas tote on the floor. "My girls were home, so it was just the three of us, but we enjoyed our time. My son went to his girlfriend's parents since he'd been home for Thanksgiving. How about you? Is that a suntan I see there?"

He laughed. "You guessed correctly. I was skiing with friends in Utah for almost a week. We had a lot of snow and sun. Perfect weather, really."

"That sounds nice." Nerves pricked as Eden considered what she wanted to tell him. He could be an excellent ally, considering his position.

"What brings you by today? Or maybe you just wanted to catch up?"

Eden gave him a bland smile, which she hoped would mask her agitation. "It's always nice to catch up, of course. I wanted to bounce some thoughts off you for a minute. Do you mind? I need feedback on something I've encountered, which may be nothing at all, or it may be serious."

He frowned. "Sure, I'll do my best, Eden. What's going on?"

"Well, I know you're the faculty contact for the Launchpad. I've done some research on past applicants and winners because it interests me to see how their careers moved forward. I like the Launchpad's goal of helping students. It might provide some inspiration for me as I think about ways to help people in the future." She shrugged, then regretted her words, not wanting to say too much about her nascent ideas. "It seems that some students who don't win later find their ideas appearing on the market, as if they've somehow been, I don't know, stolen in the process." Her word choice wasn't the best, given that she had no proof at all.

At this, Dr. Siler's face darkened into a grimace.

"I don't mean they were for *sure* stolen. I'm not accusing anyone of anything. And I know that many people can come up with the same ideas."

Dr. Siler nodded emphatically, his frown still intact. "That's just it, Eden. I was about to say the same thing. I'm sure you've had good ideas before and learned that many other people had the same ones. And if it's a business idea, a person could have the funds to apply for a patent faster than someone else. That's especially common because unfortunately, the patent process can be lengthy and expensive."

"Yes, that's true. It just seems that several of the people who had that experience were also involved in the Launchpad. Do you think it's possible that someone on the inside of that organization is taking the ideas that don't win, but are still good, and using them for their own advantage?"

He was already shaking his head before she finished speaking. "No, no. I know these people. They're upstanding members of the business community who are volunteering their time. Their only goal is to see young entrepreneurs succeed."

Eden frowned. This wasn't going anywhere. She knew it wouldn't because it was impossible to prove. "I know it's hard to prove. As the faculty contact, you could keep an eye out, couldn't you? Maybe you'll see a pattern since you're an insider."

He smiled and reached over to pat her arm. She flinched at his touch.

"I'll keep an eye out. And I appreciate your compassion for students. You're going to make a great nonprofit director one day, because your heart is so big. But in this case, meddling in the Launchpad will only create obstacles for students who are involved. As you said, it's difficult to prove, and you'll end up making a problem for nothing if you pursue your suspicions." A hard edge had entered his voice as he stared a moment too long at her. A warning? "I assure you, nothing illicit is going on. But I will keep an eye out." He finished with a wink.

Eden rose and pasted on a half-smile. "Thanks for listening, Dr. Siler. Marcus. Maybe you're right and nothing is going on. It's probably only a coincidence. I'd better get to class."

As she crossed campus on the way to her next class, a chill wind whipped up, tossing dead leaves in a ring at her feet. She pulled her knit hat down and her coat collar up. Her one idea for an ally was now dead in the water. He didn't believe her at all but had placated her as though she were a child. Frustration stirred inside. She'd hoped Marcus would be in her corner, but why had she thought that? From the start, he'd given glowing endorsements for the Launchpad. He'd never be inclined to see anything fishy in their methods, especially since everything could be easily explained as a coincidence. There was literally no way to prove anything. Then again, maybe it *was* all coincidence.

During her Business Ethics class, Eden's mind kept bouncing back and forth, one minute to the shadows surrounding the Launchpad, then to the young women who needed help, and finally back to Colin's handsome face. Like a yo-yo, her thoughts and emotions swung back and forth. Should she drop the whole matter of stolen ideas and channel her energy into the nonprofit? Maybe, but shouldn't people be warned? Without any proof other than a hunch, no one would believe her anyway.

☙ ☙ ☙

Saturday late morning, Eden pulled a pan of lasagna from the oven. A spicy tomato aroma permeated the kitchen. The clang of the doorbell pierced the silence. "Perfect timing." She untied the apron around her waist and hung it on a hook in the pantry. She opened the front door and Colin swept in, bringing a wave of cold air with him. She was on the verge of asking for his coat, but he enfolded her in a hug, followed by a deep kiss. His cold cheeks brushed against hers, but a flame lit inside her. His wind-tumbled hair invited her to reach up to stroke it.

"Let me at least take your coat."

He shrugged out of his puffy down jacket, and she hung it up in the hall closet. As she turned back toward him, he gathered her again in his arms. "I take that as permission to kiss you again." His hazel eyes held an impish request that drew her in.

His second kiss was longer and left her breathless.

"The only way I can respond to that is to feed you well."

"Gladly." He winked. "Lead the way."

Eden went to the kitchen. When she looked over her shoulder at him, he was looking around at the house as he followed her. Her home was more traditional than his. It had seemed the best kind of house in which to raise a family at the time, but back then, she never questioned if it was really her taste.

"You have a nice home. So, you ramble around all alone in here?"

"For now, yes. I've been here for over two decades. My kids grew up here, so we needed room for five. Ever since selling the restaurant, I've wondered if I should downsize, but now because of school, that idea is on hold."

"Understandable."

While she prepared a salad, he sat on the stool by the island. He summarized his week and his current projects but kept it brief. He didn't seem to enjoy talking about his work and usually urged her to elaborate on hers, saying it was more interesting than his law practice.

Eden sliced the lasagna cooling on the stovetop.

"Lasagna? You went to too much trouble. Sandwiches would have been just fine."

She waved away his protest. "It was therapeutic. And after the dinner at your house, I wanted you to have a culinary treat too. I'm not a super cook, but I have a few great recipes I rotate all the time."

"Looks and smells fabulous."

She handed steaming plates to Colin to place on the dining room table then she followed him with a spinach salad and homemade vinaigrette. He returned to the dining room carrying a pitcher of herbal iced tea.

They prayed and dug into the steaming pasta. "You sell yourself short in describing your cooking, Eden." Colin filled his fork and blew on it to cool it down.

"Probably." She hoped his statement wasn't just polite flattery. "I didn't make a dessert. I would have but ran out of time. How does ice cream sound?"

"No thanks. I'm full. I do want to hear about your progress with the nonprofit. You told me on the phone you'd done a lot of research."

"During my winter break I felt like I've moved ahead. I was able to talk to someone at the community college and the homeless shelter, you know, to get different views on the problems women might have in pursuing their business ideas. I decided that initially, since I don't have funding or a budget, I should start small. I have a lot of contacts in town from years in the restaurant business. They might be willing to do little training seminars on various topics and we could hold them at the library. They offer free meeting space for nonprofits."

"Good idea to start small. You can build as you go."

"At those community seminars, I could start an email list from the attendees, and they may become my first clients. I could learn more about what they need. As long as I have a primary goal that's clear, I can take baby steps, as you said. I won't try to do everything at once." The last time she and Colin had talked about it, they'd both assumed she'd wait until after graduating. That was likely a good plan, but Jordan's encouragement spurred her to wanting to at least get her research and first steps lined up ahead of time.

"Have you thought of a name yet?"

Eden fiddled with her napkin and shook her head. "I spent last weekend trying to brainstorm a name. I thought of boring names like Emerging Business Network, things like that. I wanted to include the idea that it was for start-up ventures for women. I liked the word *network*."

"It's a good start. To make it clear it's for women, you could use Emerging Businesswomen's Network. Or Women Emerging in Business Network."

She nodded, not thrilled by any of the options. She'd have to keep mulling it over and something would click.

Her cellphone rang from the kitchen. "I'll let it go to voicemail."

They continued brainstorming for a few more minutes. "I'll get us some more tea and clear off some of these." She stacked their plates along her arm.

"I'll help." Colin stood and hoisted the partly empty pan of lasagna from the table.

Eden set the dishes into the sink, determined to do as Colin had done the week before, leave them there to soak until after he left. She glanced at her phone to see who'd called, hoping the twins were okay. It was a mom reflex.

"How strange. Mariella called and left a message. She rarely calls me, except for that one time she called to tell me her suspicions about the Launchpad." She stopped and listened to the message. *Sorry to bother you on a weekend, Eden. It's Mariella. I just phoned my friend, Joanne. You know, the one I told you about who thinks her idea was stolen by the Launchpad. I told her I'd mentioned it to you, and you wanted to do some research on it. She was eager to talk to you and said you should also talk to her friend, Eric. He developed an idea several years ago and is convinced it was stolen by someone at the Launchpad. Joanne said you could call her directly and set up a time to meet. Just wanted to let you know. See you Tuesday at the normal time."*

Eden set the phone on the granite island. A mixture of concern and anger pinged through her body.

"What is it?"

"Mariella had more information. I told you about that girl, Joanne, who thinks her idea was stolen by someone at the Launchpad. She wants to talk to me in person. And she has another friend who's had the same experience. We're about to get some case studies, though not the kind I expected."

"I'm happy to go with you if you want. We'll be able to get more specifics and see if there's anything to this suspicion."

Could this give them hard evidence? Or were they just prying open a large can of worms?

Chapter Sixteen

"Are you ready for this?" Colin's warm hazel eyes found Eden's as they sat in the front seat of his Toyota SUV. Eden nodded and their fingers linked for a squeeze. She slipped out of the car and glanced at Joanne's home, an attractive brick ranch-style skirted by boxwood hedges.

As they approached the front door, it opened, and a woman appeared behind the screen. "Hi, I'm Joanne." She opened the door and stood back so they could enter. "Thanks so much for coming."

Joanne appeared to be in her late twenties and was about four months pregnant. Straight, dark hair framed her pale face in shoulder-length layers.

Colin and Eden introduced themselves and Joanne led them into a Colonial-style living room decorated in deep reds and blues. Eden and Colin sat on the couch, and Joanne perched on an armchair across from them.

"I appreciate your letting us come," Eden said. "I know your situation happened a few years ago, but anything you can tell us would be a help." She gave the woman a conciliatory half-smile. "I'd like to help prevent this from happening to other people, but as you likely know, it's hard to prove."

Joanne leaned forward to pour glasses of lemon water for them as a staccato laugh emerged from her throat. "Yes, I'm only too aware of that. I protested to some directors of the Launchpad, and they nearly laughed me out of their office. They told me many people come up with similar ideas, and the first one to develop and patent it wins the game, so to speak."

Colin frowned. "They don't sound very sympathetic."

"That almost hurt as much as losing the opportunity to develop my toy. I trusted these guys. From the beginning, they seemed like such supportive people." She grimaced. "That is, up to the moment that you don't win, then you're nothing." Joanne shook her head. "That doesn't really matter. They're nothing to me, but their attitudes were cold."

"Can you describe the application process for me?" Eden asked.

"Sure. I'll try to remember the order of things. I filled out an application in which I included a description of my invention, the uses and benefits of it, a drawing, and possible public who would want to buy it. I had to show that I'd researched potential competitors. All that was excellent preparation, and I was thankful to be made to do it ahead of time. The leaders of the Launchpad reviewed all the ideas, then contacted people whose ideas seemed to have merit for an interview. I'm sure they get a lot of applications for things they wouldn't even consider. They considered mine. Actually, my brother Tim and I developed it together. I had an education background, and he's a programmer. So, after about a month, I was called in for an interview. I talked to three guys on a panel about my invention. Tim came with me, and he explained the tech part of it. After another month, I got a response, and of course, it was negative. This didn't surprise me, since there are only a few slots for funding and quite a few good projects were presented."

"You must have been disappointed, though." Eden reached for a glass from the coffee table and sipped the tangy water.

"Yes, I was, but Tim and I weren't about to give up. We knew going in that there was a slim chance we'd get funding. So, we kept working on it for the next year." Joanne's reserved expression became animated. She drank some water and leaned back, laying one hand on her distended belly. "We didn't know anything about patents and figured the toy needed to be fully functional before we applied. But then a few months ago, I saw Tim's and my invention advertised online at a store called Young Minds Inc. I couldn't believe it. It was the very same toy as ours. I cried for two days."

"How much time had gone by between the time you submitted your idea to the Launchpad and the day you saw your toy advertised?" Colin asked.

"It was about three years, give or take. I'd already graduated, gotten married, moved into this house."

"Did you and your brother keep working on your idea after that?" Eden looked back up from where she jotted dates onto a spiral notepad. Heavy sadness for Joanne filled her inside. The young woman had spent years, poured out ideas, enthusiasm, investing in a dream that had splintered into shards.

Joanne shrugged. "A little bit. I admit, I lost my heart for it after that. Tim kept trying to convince me we could adapt it and still make the idea work. Then life took over, my wedding, the move. Now the baby." Her voice trailed off and her gaze wandered to the window. The rims of her eyes pinkened. She blinked and slid her stare back to the table in front of her.

"I know it must be hard to recall all those hopes and dreams," Eden said softly. "Maybe Tim is right, and you can adapt the idea so it's a bit different but uses some of the same elements."

Colin set his glass of water on the table. "Joanne, let me be devil's advocate for a minute. We all know lots of people can come up with the same idea. What is it that convinces you that your idea was stolen by someone in the Launchpad instead of simply invented in the same way you guys thought of it?"

Joanne sat up straighter and the crumpled expression on her face changed as her jaw tightcned. "That's a fair question, one I've asked myself dozens of times. First, I think Tim told the team too much during our interview. He talked about specifics of programming. There was this guy among them who was taking notes. Lots of them. We thought that was part of the interview process. Maybe it was, but the basic mechanics of the toy were in our application. Dr. Siler was there asking a lot of questions too and taking notes along with the others."

Eden's head shot up from her notepad. "Dr. Siler was there?" And taking notes?

"I guess that's because he's the faculty advisor." Joanne's eyes narrowed. "Does that seem strange to you?"

"I don't know. No, maybe not. I thought he was only the faculty liaison between the Launchpad and the students. I didn't know he was involved in the actual interview process."

"I thought the same thing, but when I saw him at the interview, I realized he was part of the team." Joanne reached for a small pillow and slid it behind her lower back.

Part of the team. Maybe that explained why he'd so heavily promoted the Launchpad to Eden. Was he getting anything out of it? Or was he simply promoting an organization he fully believed would help students?

"Was there anything else that led you to believe your ideas were stolen by someone on the Launchpad rather than just beating you in the timing?" Colin's question broke through a momentary silence.

"Mostly the fact that Tim's process was unique, and he told everything to the team. I didn't know he'd do that, and I think he regretted it afterward. I was alarmed by all the notes they were taking, but still trusted them." She let out a deep sigh. "Tim went into a sort of depression afterward. He thought it was his fault. But we learned from that, so maybe it'll help us in the future."

"I hope you both aren't planning to give up. I'm sure a lot of successful inventors have this experience in the beginning."

At Eden's comment, Joanne's face brightened. "You're right. I told Tim to work on something else and as soon as the baby's born, I'll be able to help him."

"When is your baby due?"

A soft smile stretched across Joanne's now relaxed face. "In late July. I know I'm showing my inexperience promising any help to Tim once the baby's born. I'll be over my head then."

"Yes, I'm afraid you will for a little while." Eden knew that well from experience. "If you have a passion, it can take a back seat for a few years for more pressing events, then you can get back to it. It won't go away." She met Joanne's gaze and gave her a reassuring nod.

Suddenly Joanne's expression sobered, and she turned to Colin. "To finish answering your question, Colin, another thing that convinced me my ideas were stolen is I kept hearing about other people who'd had the same thing happen to them. I mentioned one of the guys to Mariella. His name is Eric. He developed an inflatable umbrella about five or six years ago. I didn't know him at the time, since he graduated well before I did, but I met someone who knew him. Once this happened to me, I spoke to him on the phone, and he told me about his experience. I'll give you his contact info before you leave."

As Colin and Eden said goodbye to Joanne, Eden's mind whirled. They got into the car and Colin started the engine. He turned on the heat but didn't change gears. "What are your impressions?"

Eden absently clicked the seatbelt into place, her eyes still trained on Joanne's house. She shifted her gaze to him. "Everything we heard today strengthens my suspicions, but there still won't be any way to prove anything."

His breath puffed a vapor cloud into the cold car. "There may be no way to even have enough evidence to go further without patent information. It's simply unprovable. The perfect crime, you could say. Unless, by a longshot, someone on the Launchpad team applied for a patent for one of the student's projects."

"Only I don't know their names, aside from Dr. Siler. If only there were some way I could find the names of the Launchpad team."

"Are the names published on their website?"

"Maybe. I never thought to look, and I'm sure they change over time. They're volunteers, so they likely sign up for a rotating term, like board members of a company."

"Which will make it harder to find the names of those involved when Joanne or Eric applied. But we can always try. I have a lawyer friend who might know of a patent attorney I can contact. He or she might have other angles to consider." Colin gave her a sober look and reached for her hand. He held it for a moment, its warmth spreading through her chilled fingers. "Eden, it's possible that all this will be a dead end, and quickly. You know that, right?"

Eden pressed her lips together and nodded. "I know."

"But remember something. If we accomplish nothing with the Launchpad, that doesn't change the fact that you, Eden Godfrey, can start your nonprofit and help women entrepreneurs. Regardless. You can and will have an impact."

A smile crept up Eden's face, and she leaned forward to press a quick kiss on his lips. She pulled back but remained inches from him. "Thanks for the reminder. And thank you for being here with me. I really feel your support and your *friendship.* It feels good to not be alone in this. I'm no hard-boiled sleuth." She pulled her coat collar away from her neck, thankful for the heat that poured out of the vents.

Colin's expression grew tender. "No, you're not a hard-boiled *anything.*" His voice lowered. He reached up one hand to smooth a curl away from her cheek, letting his fingers rest there. "You're soft, compassionate, smart, and beautiful. You're so many things, Eden." He leaned forward and kissed her, softly, slowly, although they still sat in his car in front of Joanne's house. He pulled back, his hand still on her neck. "I love all of them. And I'm honored to walk with you through this mystery. I care about justice for students too, and I'm on board with you." He blinked, then smiled. "And now, I'll take you to lunch."

They pulled away from Joanne's house as Eden settled back against her seat. Despite the troubled cloud dangling in her mind after their conversation with Joanne, Colin's words sifted back, *I love all of them.* Was he falling in love with her? Was *she* falling in love?

ℛ   ℛ   ℛ

Eric Borelli now lived in Minnesota, but Eden was able to arrange an online video call with him the following week. He appeared to be nearly thirty years old. While he recounted the story of submitting his invention to the Launchpad, his dark eyes and facial expression blazed with frustration. The common denominator was the Launchpad, and the fact that he'd shared diagrams and technical details with the interview team. Unsuspecting students wanted to succeed. But they'd given all the details of their inventions to a team of deceptive wolves eager to exploit them. Was the whole team guilty, or just one or more members?

The video call ended, leaving Eden more convinced than ever that something illegal was afoot. She crossed her arms and rocked gently in her desk chair. It seemed like an impossible mystery to crack. *Lord, I need your help with this. In fact, would you fight this battle for me? I know it takes me a while to ask for your help, even though I do trust you. I still depend on myself too much. I think you're showing me that it's a dumb idea to not ask you for help.*

She sighed again and closed her eyes. Was she still afraid to trust him? She was much better at encouraging others in their faith. In most circles that would be called hypocrisy. She was always sincere when she spoke heartfelt encouragements to her friends and her kids. When it touched on her own life, though, that was another story.

God was sovereign, the pastor had said. Sovereign and completely good. Colin had told her that believing this provided comfort, not fear. At the time, Eden hadn't been so sure as she reflected on her early life. As for the current challenge, it seemed she and Colin were already at a dead end, even amid valid suspicions. Right about now, God's intervention seemed like the only chance for a breakthrough. And a comfort as well, smoothing the edge off her frayed nerves and troubling thoughts.

It could still turn out to be a set of coincidences. No guilty party, just pure bad luck, as other inventors happened to find the same ideas and patent them sooner. It was possible, but Eden's doubt grew stronger day by day. She'd never be convinced it was mere coincidence. She might instead be forced to let it all go because it would be impossible to prove.

ʗ ʗ ʗ

February blew in with a frosty chill that didn't top thirty-five degrees, forcing Eden to use her thick down jacket for her treks across the campus tundra. In her canvas bag was a wedding invitation she'd just received. Marissa and Jarrod would have an April wedding in Asheville. Months ago, Eden had expected to attend her wedding alone, but maybe Colin would go with her. She smiled, despite the razor-sharp cold hitting her cheeks. She and Colin could attend the wedding as a couple.

If she'd known how much she would enjoy being a part of a couple, especially with Colin, she might have tried to meet someone years ago. For the first time since she could remember, Eden had enjoyed Valentine's Day in male company. Even during her marriage, the lovers' holiday usually passed unnoticed because of the demands of the restaurant. Always the restaurant.

Colin had found a new restaurant in Muncie. For one romantic evening, Eden's thoughts were far away. Far from the Launchpad mystery and far from the pressures residing in her current life. Instead, she relished the oasis of a romantic evening with the handsome man across the dimly lit table in a hushed and tastefully appointed dining room. For that slice of time, she blocked out her concerns and enjoyed being a desired woman dressed in elegance, the object of Colin's admiring gaze. His focus was attentive, his eyes intense, nourishing her feminine soul. It had been a long time since she'd felt that way. A long time since someone had looked at her like that. During the exquisite dinner, they avoided all discussions of the Launchpad or the nonprofit, as if by silent agreement. It was *their* time as a couple, and she wouldn't taint it with darker thoughts.

By the following week, though the memory the Valentine's dinner left a splash of pleasure in her mind, the questions evoked by Mariella and Joanne seeped back. Meanwhile, her progress on the nonprofit stalled and sat idle, a stack of papers in an untouched folder on her desk. She'd struggled for weeks to find an appropriate name, but every idea that came to her fell flat, nondescript and lacking sparkle. Without a name, she had to delay promoting the organization to prospective board members. Aside from that, she hadn't yet filled out the legal paperwork, often feeling confused about what she should do first. Despite that obstacle, the nonprofit's purpose of helping women start in business remained clear in her mind, though its urgency was currently upstaged by the deepening Launchpad puzzle.

Eden sat alone at the corner table of the campus coffee shop where she normally met with her school friends. It wasn't their usual day, but she'd craved a hot drink and some alone time. Life was getting complex between Colin, the nonprofit, and the developing web of stolen ideas. Not to mention her school assignments. She hadn't even talked to the twins in a week and her girlfriends even longer. How to catch everyone up on the current dramas?

The hum of conversation and the whoosh of the espresso machine filled the air with comforting background noise. The coffee shop was adjacent to the library. As Eden idly watched student traffic back and forth through the doorway, she saw Dr. Siler enter the shop and stand in line at the counter. He bought a bottled drink and turned back toward the library door but stopped to scan the room. He met Eden's gaze and approached her table.

"Hello, Eden," he said with a tight smile, unlike the warm greeting he'd given her the last time she stopped by his office. "Do you mind stepping into the library for a minute? I'd like to ask you a question and it's a bit noisy here."

Surprised, Eden reached for her tote bag. "Sure, Dr. Siler." Her heart pounded as she rose to follow him to the library. She couldn't imagine what he wanted from the grim expression on his face. Aside from their terse conversation about the Launchpad a month earlier, she'd had no contact with him since she wasn't in any of his classes that semester. She hadn't called him Marcus since ending their social relationship. Maybe he'd noticed. That day, he seemed cool and formal, walking a few paces ahead of her.

Dr. Siler led Eden to a row of bookshelves, noticeably quieter since few students were browsing there. "I wanted to reassure myself that you'd left the Launchpad inquiry alone, as I'd encouraged you to do."

A moment of shock was quickly engulfed by fury as she thought of the Launchpad victims. Joanne, Eric, and others. Innocent students whose creativity had been exploited. She had to be onto something. Otherwise, Siler wouldn't have dragged away during her personal time. She needed a sufficiently vague and misleading response but had no time to compose one. "No, Dr. Siler. I mean, yes, I haven't pursued anything. I have too much work this semester to think about that."

His eyes narrowed and his expression darkened. Wrong answer, since it implied she'd resume her investigation as soon as she had time.

The slight lie she'd told twinged inside her, but she knew she couldn't answer honestly. So far, he was under suspicion, as was everyone else associated with the Launchpad.

A menacing gaze from behind his glasses met hers. "Does that mean you've abandoned your distrust of the Launchpad?"

"I understood your feelings about that. You told me you'd look into it, and I believed you. I wouldn't want to block any students from a good opportunity." She couldn't stop herself from adding, "If that's what it is."

Dr. Siler's jaw tightened. "It's a valid organization doing good work. The last thing it needs is a misguided activist tearing apart what they'd taken years to accomplish with students. Do you understand?"

The ferocity of his tone took Eden aback. Her scalp prickled, but she didn't whither beneath his stare, as he likely expected her to. "I do."

"If you don't, I'm afraid I'll have to take action against you."

Her eyes widened and she fought to harness her anger. "Really? Are you threatening me for simply asking valid questions based on some observations?"

"I'm threatening you if you try to destroy an organization that does so much good for students. I'm concerned enough about the students you'll harm if you continue with this preposterous witch hunt. There have to be consequences."

"That's a bit strong, don't you think?" Her initial rage seeped away. Maybe she'd just push some buttons and see what she got. "*Destroying* an organization? I'm hardly doing that." Eden's throat tightened as she detected a wild cast to his eyes. *Back down, Eden.*

The warning whispered in her mind. Yet, it was an ideal moment to test him, wasn't it? "What can you do to me, Dr. Siler? Just by curiosity."

His sneer deepened. "You want to get your degree, Eden. You told me it was one of your dearest desires, a lifetime goal. I can stop you."

Her mouth went dry, and her heart began thumping against her ribs. "You can? You *would*? How? My grades are great." She couldn't let him see her fear at his words. She drew her shoulders back, though it didn't change the fact he towered over her.

A sly smile stretched his lips and his eyes remained cold, like a shark or a snake. "You need one final class to graduate next fall, remember? Management Economics. I teach that class. I can find a way to bar you from enrolling." He shrugged. A bored blandness replaced the previous intensity in his expression. "Or fail you. Wouldn't be that hard."

Fail her? Eden had never failed at anything academically in her life. Not as a child, not as an adult. That had been her means of escaping her family, and it had worked for a while. Academic success was something she knew she could control. She was smart, worked hard. But Dr. Siler could pull the rug out from under her faulty foothold without a second thought.

Despite the fact that her legs felt like jelly, Eden was emboldened by the outrage that crawled up her throat. She kept her tone even. All she had to do was get out of this confrontation. "That's unethical, you know. I'm not saying I would do anything against the Launchpad you care so deeply about. It doesn't matter that much to me. You know I want my degree, so I can easily back down. I won't jeopardize it. But you are a bully, Dr. Siler." *And you must have something to hide.*

His jaw slackened as he visibly relaxed. "Backing down is an excellent idea. You're as smart as I thought you were, Eden." His voice lowered to a gravelly scrape. "Yes, I'm protective of the Launchpad because I've seen the good it does for students."

Eden continued to stare at him, her lips pressed together. *Don't say another word. Turn and go. Just go.* She turned and left the library, taking pains to hide the fact that she was trembling from head to toe.

Chapter Seventeen

Colin and Eden sat in the front seat of his Toyota on Saturday morning. The buds of early spring had pushed out of the branches of bare trees seemingly overnight, though a sharp chill still laced the air.

"Is this the right address?" Colin held up his phone to show Eden.

She leaned from the passenger seat to peer at the GPS. "Yes, that's the one I found." Her search in the faculty directory had yielded nothing on Dr. Siler but an office phone number and campus address, as she'd expected. But the internet had been more cooperative. During her one restaurant date with her professor, he hadn't talked about where he lived, nor much else about his personal life. She regretted not asking more questions when she had the opportunity. His answers would come in handy now, although the few she had asked had yielded sketchy responses. The man was a closed book even before she'd gotten on his revenge list. "This might be a wild goose chase, of course."

Colin's face sobered. "Yes, it may very well be. We're just going for a drive together, right? If we don't learn anything new, we've had a nice Saturday morning outing."

She nodded and looked down at her hands, ignoring the heaviness that fell like a blanket.

"Hey." Colin's voice softened, and he tipped her chin up so she looked into his eyes. "Are you okay? You were pretty shaken last night when you told me what happened in the library."

Unbidden, her eyes filled. She blinked the tears away, but they slid down her cheeks. She swiped in frustration at her cheeks. "Yes and no. I think he'll make good on his threat if I keep going. So, I have two bad choices. I let this criminal dirtbag get away with whatever he's doing so I can get my degree, or I become a crusader and lose everything I've worked for this year."

"There's a third choice." Colin paused, making sure he had her attention. "We trust God's sovereignty to work this out."

Eden nodded without responding. Yes, there was that. She sighed. Lately, that hadn't been her first reflex.

"And would not getting your degree really be the end of the world?"

"No, not the end of the world. You know it's important to me. Maybe we'll just hit so many roadblocks the decision will be out of my hands. I won't have the option of being a crusader."

Colin's face was earnest. "Maybe not this time. Eden, you're a crusader in your heart, whether you admit it or not. You love the underdog, especially the young women who struggle." His voice softened. "I love that about you. But how about we take one day at a time and not assume the worst, okay?"

She smiled then. "Okay. I'm with you and you're in my corner. How bad can it be?"

"Right. And even better, God's in your corner. He's *for* you."

"Yes, he's *for* me," she repeated, willing her heart to believe a little deeper. "I got really mad with Dr. Siler, though I tried not to show it to give him the upper hand."

"Your anger was justified, Eden."

"I know, but ever since discovering my fear of being controlled and the connection with the past, I find myself getting angry more easily. I've never thought of myself as an angry person. I don't like what it's stirred up in me."

"I wouldn't call you an angry person. Your anger over past events has been brought to the surface because you're healing from them. The anger doesn't define *you*. It's like a wound that was ignored for years, then was opened. Now it can heal."

Eden swallowed, though it felt like sand in her throat. She turned to Colin. "You think it's because I'm healing that all these ugly emotions are coming out?"

"I believe so. Are you taking it to the Lord?"

"Trying." How had her faith gotten so tattered? Even so, her admission opened a small door to a trickle of calm. She looked back at Colin and offered a small smile. The idea that the surfacing of anger was part of her healing made her feel less guilty. Not that she'd let rage run unbridled. Instead, she'd let it remind her to take it to God each time, assured he was healing her.

"Okay, Sherlock. If you're ready, I'm ready." Colin pulled away from the curb in front of her house.

The Saturday morning traffic was picking up, though not yet too thick. Overhead, a crystal blue sky belied the prevailing cold. The previous evening during a phone call with Colin, Eden had suggested they drive by Dr. Siler's house. Wouldn't hurt anything and they might get some clues. Nothing had proven Siler's guilt, but his reaction toward her made him a prime suspect, either as a perpetrator or as an accomplice.

By the address, she didn't know if it was a chic neighborhood or if anything else on his property would betray a higher income than a college professor would normally have. Maybe he'd have a fancy car or boat. Then again, if he had spoils from any underhanded activity with the Launchpad, he could have easily hidden them in stocks or other investments they'd never learn about. And none of that would even prove anything but doing something felt better than doing nothing.

"I forgot to tell you." Colin eased the brakes at a red light. "I spoke with my attorney friend, Jason. He's an intellectual property attorney but is involved less with patents. As I hoped, he knows a couple of patent attorneys he deals with in some of his cases. I briefed him on the situation, and he said he'd reach out to one he thinks might be sympathetic."

"That's wonderful news, Colin. It'll be so good to have someone on our side who's also knowledgeable about patents. The research I found online is contradictory and complicated." She shook her head. "I'm sure glad *I'm* not trying to invent something. It's not an easy road, with or without something like the Launchpad."

"I'm sure that's true. It's long and expensive, apparently. There are different agencies that can help would-be inventors. At a price, of course."

"Of course."

The GPS gave clipped instructions to enter a highway. Colin flipped his blinker and eased onto the ramp. "We'll be there in another twenty minutes."

"I'm surprised Dr. Siler lives that far from campus." Though probably a lot of school employees had at least a thirty-minute commute. Didn't mean anything.

When they arrived in the town where Dr. Siler lived, Eden noticed an ordinary-looking main street with storefronts and chain stores on either side. "So far, looks pretty normal. Maybe he got a good deal on a house out here."

Colin focused on the voice of the GPS, who suddenly had a lot of instructions. Left turn, two blocks, right turn. Finally, they entered a neighborhood with two large signs at its entrance. He slowed the car to twenty-five. A left turn, another right. "This is his street. The house is up ahead on the left."

Eden leaned forward. "Are you sure that's his?" The sprawling house, flanked by immaculate landscaping, sat back a short distance from the street. The right side of it had two stories, and the rest stretched out into the emerald-green lawn that was surely maintained by a professional service. She let out a whistle as Colin slowed the car to a crawl. "He has *this* on a professor's salary?"

"Pretty sweet, eh? Maybe in my next career I'll be a college professor." Colin's tone was dry as he smirked. They idled the car in front of the house.

"I guess I shouldn't judge. Maybe he got a fixer-upper years ago and made it look like this." Eden stared at the property. However he obtained it, at least the man had good taste.

"Don't believe that. I can tell by the other houses that it's a pricey neighborhood. In fact . . . " He picked up the phone from the console and tapped the screen a few times. "Says here the property value is over seven-hundred thousand."

Eden's mouth dropped open. "Wow," she managed. Did he inherit money? Did he publish a bestseller? Or had he stolen ideas and sold them?

As she sat almost in a trance, the front door opened, and Dr. Siler emerged. "Oh, no." Eden slid down in the seat and frantically pulled her hood over her head. Dr. Siler would recognize her bright blond hair in an instant. "Drive, Colin," she hissed as she folded herself even lower into the passenger seat.

Colin accelerated, though not too quickly as to raise suspicion, and turned the corner to the next street. Seconds later he pulled to a curb and idled.

"Do you think he saw us?" Eden pulled herself upright from the floor and resettled in the passenger seat. Colin snickered.

"You're laughing?" She swiped at a lock of hair that still hung in her face.

Colin's laughter filled the car. "You're so funny crunched down on the floor. I couldn't help it."

"You *do* realize, don't you, that he could have recognized me in the car and accused me of stalking him?"

"I know. But it's still hilarious. In answer to your question, he looked up and saw us moving slowly. I'm sure he was curious, but he didn't see us parked. He doesn't recognize me or my car, so that's good."

Eden refastened her seatbelt. "I hope he doesn't make more trouble for me. He can't prove anything. But what we saw was evidence. Not evidence that proves anything, but suspicious, all the same."

"I agree it's odd but doesn't prove anything."

She sighed. "Yeah, we're back to that."

ಞ ಞ ಞ

The following Wednesday after classes were over for the day, Eden finally had time to plop into her desk chair at home and pull out her file on the nonprofit. Amid mounting circumstantial evidence against the Launchpad, new semester assignments, and mundane matters of house and life maintenance, she'd neglected it. She was only in the research phase, so there was no self-imposed deadline looming. It was more of an expectation she'd put on herself to keep all plates spinning at once. She knew that was counterproductive but couldn't stop herself from trying.

She opened the folder. On the top page were three names of potential board members. She sought experienced men and women with skills that could contribute to her goals and share her vision to help young women starting businesses. None had responded to her initial letter yet. Had she been premature? Probably.

She still didn't have a catchy name she loved. She'd settled on a working name, Women Emerging in Business. She liked its acronym, WEB, which could also convey the idea of a network of helpful resources. Colin had affirmed the name, saying, *As a name, it's not sexy, but it's clear. And that's what you want, right?*

She'd agreed that clarity was most important, as long as the name wasn't clunky or generic sounding. At least with a name she could live with, she'd be able to fill out the paperwork and request a nonprofit status. She'd already done her basic assessment of needs in the community, though it was likely the tip of the iceberg. She'd also drafted a mission statement.

There wasn't a lot more she could do prior to receiving a nonprofit status, but she hadn't filed her request yet. She wanted to be ready, but hung back, in case she was overlooking something. That prospect nibbled at her mind, leaving discomfort in its wake.

One thing she could do was call an old associate, Clint Ward. She'd known Clint during her restaurant days and through Gerry. They'd both attended chamber of commerce meetings back in the day.

"Hi, Clint, sorry to disturb you during the workday," she said cheerfully when he picked up the phone. "I hope you had a great holiday and a good New Year so far."

She hadn't spoken to him in over a year, so they caught up on family and personal news. He commended her for wanting to complete her degree.

"I received your letter about the nonprofit, Eden. I haven't had the time to get back to you. It's a good idea, I suppose. I'm not that knowledgeable about the needs you spoke of. I like your idea of hosting seminars initially to get the word out."

"Thank you, Clint. I was thinking the community seminars would be a great thing to continue, even once the nonprofit is established. Free sessions to benefit people in the community, but also to stay visible." A rush of satisfaction at his response pushed away her prior doubts. He was on board with her, at least in theory.

"I'll be honest with you, Eden. It appears to me you're rushing this process. Do you have all your forms filed with the secretary of state? Have you got your entity in line?"

Her buoyancy popped like a balloon. "Um, I'm in the process of doing that. I wanted to give initial information to you and others who might know of needs and resources." She spoke truth, but so had he. She *was* rushing. "In view of needs I've already observed, I felt compelled to start gathering like-minded partners. I don't mean financial partners necessarily." Heat filled her face. She sounded like she was passionate about needs but hadn't done her homework. Hadn't set her foundation.

"How about this, Eden." Clint's voice was compassionate, like a grandfather. "Why don't you get all the administrative parts put together? Your potential donors and board members will want to know the state has already approved you and you exist as an entity. Once that's done, get your website up, your other marketing in place, some initial clients enrolled or whatever. Piece by piece, that's how it's done. Then you'll reach out to people who can help you."

Eden nodded, feeling chastised like a child, though she recognized his wisdom. "That's good advice, Clint. I knew I needed some board members early on, so I rushed to get the word out. And I was moved by the situations I'd seen, women trying to go forward, but hitting obstacles. I guess I'll be more help to them after I put the foundations in place."

"Exactly. And you haven't finished your degree yet, so why not do that first? Take it slow, finish your degree, then you'll have more time and clarity for all this. Running a nonprofit isn't a hobby. It's as much work as running a company, with a few extra pieces, like fundraising and additional tax-related steps the government requires." At her pause, he added, "Keep me posted as you get things put together."

"Absolutely."

Clint had pointed out the obvious. Why didn't she finish her degree before leaping into creating a nonprofit? Another thought brought a chill along with it. What if she didn't finish her degree? What if Dr. Siler learned she was continuing her research on the Launchpad and stopped her from graduating? Colin had pointed out that she could have an impact without a degree. Though that was true, she'd still feel unfinished. How would it look if the founder of a nonprofit didn't have a college degree? She knew several founders of large companies who hadn't finished college, so why would *she* feel like a pretender without one?

As for the nonprofit, was she thinking the whole thing through step by step or just jumping in too quickly from a wellspring of compassion and need, or even selfishly seeking her own legitimacy?

She sat still at her desk, staring out the window where a still naked tree trembled in the winter breeze. Why was she in a rush? Was it because of Jordan's urging, that time would slip by? Was she trying to have something in place already when she finished her program so she wouldn't again be facing an uncertain future? As Marissa said, there was no growth in certainty. And certainty was a myth.

It stared down at her again, that helpless feeling she hated. Reminded her of those first panicky months managing the restaurant herself after Gerry's death. Those had been long, frightening days, when the learning curve seemed like Mount Everest, but she'd been determined to succeed. And she had.

She thought she could do the same thing now by sheer will. Maybe her own will wasn't enough, as she fought the battle against injustice and against the Launchpad. Her quest to create a nonprofit and her drive to expose the Launchpad might not be God's timing nor even his goal for her. As a child, she'd been too small to fight back. Yet somewhere along the line, she'd become too confident in her own abilities.

Eden closed her eyes. *Lord, doing all this with my own strength and determination isn't going to cut it. And even if it could, I wouldn't want to do it without you at the helm."*

Her mind went back to her conversation with Colin that day at the restaurant. He'd insisted God's sovereignty was a comfort. She saw it as a source of fear and helplessness, but in Colin's worst moments, he'd drawn comfort from that certainty. The *only* certainty that existed. Her situation wasn't as dire as his had been. Yet she'd struggled with anxiety all her life. What if . . . The lists were always long. Wouldn't complete trust in a loving God, really letting go, be better than this? Could she bring herself to do it fully, instead of only in the simple things? A parking place, a good night's sleep?

Eden's phone pinged. A text from Colin. *Good news. My attorney friend's colleague is happy to help any way he can. Seems his nephew had a similar thing happen to him when he created something. So, he's eager to help us. Just wanted to brighten your day with that. Hope your Wednesday is going well. Save me Saturday night, okay?*

A smile curled her lips. Colin was a sunny spot in her life for sure, but he also bore excellent news. This patent attorney would join them in their quest. Without that, they might have to halt everything. Even with the man's help, it may lead to nothing, and she had to prepare herself for that.

She noticed another message on her phone, a call from Brent. That was unusual, since he was rarely in touch, and even then, only by text. She hoped nothing was wrong. She input her code as her heart pounded.

At the sound of his first word, *Mom*, terror filled her soul. He sounded anguished or hurt. *Kelly broke up with me last night. I bought a ring so we can get engaged, but she broke up with me. She said I wasn't supportive of her, and it was all about me. Where did she get that idea, Mom?* Eden cringed at his accusatory tone. *When we visited you at Thanksgiving, you must have said some things to her that set her against me. You don't need to control my life and my relationship. I'm a big boy and I can handle this.*

What? Eden searched her memory. What had she said directly to Kelly? She'd showed interest in her work, made a comment about children versus career, but nothing too bold or pushy. She shook her head. This was a mystery, but a cold spear thrust through her insides. Her lastborn child was furious with her.

Eden dialed Brent's number, her shaking hands slowing the task. He didn't answer. Of course, he'd be at work. "Brent, honey, I just got your message. I'm so sorry Kelly broke up with you, but I have no idea what you mean about me setting her against you. I'd never do that, and I'm sure you know that. I thought she was lovely, and I can see you together. But I barely know Kelly and had no contact with her other than that weekend." She groped for more words that might convince him. "I spoke to you alone about your relationship just to encourage you to make it about *both* of you. I wanted to help you *avoid* a problem so that it *would* work out between you, do you see? It's important for a couple to validate each other. But I'd never try to set her against you." She swallowed a sob. "It breaks my heart that you would say that to me. Please call me when you can, and we'll talk about it."

He wouldn't. She knew her son. He'd stew in his misguided beliefs.

Tears gushed from her eyes and a whimper escaped her throat. Had she said something offensive without realizing it? Or had there been other events since Thanksgiving that had occurred between Brent and Kelly, which caused the breakup? She was almost certain it wasn't anything she'd said. Brent was hurting and lashing out instead of considering something *he* may have done.

Just like his father.

Chapter Eighteen

Eden sat in her car in Colin's driveway on Saturday evening. Eagerness to see him swirled against a pervasive impression that her life hung in midair. Her degree was uncertain, as was the future of her nonprofit. Who was she kidding? She couldn't even finish a year of college, let alone run an organization. She hadn't taken the proper steps, but was rushing to get something established, as if the opportunity would vanish if she didn't grab on and control it. As if it were completely up to her to make it all happen.

No wonder she felt anxious. And tired.

With a heavy sigh, she slid out of the car. The wind had picked up again, and she tightened her scarf around her neck for the short walk to Colin's front door. As she approached, she recalled the first time she'd come and, despite her dark mood, couldn't stop a smile from tugging at her lips. That was the night they'd talked about their relationship, their first kiss. The night they'd become a couple.

Lately, most of their conversations had been about the Launchpad and the nonprofit, leaving her with the feeling they were business associates. That wasn't what she aimed for as she sought a partner, and it was her fault she'd let it go there. Guilt and regret twinged inside. Colin was too good a listener to pull her back to the fact that it wasn't all about her. And he deserved better.

Colin opened the door at her knock and swept her into a warm embrace, followed by a light kiss. "I've missed you, Eden." True, they hadn't found much time together since their drive to Dr. Siler's house the previous week. No word yet from the attorneys working with them. Time to put that aside for a few hours.

"I've missed you too." She managed an apologetic smile.

He took her coat and led her to the kitchen, just as he'd done the first time she went to his house. She settled on a stool at the counter, already feeling at home. In front of her sat a cutting board covered with chopped tomatoes and cucumber and something simmered on the stovetop. "Smells wonderful. Italian?"

"You guessed correctly. But why wouldn't you?" He lifted his brows. "I strive for culinary excellence when you come for dinner, not only to impress you but knowing you must have high standards." His playful expression told her he was at least half-kidding.

"Don't you believe it. Owning a restaurant doesn't make one an expert at food. In fact, I must admit I'm not that good of a cook."

Colin's gaze lifted to hers as he continued cutting the tomato. "You said that the other day when I was at your house. Who told you that? I think you're a fine cook."

Eden shrugged. "Gerry always told me that. He'd make these little jokes about my cooking, but they hurt. I never let on how much, except once, and he told me he was just kidding, and I was being too sensitive."

Colin grimaced. "Maybe he was the one with insecurities, so it made him feel better to put you down." He paused. "I'm sorry, Eden. It's not my place to criticize your late husband."

"It's fine, you're right. I did figure that out after a while and thought maybe he needed to do that. Anyway, I didn't mean for the conversation to go there. We can keep it light." To underscore her statement, she forced a smile. After all, Gerry was gone, so she should let go of his faults too.

Colin looked unconvinced, but then his expression changed. "Wine? I have a red blend from Washington State."

Eden nodded. "Please. I'll get it, you're busy." She rose and went to a bottle he'd already opened. "In fact, I can certainly help. I forgot to offer."

He pulled a pan from the stove and gently spooned its contents over steaming pasta. "All done. Just relax and enjoy. I heard from Jason, my attorney friend," he said without looking up. "The patent lawyer is called Robert, and he went through some patent data bases present and past but couldn't find the name Marcus Siler."

Disappointment pooled inside Eden. "Oh." Then her head shot up, and she met his gaze. "Oh, wait. His real name is Eugene. I remember now."

"Eugene? But he goes by Marcus?"

"Yes, he told me that one night at dinner."

Confusion crossed Colin's face. "At dinner? You went to dinner with your professor?"

Heat rushed up Eden's neck. "Uh, yes just once. He asked me out a couple of times before you and I met up again. We went once to a restaurant, and we were sharing things we think few people know about us. I guess, as an ice breaker of sorts. He said his real name is Eugene. He goes by Marcus, which is his middle name, apparently."

"In all the times we've talked about Siler, you never mentioned you'd gone out with him." Colin didn't seem angry, but less laid-back than usual.

"I'm sorry. It wasn't deliberate. It was past history, so I didn't think of it. I don't know why I went out with him, honestly. Maybe I needed a boost and his attention felt good. I don't know." Against her better judgment, she'd accepted his invitation not once, but twice. "But I cut it off quickly. I saw he wasn't a believer. Also, we had little in common, aside from an interest in business."

The troubled expression eased away from Colin's face. "And maybe he's a thief too." He turned to scoop the cucumber and tomato mixture into a bowl, then added feta cheese chunks.

"That looks good." Her stomach rumbled just then as she realized she'd missed lunch. A result of her preoccupation with Brent, which still hung heavily in her mind.

"It is. I'll add some fresh mint. I had this once at the home of a friend from the Middle East and it became a favorite. Easy to make too."

Apprehension eased inside Eden as Colin's attention seemed to move away from her previous relationship with Dr. Siler.

"Eugene," he muttered as he walked to a small built-in desk in the corner and pulled out a pad of paper. He jotted the name and returned to the counter. "I'll let Robert know. This is almost ready, so you can help take things to the dining room."

She rose instantly. "I can set the table."

"It's done, so just grab the salad and I'll get the fettuccine and sauce."

They settled at the table, adorned with candles, and set with matching dishes. Eden loved that Colin always paid attention to the ambiance, candles, gentle jazz in the background, appetite-provoking smells emanating from the kitchen. Coming to his home felt like an haven from her crazy life. "This is lovely, as usual." She reached for his hand and squeezed it. A small sweep of melancholy whisked by and then disappeared. Where had that come from and why? She didn't know, except she missed these moments where their focus wasn't on mysteries to solve. She sensed that their current contentment was somehow fragile.

"Before I forget, you remember I told you about my friend Marissa?" she asked after he'd prayed for the meal.

"Of course. One of the famous four from college days, right?"

"Yes, the very same. She's getting married in April and I'd like to invite you to come with me to the wedding. If you want to." She hesitated. "If you're free."

Colin reached out for her hand with both of his. "I'd be honored."

"You're more than a plus one, you know." She softened her tone, suddenly feeling shy.

"Thanks. I feel reassured."

He winked and though there was humor in his voice, his statement sunk heavily in her stomach. Did he mean anything by that? Was he unsure of her? She'd hoped for a different response.

Eden didn't have the energy to pursue it, preferring to enjoy their peaceful evening. "The wedding is the second weekend in April in Asheville, North Carolina. We should fly, don't you think?" She didn't wait for his answer. "I can't wait for you to meet my friends." For the first time, all four of them would be together with husbands and significant others. She hoped the pairing up of the women wouldn't lead to the end of their supportive bond. That they hadn't met in November had been a unanimous decision since they'd seen each other in August for Julia's wedding. Their April reunion might get them all back on track. They wouldn't abandon the four of them, as Sydney had promised almost a full year ago.

"Suddenly, you look lost in thought."

She smiled and looked at her hands. "Thinking of my friends. We used to meet twice a year and now all four of us have men in our lives. I hope that won't change our friendship."

"Those men, they get in the way sometimes." Colin pushed his plate away.

"And aren't we glad of that." Her tone matched the humor in his. "But I'd still hate to see us fade away as a girls' group. It's meant a lot to all of us."

"Then it should be preserved. There's no reason to let life changes stop you from continuing to get together. I'm looking forward to meeting these friends you've raved so much about."

During the meal, Eden made a conscious effort to avoid talking about school, the Launchpad, and her nonprofit. After dinner, they lingered at the table. Colin refilled her wine glass halfway. "Do you have any news about Brent?"

She stiffened at the mention of his name. After receiving her son's text message, she'd later called Colin to tell him about it. It was amazing how quickly Colin had become her rock. Eden shook her head. "I asked him to call me but, of course, he didn't. He's probably stewing and doesn't want me to explain. I've given it some thought, and I might have come across too strong. Not so much with Kelly, but with him." She bit her lip. Not the first time she'd tried to run interference to spare her children something she feared. The incident with Brent had come at her like a flash flood, taking her off guard. She couldn't begin to make him understand what she'd experienced and the reason she didn't want him to repeat history.

"You said you confronted him about behavior you observed. Aside from that, you showed interest in his girlfriend's work. That all sounds positive to me." Colin paused and drained his wine glass. "Is there more?"

Her shoulders sagged. "He accused me of trying to control his life and relationship. That was unfair. Of course, I don't want to control his relationship. But I've never learned the best way to talk to him, so that he understands I'm only suggesting. He thinks I'm mothering him. Maybe it's a guy thing." She paused. "I just don't want him following in his dad's footsteps by getting all wrapped up in his own life and forgetting the desires of his wife. But he might have felt I was pushing him. After our conversation that day, he seemed okay. But I know from experience that sometimes he'll look fine on the outside, but after stewing on something, he gets angry." Oh, how she hated that. Not knowing where she stood. Having to guess and watch her steps.

"He might just need a scapegoat for his pain." Candlelight cast a dancing glow on Colin's shadowed face. "If he's open, though, it can only make things better between the two of them."

"If it's not too late." Despair spiraled through her chest. "That depends on Kelly. And if they don't get back together, I wonder if he'll stay mad at me forever."

Colin reached for her hand, a gentle smile on his lips. "Now, don't catastrophize in advance, Eden. You'll likely be able to talk it over with him soon."

She nodded. "I hope so." She offered a sad smile, then closed her eyes briefly to recalibrate her thoughts with the mellow notes of instrumental jazz drifting from the living room.

Colin withdrew his hand and fell silent for several minutes. "I'm glad you have the view that couples should support one another."

Something Eden couldn't identify hung in his words. "You've been so supportive of me in our Launchpad mystery and the nonprofit, and I want you to know how much I appreciate that. But I want to support you too, but I'm not always sure how. You haven't shared a lot about your work, other than you're bored with it and wanted to change. Or maybe there are other areas where you'd like support." She paused and searched his face, which was unreadable just then. "Are there?"

The way he blinked and didn't respond right away caused a wave of dread to ripple through her.

"I do want to be there for you, Eden. And I want you to be there for me too."

Eden's mouth fell open slightly as she mentally spooled through their weeks and months together. She blinked as tears threatened to fill her eyes. "Are you speaking in general, or do you think I'm one-sided like my son Brent? Do you think I think it's all about me?" Was that even possible? She'd spent her life doing for others, supporting them, ignoring her own needs. But that didn't give her the right to become absorbed in her own priorities.

A partnership wasn't one-sided, nor was a romantic relationship.

He remained silent.

"When I asked you about your work a few times, you didn't want to talk about it. Remember?"

"You're right. At those moments, I was tired and didn't want to explain the cases I was dealing with. It's true that we haven't talked much about my desires or what my goals are. I'm not blaming you,

Eden. I *wanted* to talk to you about your concerns. But as I mentioned to you once, sometimes I go along for a while and don't talk about what I'm dreaming of or what I want. That's my fault. I can't blame you for that."

"I guess we got caught up in the Launchpad stuff and the nonprofit. I apologize if I haven't been there for you as much as I should have."

"Don't get me wrong, Eden. I *love* supporting you," he said. "I haven't regretted it for a minute. But there *are* times it seems like we talk too much about it. I'd like us to lighten up more often and focus on each other more."

The muscles in his jaw tensed, unlike the laid-back Colin she'd gotten used to. Was there another side of Colin she hadn't seen?

Yet his words echoed her own desires. "Yes, of course. I'd like that too. And I'm sorry I've talked so much about my burdens. I'll try to find the balance. From now on, say you'd like to change the topic, if that's what you want." Her eyes raised to his again. Colin's face had relaxed. "Can you please tell me things you wanted me to ask you about?"

"I don't want to make it about me, either. I think of myself as a pretty laid-back guy, but I also need to be more open with you. I care about you so much that I hesitate sometimes to speak up. My ex-wife Adele sometimes used things I shared against me when we had a fight. That reinforced my weakness just as I was making progress with it."

"That sounds unloving and cruel on her part. I think it was normal for you to share things with her. That's part of intimacy."

"True. But intimacy is tricky. The person has to be ready for it."

Confusion tumbled in Eden's mind. "But in a committed relationship, it's necessary, whether or not it's comfortable. Don't you think?"

"I agree a hundred percent."

"Colin, do you want to tell me something you don't think I'll be ready to hear? I sense there's something you're not telling me." Her heart began thumping in her chest, but she kept a calm expression on her face.

A long pause followed, as if he were constructing the best way to let her down. She braced herself but knew that would do nothing for her.

"Maybe. I'll just say it and see what you think. Better now than later in our relationship when things get more serious between us."

"You're scaring me now, Colin. Spit it out. What am I going to be terrified to hear?" In her mind, they were already serious. But not in his? She swallowed the dry lump that had formed in her throat.

"Okay, here goes. You already know that for a few years, I've been getting increasingly unhappy in my work. I couldn't change because of the kids, as I told you. Now, with April graduating in a year, I'm revisiting that idea."

Eden laid her hand on his forearm. "I'd encourage you in whatever endeavor you wanted to do, Colin. Do you know what you'd like to do?"

"Yes." He answered without hesitation, but his forced smile took on a veil of sadness that caught her breath. "I've thought about it a lot, but recently, I concluded that I want to take an early retirement and do something completely different."

As he spoke, she noticed a new fire emerged in his eyes, a challenge of life. "I'd like to move to Colorado."

Her eyes widened, and she fell back against her chair. A sudden force pressed down on her chest and lungs as she struggled to take a full breath. "I, um, don't know what to say." When an ache replaced the numbness of shock, a sting began in her eyes. She blinked and stared down at the chandelier's reflection on the silverware. "I don't know what to say," she whispered. After twelve years of hiding out from men, she'd finally found one who evoked feelings she'd forgotten. One she could see in her future. And he wanted to move across the country. Out of her life.

Colin leaned toward her. "It's not for tomorrow. I'm thinking about it and wanted to let you know that's a desire I've had for a while. A strong desire. Do you remember I mentioned it once when we first started seeing each other?"

"No, I don't remember." Her voice emerged in a whisper. She couldn't stop a few tears from squeezing through her eyes. "I do remember you talked so glowingly about Colorado. But it didn't occur to me—"

"Come with me, Eden."

Eden's mouth fell open. "To Colorado? But you said you were just thinking about it. Is this definite?"

"No, of course not. But I want to know how open you'd be *if* it moved in that direction. Maybe after April graduates, or the year after that. I don't know, I'm just thinking about it. Whenever I come back from a trip to see Davis, it hits me how much I love it out there. It suits me, the wide-open spaces, and mountains all around in the distance. The weather's great too. Sunny most of the year."

"And snowy," Eden couldn't help but add.

"It's not the same. There is a lot of snow, but the humidity is much lower, so it melts quickly and doesn't even *feel* as cold. Not like the snow here."

"Sounds like you've already decided." Waves of darkness swirled around her. Why wasn't it ever her turn? Colin seemed perfect for her, though not with a country between them. And not when the specter of his leaving would keep them from building anything further in their relationship. Was she overreacting? Yet, she couldn't lift the heaviness in her chest.

"Eden, I wanted to be up front with you because it's in my mind and it's growing. Every time I visit out there, I come back wondering how I can work it out financially to retire. Life is short. I keep thinking about that. But I want to know how *you* feel because my feelings for you are growing too. You're important to me. I see you as a part of my future."

She couldn't allow the significance of his words to warm her. The future he described wasn't possible. She was already shaking her head. "What about the non-profit?"

"Colorado is a fantastic place for nonprofits. Didn't you know that? And needs are everywhere, not just here. If I took an early retirement, I could help you with it."

Eden pressed her moist hands together, his words pulling a tug of war with her panicked thoughts. "My kids are here. My girls, at least."

Colin let out a patient sigh. "April won't stay in the area after she graduates. She's already told me that. She's heading to Chicago, where she can get a job, live in the big city, and be near my sister. Our kids'll leave, you know that. The twins may move as soon as they marry someone. Brent's already gone. Geographically, I mean. Just think about it, Eden. They can visit you wherever you might go."

Her hands trembled. She pushed them down in her lap. Of course, her objections were easy for him to answer. The real issue wasn't so simple. "Change is so hard for me. So *hard*." Her voice trembled. The walls of her security were cracking, crumbling with an almost audible splintering crash. Once again, her foundations were being pulled from beneath her.

"But you told me you packed up and went all by yourself to North Carolina for college." Colin's voice took on a buoyant tone, though Eden kept looking at her whitening hands. "That took courage, and it was a big change. An adventure."

A humorless laugh escaped her throat as he met his gaze. "*Not* an adventure, I assure you. I was terrified. It was survival. It was my escape from a miserable home life."

"And you told me you loved it." Colin paused, his steady focus trained on her. "Have you ever had an adventure, Eden?" His tone became gentle, inviting.

Eden shook her head. "Not really. I was always escaping something. Even my marriage was an escape of sorts. Then the kids came, and the rest is history."

"It's not the end of your life. You have your future ahead. Your empty nest future, don't you see? It doesn't have to stop there. Please think it over. Pray about it. It may never happen. I might change my mind. But as we grow closer in our relationship, I want to know whether you'd at least be open to it."

Eden's tears began again as her heart tore apart. She rose. "Colin, I need time to think about this, okay? I need to process it."

He stood at the same time but remained at a distance, as if a dry, howling canyon lay between them. "You've told me a couple times how hard change is for you. I get that, given your background. But don't try too hard to control your own life and miss out on something so much better that God might have for you. He may be opening a door for us. Ask him and I'll do the same. Maybe we're not supposed to be together, I don't know. But maybe we are. It's part of the faith thing, Eden. He can guide me to stay or you to go if he wants us together. He can change our desires to fit his good plans for us."

She nodded, blinking away fresh tears, and stepped toward him. His arms went around her. He held her more tightly and longer than he'd ever done before, pressing his lips into her temple, stroking her hair with one hand.

As if he were already saying goodbye.

Chapter Nineteen

Eden awoke to a gray, drizzly Sunday morning. Before she could fully open her eyes, the memory of the previous evening with Colin—and his bombshell—rushed back to her with the force of a tidal wave. She groaned and tears pricked through the sand coating her lashes.

What had begun as a romantic evening had ended like a train wreck. And yet, throughout dinner, she sensed tension she hadn't been able to put her finger on. How long had he been sitting on his secret desire? And why had he told her just then? Clearly, he'd sensed their growing commitment to each other, as she had, and he wanted to make sure it wouldn't split apart down the road. A wise thought, but how painful the result. Pain soon or pain later, both options agonizing.

She should have known it was all too good to be true, finding love again at her age.

With a long groan, she pulled herself from the suffocating wrapper of bed sheets and stumbled to the bathroom to wash her face. Sure enough, she looked like she'd endured a round or two in a boxing ring. Her blond hair spiked up at odd angles and her puffy, red-rimmed eyes looked ready to burst into tears. No question about skipping church that day.

Once she'd showered and gotten her coffee, she sat in the recliner that occupied the corner of her office too exhausted to move. She'd expected to feel better with a shower and caffeine, but a fresh wave of grief rolled over her. Crushed her, in fact, if she combined Colin's news with what was happening at the Launchpad and with Brent. And after all her hard work that year, it was unlikely she'd receive her degree or be able to continue classes. Dr. Siler would make certain of that. As icing on the quickly disintegrating cake, she hadn't progressed with her so-called passion project, the nonprofit.

But her conversation with Colin weighed the heaviest in her mind. She already missed his arms around her. She longed to call him. But what would she say? She needed time to sift through his news and the implications.

It was as though her life lay in pieces at her feet. A multitude of dreams had collided and not survived the impact. Would anything remain?

Eden shook her head and pressed her eyes shut. She was being dramatic, wasn't she? Of course, she could pull herself up. She always had, hadn't she? When she was dragged back from North Carolina to appear the doting daughter in a sick family system. When she found herself pregnant with twins shortly after being married, she'd coped. As she did years later, a widow responsible for three teenagers and a thriving restaurant. She could move forward somehow.

But it wouldn't be the same without Colin. She was used to facing life alone, but she was tired of it. At Sydney's wedding, Eden had felt longing for a male relationship for the first time in years or maybe ever. *What are you trying to teach me, Lord? Do I need to be ready for a radical shift?* She stared up at the ceiling, aware that it had taken her too long to ask. Conscious that the Godward question hadn't pierced her heart because part of her wanted to back away from him.

What did it mean that she'd ventured into dating only to hit a wall? She returned to college only to hit another wall. Was there a rhyme or reason to her life? *Please show me, Lord, in spite of my stubbornness. Are you trying to break my will? And am I having a major pity party? It's all so messy and complicated right now. I'm afraid.*

Silence filled the room, loud in Eden's ears. She leaned toward the desk and snatched her phone to call Marissa's number. Processing with her friend would help, wouldn't it? Only Marissa didn't answer. She was probably already at church. Eden didn't leave a message. Her daughters? No, they were likely either at church or doing weekend tasks they didn't have time for during the week. Seemed like a while since she'd had any more than a quick life summary greeting with them.

No, it was just her and God. He was probably waiting for her to drop everything now. She'd put it off long enough. She grabbed the worn Bible sitting on the table beside her and flipped to two, then three of her favorite Psalms. The comfort began to drip, slowly at first, into her bruised heart. She still needed to speak. To him.

God, my loving Father. She stopped. He'd see the hypocrisy in her heart right away. *Okay, honestly, I want to see you as a loving Father. I don't know what that looks like. The words father and loving don't go together for me.*

Her voice broke as her words triggered a surprising wave of grief. Tears surged, drops followed by a flood. She wept for a few minutes, unable to do anything else, as the full force of being an emotional orphan struck her. When her shuddering stopped, she breathed deeply and mopped her face with a tissue.

She sat still, silent for several moments until she was ready to talk to him again. *That's my earthly experience, Lord, but you're so different. You've always been a different kind of father. Full of love, always reaching out to me. I wish I could see you that way instead of conjuring up my drunk earthly father. You're not like that. You've never ever been like that.* Her words emerged in a whisper, choked by renewed tears.

Her insides spasmed as she absorbed the impact of her childhood pain, the rejection, the unmet thirst for love and understanding. Finally, as though a giant, cruel hand abruptly released its grip, stillness flowed in its wake. A flicker of peace. She was loved, her head told her. Her heart was starting to catch up, but it would take consistent and stubborn believing before that truth put roots down to her fractured soul. But it had begun. The picture that came then to her mind was that of a child covered by the arms of a loving father, one who loved perfectly, and whose sovereignty was completely good and wise.

Eden glanced out the window. The drizzle had stopped, and the sun was elbowing through a blanket of clouds. The day was slightly warmer than the previous week. Though it was still chilly, it was mild enough to get out of the house, which she desperately needed to do. She bundled up in a parka, pulled a knit hat over her head, and wrapped a scarf around her neck. She got into the car and headed to a nearby park.

It was almost deserted, which was fine by her. She ought to be doing some of the substantial homework that awaited her, but her mind would never go there until she worked through the main issues that had become her life. A concrete loop wove through the trees and passed a mirror-still lake. She breathed deeply of the chill air and felt her spirits slowly lift.

Colin hadn't said he was definitely moving to Colorado, but he might want to do it after April's graduation. Another year away. He'd also said he could change his mind. Of course, he'd want to know Eden's response before getting in too deep emotionally with her. Despite the chill that threatened to invade her down jacket, it warmed her inside to admit Colin considered her part of his future.

But what good was that if they'd have to separate as he moved out west?

Here I am again, Lord, trying to figure everything out so I can have certainty and control. You're all powerful and wise, but I try to muddle through on my own. I felt like you brought Colin into my life, but now he's going to Colorado. I don't understand why I even met him if he's going away.

But he'd asked her to go with him, almost as if he'd whispered the romantic words, *Run away with me, Eden. Let's go together.* A flush of joy bumped against her despair.

She let out a long sigh that puffed a cloud into the cold air. Giving up everything she knew in Wadesboro seemed an unfair exchange for keeping Colin in her life. But if she clung to her history and her current comfort, she'd likely lose him. *Are you telling me to go to Colorado with Colin, Lord?*

Not yet. God's fingers were pressing in a different place. Had her control of her own life already cost her opportunities God would have given her? She might have met someone years earlier, but it had felt too risky. Her faith was anemic because she held the reins in a death grip to stave off anything resembling the chaos of her youth. In so doing, she missed the vitality God offered her. Vitality that emerged from standing on the edge of a cliff, staring out at the unknown. Scary, yes, but what a view he promised her.

A protest spiraled up from the hurt child within her. Hadn't God allowed her life to be derailed so many years ago? She believed him for her eternal salvation, but could she *really* trust him with her future? *It's crazy, isn't it, Lord, that I trust you for eternity, but I can't seem to trust you for next year?*

She had a reason to fear God's complete control over her life, didn't she? What about her abrupt return to Indiana when her heart's desire had been to stay in North Carolina? What about getting pregnant too quickly after her marriage so that she was unable to settle in as a wife, finish her degree, find her bearings?

With a flash of understanding, she knew that *she* had made certain decisions herself. *She* had decided to return home. Yes, she'd been guilted, coerced by her mother, but caving in had been easier than fighting for what she wanted. She didn't think she had a choice back then, but she had. She could have made a different decision. How had she never seen that *she'd* made those decisions herself? Why had she blamed God for re-scripting her life when it had been *her* choice, motivated by guilt instead of faith? Then, after her marriage, she hadn't taken enough precautions to avoid getting pregnant so quickly. She'd done that because of Gerry's pressure about wanting to be a father. She hadn't stood up for what she'd wanted, but had been weak and caved in. As a result, she hadn't finished her degree. Again, her responsibility.

Yet, despite all the choices she wished she'd done differently, her life had turned out pretty well, hadn't it? She had three beautiful, successful children, even if one of them wasn't speaking to her. She'd had a reasonably satisfying, though imperfect marriage. She'd learned to run a restaurant. That had built her self-esteem and provided for her family for many years, as well as possibly prepared her to run a nonprofit. Was it really that bad?

No, God had given her a good life, *despite* her misguided decisions. He'd made all things work together for the best, as he promised. Suddenly, she began to see her whole life differently. Sure, she hadn't traveled much or done anything besides raise her family, but that had been a worthy choice. And her life wasn't over. She had her future.

Maybe a future with Colin.

Her pace increased, and not only from the cold that chilled through her scarf and hat. Inside, a fire had been lit. The smoldering warmth rose to flames. It was suddenly so clear. God's hand had been on her all her life.

He'd protected her within her dysfunctional family. He'd led her to faith at a young age. He'd allowed her to attend college in another state. He'd provided a decent man as a husband and had given her children. And opportunities to learn and to encourage other women. No life was perfect, but he looked out for his children according to the promise he'd made. According to his character. Yes, his children made bad decisions once in a while, or just misguided ones.

That was the beauty of sovereignty Colin had spoken about. She remembered that day when they talked about it at the restaurant. He'd made it sound so appealing, so perfect, when all the while she'd been squirming. He'd spoken of it as his lifeline after his wife walked out, his assurance in the dark that everything would eventually be fine. If only Eden had that assurance at the time. For years, God's wise sovereignty had frightened her, but now, she had to admit, it resembled freedom.

Inside her, it was as though she heard glass breaking and tiny shards falling, a musical sound as the old lies hit one another on the way down. Protection. Self-protection and control had robbed her of so much, mainly a peaceful walk of faith. Was her commitment to controlling her own life robbing her of a man she was growing to love?

Suddenly, from a deep place inside her, laughter erupted. She wasn't sure why, but she felt joyful, buoyant, like a child with no cares, because of her loving parent. She still had riddles in her life—Brent, Colin, the Launchpad, the nonprofit—but it wasn't *her* burden. A phrase echoed in her ears, seemingly from nowhere. *Though they stumble, they will never fall.* Where was it from? A Psalm? She didn't know. Maybe God would show her.

Eden left the park, the cold air forcing her to a nearby coffee shop. She grabbed a small book of Psalms she always kept in her glove compartment and went inside. With a steaming mug of hot chocolate, she settled in a soft leather armchair and opened the booklet.

Where was that verse? She flipped through the Psalms for a few minutes, scanning her favorites, pausing from time to time to sip the beverage, which burned a comforting path down her throat. As she turned a page, her eyes stopped, riveted on the same verse that had teased her mind a while ago. It was Psalm 37:23 and 24. *The Lord directs the steps of the godly. He delights in every detail of their lives. Though they stumble, they will never fall, for the Lord holds them by the hand.* Though they stumble. Yes, she'd stumbled, but he hadn't allowed her to fall. She was still there, and he was still holding onto her hand.

Her future with Colin wasn't resolved, but she felt lighter. She'd shifted the burden. *Lord, thank you for your sovereignty. You do the best for your kids even when they mess up or think they're making the best decision when maybe they're not.* No reason to fear and no reason to control her life, her kids' lives, her future.

An hour later, Eden pulled into her driveway. She idled the car for a moment as she stared at the house where she'd lived for over twenty years. Not that long ago, she'd considered selling it. Why was it now so important? It was a lot of space to keep up with. She'd loved hosting holidays, having the kids come back. Twice a year.

She got out of the car and went in the front door. Disabled the alarm. Stood in the silence. Apart from twice a year, this is what she lived with every day. Silence. Unused space. Somehow, it looked different to her than it had a few hours earlier.

For a few more moments, Eden stood in the foyer listening to the silence. Then, a need for connection, to share what God had told her. She pulled out her phone and dialed Sydney. No answer. Eden left a message. "Just wanted to say hi and catch up, Sydney. I miss you and hope all is going well." Generic message, but her friend would call back later. Eden called Julia and left the same message on her answering machine. Lastly, she called Claire and Jordan's landline. No one answered in the apartment.

Eden shook her head, but a smile crept onto her face. Clearly, they were all out living their lives. And she needed to live hers.

It was mid-afternoon. Brent's number rang and rang. His recorded voice filled her ear, causing a stab of grief. "Brent, honey, it's Mom. I miss hearing from you. I only want the best for you. I hope you know that. I'd wanted to encourage you to talk more to

Kelly about what she needed and wanted, and I still think that's vital. It's the way forward, sweetie. I hope and pray you'll be able to talk things out together, find out what you both want in the relationship, and come to an understanding. I'm praying for that and for God's will for you both. I regret any part I may have unwittingly had in your conflict. I love you so much." She blew out a breath of tension. She'd still stand by what she told Brent, but having said her piece, she needed to back away. And entrust him to God.

Next, Colin. That would be both harder and easier. She hungered to hear his voice, even though it had been less than twenty-four hours. The way they'd left things the night before made it feel like two years.

His phone rang and, true to her pattern for the entire day, he didn't answer. "Hi, Colin. I've spent the day thinking and praying about our conversation last evening. I admit, it was a shock for me, and I know I didn't react very well. I'm sorry for that. I'm so sorry I missed references you made about it previously, and I regret you didn't feel free to talk about it sooner. I don't want you to tiptoe around with me. You can always tell me what's on your mind." She took a breath, wanting to take her time, but knowing the recorder would soon cut her off. "I just want to say that being in a relationship with you is more important to me than staying in my comfort zone. Wherever that leads me. Wherever that leads *us*. I want you to know that. Please call me when you feel ready to talk."

Her hands were trembling. *Okay, Lord. I'm ready to trust you with this. And all the rest. And no one is answering the phone today, so I guess it's just us. You and me.*

Her trustworthy safety-net Lord wanted to hang out with just her. And for the first time in a while, so did she.

Chapter Twenty

The nutty smell of coffee beans and the whoosh of the espresso machine filled the coffee shop, blending with the rumble of students talking and laughing. Eden settled into her seat at the corner table and glanced at her watch. She was a few minutes early to meet her school friends. Though she was thankful for their regular Tuesday meetings, having a few minutes to herself allowed her to catch her breath after walking across campus.

Her mood was an odd mixture of jubilation and trepidation. On the one hand, she'd spent the weekend cleaning house in her relationship with God and she felt like a new woman . . . hopeful, adventurous, unencumbered. On the other hand, Colin hadn't called her back. Not Sunday. Not Monday. She'd laid out her heart in her phone message, her fears, and her willingness to step out in faith with him. She chose *him*. Her message was clear, she was sure. So, why hadn't he responded? Was he angered by her initial response? Did he even receive her message?

A heavy weight sat in her stomach as she pressed her lips together. She couldn't think of one rational reason why he hadn't called her.

"You look worried, Eden." Tara's voice broke into Eden's tangled thoughts as she pulled back a chair with a scrape and sat down.

Eden pushed her concerns to the back shelf of her mind and smiled at Tara. "Hi, Tara. Just thinking about . . . different things. How was your weekend?"

Just then Mariella arrived. Their conversation became animated as everyone talked at once. Eden chuckled. "I've missed you two. I know it's only been since last week."

"Me too. I wish Cheyenne were here with us." Mariella frowned. "I miss her too."

"Yeah. Bummer." Tara slipped her coat over the back of the chair.

"I forgot to tell you," Eden said. "I contacted some people from my church to see if anyone knew of a babysitter who could help Cheyenne. I'm waiting for one of them to get back to me, so keep fingers crossed."

"That's a great idea. We should put the word out too." Mariella nodded.

Tara offered to get their drinks and left the table to join the queue. "I have some updates for you about Joanne and the Launchpad." Eden lowered her voice. "We're still working on it, but I think it's moving ahead."

"Oh, that's good news." Mariella's dark eyes looked eager. "I can't wait to hear. If we don't have a chance to talk privately, I'll call you at home this evening. Is that okay?"

"Sure. I should be there." Unless she had an invitation from a certain lawyer in town. Didn't seem to be much chance of that.

Tara returned with the drinks. "It's only March. Spring break is weeks away and all the profs are going crazy on us. You wouldn't believe the homework, as if theirs is the only class I have to think about."

Eden and Mariella murmured agreement and the women started talking about spring break, and all the exams and projects they had to complete before then. The break would miss Marissa's wedding by about a week, but Eden planned to skip her Friday class and go on Thursday so they could all get a sliver of girl time. Without a response from Colin, she didn't know if he was still planning to attend with her. They'd soon have to make plane reservations.

The conversation drifted from spring break to summer plans. Summer seemed another lifetime away. Eden could no longer imagine a stretch of time free from academic pressure. Her attention wandered as she scanned the surrounding tables, each one filled with noisy groups or a lone student with earphones and an open laptop.

Her gaze paused at the doorway. Colin. He stood inside the entrance, scanning the tables as she'd just done. Their eyes met, but she kept her face stoic until she saw his eyebrows lift and a smile spread across his face. She rose from her seat and gathered her canvas tote and purse from the floor. "Girls, I need to go talk to someone. I'll catch you soon, okay?"

She snagged her coat from the chair and heard behind her, "Is that your guy, Eden?" She hoped he was still her guy.

Eden reached him at the doorway, and they stood still, facing each other. His eyes locked onto hers. "I got your message late last night."

"Just last night? What happened to your phone?"

"It's a long story. Can we go somewhere quieter?"

"Of course. I said goodbye to my friends when I saw you so I can leave with you."

They both glanced toward the corner table where the young women still watched them with wide grins. He waved to them, and Eden smiled.

"I know another coffee shop off campus," he said. "Can you drive with me, or would you rather follow in your car?"

"I can go with you. I have one more class this afternoon, so I'll need you to bring me back to campus. But I have a couple of hours."

They walked half a block to where he'd parallel parked close to the coffee shop. Students meandered or rushed on the sidewalks and crossed the streets as they changed classes. Colin opened the passenger door. Eden leaned to get in, but he touched her shoulder. When she turned back to him, he pulled her toward him and kissed her. His mouth probed hers as a man searching for long-lost love, fearful of losing her. She melted against him and curled her arms around his neck, savoring him, unmindful of student voices nearby.

He pulled back, but his hands still on her shoulders. "Eden—"

"Let's talk in the car." She pulled her collar closer at her throat.

"Sorry, it *is* cold out here. And too many spectators."

When they'd settled in the car, he started it and adjusted the heat. He turned to her. "I can't tell you how happy your phone message made me. I didn't expect you to say what you did." His voice was soft as his eyes lingered on her face. "I was amazed and frankly humbled by the way you laid down your fears in favor of our relationship. It meant so much to me." He took her hand and pressed his lips there. "Like I told you the other night, it isn't for sure that I'll move out there, but just knowing that you're putting us first, regardless, well, it's like a stone lifted off my chest. And I want you to know I'll do the same for you."

Eden shifted in her seat. "No, you don't have to—"

He shook his head. "I'm not sure I could go there without you, Eden."

She laid her hand on his arm as the impact of his words brought a sudden gush of tears that filled her eyes. "You couldn't?" She swiped at her cheek. "You have a way of making me lose my words." She laughed. "And I hardly *ever* do that." He joined her laughter. The meaning of his statement struck her like an arrow. "You don't have to give up on your dream for my sake, Colin. We'll figure this out together."

He nodded as the ghost of a smile crept across his face. "I'm sorry I didn't phone you yesterday. I'd taken the day off because some old and dear friends of mine were in town on their way to Illinois. I hadn't seen them in a long time. I didn't check my text messages because I didn't expect to hear from you that soon. Then halfway through Monday, I saw that you'd left a message, but didn't have the courage to listen to it. I thought I knew what you'd say, and I didn't want it to spoil my time with my friends." He shrugged. "So, Monday evening, I knew I had to man up and check my message and, well, you made my day. I wanted to talk to you in person. I remembered your Tuesday coffee shop appointment with your friends, so I decided to crash it."

She swallowed and her eyes latched onto his. "I'm so glad. I missed you. I hated that I didn't feel close to you for a couple of days." She paused. "Colin, how about for now if we don't think too much about Colorado and all the what ifs? We haven't known each other all that long, so let's focus on *us*. We'll listen to God and see where he leads us in our relationship and geographically."

Colin reached up to run his fingers down her cheek. "You're not only gorgeous, but you're so wise. That sounds like a perfect idea. One day at a time together." He leaned forward and kissed her again, this time softly, lingering.

"I still want to take you to a coffee shop or else to lunch," Colin said as he pulled away. "Have you eaten?"

"It's in here." She pointed to her canvas bag on the floor. "Lead on, culinary director."

"We can go someplace fast since you have a class soon. After we get our food, I want to hear your thoughts leading you to what you said on the phone, because I sensed you were not at all in that frame of mind when we talked Saturday night. Am I right?"

"Ha, no, I wasn't. I was in shock, really. But God met me in a special way. Wow, did he ever. I'll tell you more after we order."

"And I also have some very interesting news for you about our Dr. Siler."

She sat up straighter. "Oh? You're looking like you swallowed the canary. I can't wait to hear."

"You will. But one thing at a time. We'll go to that sandwich place over there if that's okay with you. It looks pretty quiet." He gestured to a strip mall and pulled into the parking lot.

They went into a small storefront restaurant with white walls and furniture and lime green lamps hanging over each table. Eden looked around the sterile room. "Looks a bit like a laboratory. But it's quiet. Hope the sandwiches are good."

And they were. As they ate, she enjoyed telling Colin about her encounter with God and her realization that he had continuously directed her steps despite her choices. It still seemed like the earth had shifted under her feet and changed her perspective on her whole life. She felt the Fatherhood of God in a way she'd never known. Loving, wise, completely on top of things. "From one minute to the next I went from feeling like I'd had an awful life to seeing all the ways God protected me, provided for me, and guided me."

"See what I mean?" Colin's face showed certainty. "The sovereignty of God is wonderful news. It's the best insurance policy ever."

"Yes, I know it now." She chuckled at his enthusiasm. "Makes me feel so much closer to him. I'm now a believer in *his* leadership. And what peace I have. I can't describe it." She lowered her head as new tears of gratitude stung her eyes and a wave of fresh emotion flooded her chest. But she was smiling. If only she'd realized this four decades ago.

A couple of young people, probably students, sat two tables away from them. Colin lowered his voice and drew his head toward hers. "I'll just tell you this briefly since it's not the most private place. When I was on the way to meet my friends, I got a call from Robert, the patent attorney. He did the research on—I'll call him Eugene for now—and found *three* patent applications in his name going back between three and six years."

"Three! I knew it. No wonder he has such a nice house. He's getting income from his stolen inventions."

"Three were listed, but there may be more. It takes eighteen months to make the names public, remember. That means he could have a few in the works from the last year or two."

"I *knew* he was guilty," she whispered. "Why else would he have threatened me if he didn't stand to lose something?"

"Not only lose what he has, but possibly risk going to prison. What he did was a crime. It's hard to prove, but we have more evidence now than we did a week ago. I asked Robert about the wording of the applications and he's working on getting that together. We'll need Joanne's copies of her descriptions and Eric's, then we can compare them to the official applications."

"Amazing." Her voice emerged in reverent calm. "We've come a long way in this. I don't know what we'll do if we get a match on the descriptions. Where will we go with this information? I don't think we can go to the Launchpad board, because one of them is probably complicit too."

"Or all of them. We just don't know. You're right, we can't trust them."

"Maybe the college president? I wonder who would be interested in all this and want to protect the students. Or the dean of the business department."

"Not sure the president will believe us or even the dean, but I can't think of anyone else. We can't go to the police because they wouldn't take us seriously either at this point."

"I bet they wouldn't. Well, let's wait to hear from Robert on the drawings and descriptions. Meanwhile, we'll contact Joanne and Eric to get copies of what they have."

Colin leaned back. "I assume Joanne still has her original designs to compare. Then we'll see if we have a match."

"They *have* to match. I'll call Joanne this afternoon and tell her what we found. The biggest thing is Eugene's name, right there on the application. That's a smoking gun. Did Robert make copies of all his findings?"

"Yes. He's scanning them to me today." He paused and stared at Eden. "Eden, how are you feeling about your degree? Just in case Eugene follows through with his threats."

Eden let out a breath. "I know in my head that a few courses and a diploma don't validate me. I'd be disappointed to not get my degree, but it's far more important to me to stop a thief and protect students who are being exploited."

"That's my girl. It wasn't even a contest, was it?"

She shook her head. "You know where my heart is. I'm for the underdog. Always have been. I'll risk being thrown out of school. I don't care anymore. Well, not as much as before." She gave him a crooked smile.

"And if Siler makes this ugly? I want you to be prepared."

"God makes me bulletproof." She lifted her head and her fist in defiance. Felt good. "Standing for justice can't be the wrong thing to do, can it?"

"Definitely not." Colin took her hand and pressed his lips into her knuckles. "That warrior talk is so sexy." They laughed.

"A warrior I am not." Eden looked back at him, drinking in the renewed closeness, the defined commitment they now had. "I can tell you all the self-protective, fearful things I've done, decisions I've made. It's amazing I'm still here. Except that God saved me from myself."

"Yeah, he likes to do that. Isn't it great?"

Eden smiled, then glanced at her watch. "Time's going too fast, Colin. I'd rather hang out with you than go to class."

He leaned forward and grabbed her other hand. "How about this. I'll drop you off on campus. I need to get back to work too, but I'll phone Eric this afternoon and tell him what we found out. I'll ask him for a copy of his design. You can ask Joanne for hers. I'll call you tonight, mainly because I want to hear your voice."

"And I want to hear yours."

"Can you get the contact info for the dean and the president? We'll have to talk about which one we should approach."

"The dean will be a good person to start with. I don't think he's in on it because he's known for his integrity and involvement in the community. Then he can open a door to the president if we need to take it further. And as a student in the business school, I'll have easier access to the dean. What do you think?"

"Yes, definitely. Let's go, Sherlock."

Colin dropped Eden off in front of her building. He planted a firm kiss on her lips before she slid out of the car. She regretted having to say goodbye to him, but at least they were back on track in their relationship.

Though the nonprofit sat firmly on the back burner and her diploma hung by a thread, the revelation about Dr. Siler powered a renewed purpose inside her. And her redefined bond with God felt like rocket fuel.

Chapter Twenty-One

A week later, Eden and Colin exchanged a pensive glance as they sat in silence in the reception area of Dr. Franklin Boswell, the business dean. The dean was running late for their appointment and with every passing minute, Eden's stomach tightened like a fist. The secretary, having seated them, continued with her work. Eden could hear a male voice through the partially open door behind the secretary's desk.

She reached out and brushed Colin's hand with the tips of her fingers. He grasped them and met her eyes with a smile. He'd come for dinner the previous evening and afterward, they'd gone over the sketches and prepared what they would say to the dean. They'd prayed together for the meeting, which was a first aside from mealtime prayers. A vital and natural step, given their conversation about God's sovereignty and guidance for their Launchpad quest as well as their relationship.

Ten minutes later, the secretary looked up. "Looks like he's finished with his call. I'll let him know you're here." She rose and poked her head into the dean's office then gestured to Eden and Colin. Eden's chest tightened as she and Colin went inside.

Dr. Boswell was a tall, bearded man in his late fifties, with a ruddy face and a gaze that instantly spoke of influence. "Good morning. Eden and Colin, is it?" He looked at his agenda as they echoed his greeting. "Have a seat. What brings you in today?"

Eden and Colin sat in two leather wingback chairs facing the dean's desk. "Dr. Boswell," began Eden. "Thank you for seeing us. I'm an undergrad student in the business program, an advisee of Dr. Siler. Colin is an attorney but is here today to lend his support as my friend." She took a breath and Colin handed her the file containing copies of their evidence against Dr. Siler. "Early in the fall semester, Dr. Siler told me about an organization the school partners with known as the Business Innovation Launchpad. He is the faculty advisor for this organization."

"I'm familiar with the name and what they do." Dr. Boswell steepled his fingers on his desktop.

"Yes, of course you are. So, you know students present inventions and business ideas to the Launchpad committee hoping to receive funding for startup costs. To my knowledge, they aren't given the opportunity or encouragement to complete a nondisclosure agreement to protect their inventions prior to presenting them. And of course, none of the students have patents, either."

The dean's graying brows gathered, and his eyes narrowed.

"Through a series of circumstances over the last several months, we've become aware that a few ideas presented by past applicants may have been stolen by someone associated with the Launchpad. Someone who heard their ideas saw an opportunity for exploiting them."

At this, Dr. Boswell sat straighter in his chair. Bushy eyebrows drew together, and his frown deepened. "Go on."

"We know of at least three students who presented inventions to the Launchpad over the last six years who believe this happened to them. They weren't awarded funding for their ideas and years later, saw their invention marketed and sold by companies. We know that alone doesn't prove anything, since people can come up with the same good idea and the first one to get a patent produces it."

"Yes, I was about to say the same thing. It's common sense that if someone doesn't have a patent or an NDA, their invention is fair game for anyone else who has the same idea."

"Exactly, Dr. Boswell." Colin's voice emerged steady and strong. "However, in this case, we have proof that the ideas may have been stolen by someone on the faculty of this institution. The only faculty member to have close involvement with the Launchpad."

"Siler?" Dr. Boswell's disbelieving tone sliced the air.

"Yes, Dr. Marcus Siler," Eden said. "He was a member of the panel that examined the ideas. He was there, taking notes. One applicant told us that."

Dr. Boswell shook his head, his expression closed. "Dr. Siler is well respected and has been on the faculty for going on ten years. He's a good man. If what you say is true, it might be someone else on the board of the Launchpad. Can't be him."

"Dr. Boswell," Colin said. "As an attorney, I have law contacts in the community. A patent attorney acquaintance did some research at my request into the patent applications of several inventions. Some patents are still pending, but the names of the applicants have been published. Dr. Siler's name appeared three times in the last six years. We believe he stole students' ideas and receives income for them."

"This is preposterous," Dr. Boswell spluttered. "A conspiracy theory. That's what this is."

"We have proof in this folder." Eden's heart thudded more strongly at Dr. Boswell's outburst, despite her vain efforts to prepare herself for opposition. She tapped the folder in her lap, unable to stop the insistence from creeping into her voice. "Not only does Dr. Siler's name appear three times as the applicant for these patents, but we have seen the diagrams and details on the patent application and compared them with the students' notes for the Launchpad. They're nearly identical. Don't you find that too coincidental?"

"Dr. Boswell," Colin prodded before the man could respond. "Do you know Dr. Siler as a man who invents things?"

"I can't speak to that." Dr. Boswell's mouth sagged into a grimace. "I know Dr. Siler mostly in a professional context. We respect each other as colleagues, but I know nothing of how he spends his free time, whether he tinkers in his garage on weekends inventing things or prefers to play golf."

Eden threw a glance at Colin, whose jaw was firm as he stared back at Dr. Boswell.

"As a member of the faculty," Eden continued. "Dr. Siler's books and journal articles are public knowledge in the college *and* the business community. If he were an inventor and had acquired three patents, wouldn't those achievements also be known? The reason they aren't is because he stole them from students. He doesn't *want* them known."

He leveled a stare at Eden. "That's quite an accusation you're making."

"We only ask that you examine these documents carefully." Colin took the folder from Eden's lap and slid it across the desk. "Please study them and see what you conclude. We've made these discoveries over several months and you're the first person we're approaching with them."

Eden's heart seemed to stop as she awaited the dean's reply. He stared at the manilla folder in front of him. "I'll take a look at these and get back to you. Did you leave your contact information?"

"Yes, my email and phone number are both there on the top sheet." Eden gestured to the folder.

"I'll get in touch. But my stance is to call Siler innocent until proven guilty."

"This folder will give you all the proof you need to at least *suspect* him of what we're saying," Colin said. "Of course, if you speak to him about it, he'll deny it or make excuses. Personally, I don't recommend that. After you read the file, you may wish to take it directly to the president."

Dr. Boswell didn't respond, but he took the file and placed it onto a pile of documents and folders. Then, as a second thought, he slid it underneath. Eden hoped it wouldn't stay buried indefinitely.

They thanked Dr. Boswell for his time and left the office. For a moment, they didn't speak. When they reached the hallway, Eden collapsed against Colin as her tension spun out of her all at once. His arms went around her. "You okay?"

She blew out a breath of air. "He didn't believe us."

Colin lowered his voice. "Maybe he didn't want to *appear* as though he believed us. He has some kind of professional friendship with Siler, so doesn't want to believe it. Let's give him time."

"I hope he'll look over the file carefully. I don't know how he can conclude otherwise, Colin. Unless he turns a blind eye."

He led her toward the wide staircase. "He may very well do that. We knew that from the start. It may end up being a wall."

His words rang in the hollow that opened inside her. All that for nothing.

"Then we'll just go to Plan B," he added.

She looked up at him. "What's Plan B?"

Colin shrugged. "We'll figure it out."

Despite the discouragement she felt, Eden smiled.

Ten days went by with no response from Dr. Boswell. "I guess we're dead in the water," Eden glumly told Colin on the phone after a long day of midterms. "Let me know when you think of that Plan B, okay?"

"I will. Nothing comes to mind unless you want to go to the president."

"That might be a good next step. But—this may sound cowardly on my part—if we *do* go to the college president, I'd like to finish my finals first. Just in case Siler makes good on his threats, he won't be able to touch my spring semester. Then I'll only need one class to finish and maybe I can take it later when things calm down."

"You're optimistic. I like that, but don't get your hopes up that Siler's going anywhere. Might be better to think about taking the course online if you can. I don't know if it's the kind of class that's available online at another school. Let's take one day at a time, okay?"

"Yes, I will. We'll relax about this and trust God. I'm glad we went to Dr. Boswell, since at least someone in a position of authority has the details on Siler. If there's nothing further we can do, he knows the facts."

"Exactly."

"Well, I'm beat after two midterms. I'm going to bed early tonight."

"Good idea. Sleep well, Eden."

She got ready for bed. As she brushed her teeth, she remembered she hadn't checked her phone or email since that morning. Just in case Brent or one of the twins had texted. Eden turned down the comforter and picked up her phone. No new text messages. She scrolled through her emails and saw a message from Dr. Boswell.

And one from Dr. Siler.

Her heart ramped up and suddenly she wasn't tired anymore. She hadn't heard from Dr. Siler in months, so his message signaled that Dr. Boswell had likely spoken to him. If he had, that was the worst thing that could have happened.

She read Dr. Boswell's message first. *Eden, please excuse the delay in getting back to you regarding your inquiry. I was called out of town for several days, but I had the opportunity to speak with Dr. Siler."* Eden cringed but kept reading. *"I learned something that you hadn't told me, that you and he had a short-term romantic relationship. He feels your research into the Launchpad is an effort to discredit him as revenge for his ending of your relationship.*

"What?" Eden shouted aloud toward the phone as she bolted up on the side of the bed. "That snake!" She continued reading, despite the churning inside her that threatened to boil over. *Although this puts a different light on your accusations, I looked at the reports you gave me and noticed his given name, Eugene Marcus Siler, as the applicant for those patents. I asked him about his inventions, and he told me he'd been inventing things since he was young.*

"What?" Eden said again. "He has *not*." Or had he? Could she and Colin have been wrong about Siler? If so, why had he never talked about inventions, nor sought any recognition?

Because the inventions weren't his. The fewer people knew, the better. Still, a sliver of doubt remained in her thoughts. And he'd successfully planted doubt in the mind of Dr. Boswell, their only potential ally, regarding Eden's motivation.

Dr. Boswell's email continued. *When I asked him why no one knew about the inventions, he stated he had personal reasons for keeping them separate from his academic profession. So, there you go. I hope that satisfies your quest. If you have further questions, don't hesitate to contact me.*

Eden fell back against the pillow. How was it possible that Dr. Boswell had swallowed Siler's lies about his *private* inventions?

Before stewing further, she glanced at the ceiling and murmured a brief prayer. Then she read Dr. Siler's email. *Eden, I see you didn't heed my recommendation to drop your investigation into the Launchpad."* Her pulse ratcheted up once again as she read his words. *"And now it's no longer the Launchpad you're targeting in your witch hunt. It's me. I've only tried to be kind to you, since you'd returned to the academic realm later in life from being a housewife, but this is how you repay my kindness. After less than a year, you don't even have basic business skills, yet you're attacking my entire career. Since you've taken this to a more personal level, I will have no choice but to make good on my threats to bar you from my class in the fall. It's fortunate Dr. Boswell didn't believe your insane accusations. He asked me about them but understood perfectly when I explained everything to him.*

She could almost hear him smoothly talking as he made her sound like a vengeful, jilted lover who'd just arrived on campus from her minivan full of groceries. Not even basic business skills, he'd said, when she'd run a popular restaurant alone for ten years. Anger flared inside.

His message finished with, *I suggest you let all this die down, or you'll bring even more humiliation on yourself. I wouldn't want that for you, despite how you have tried to discredit me. Marcus.*

Instantly, she dialed Colin. "I'm sorry if I woke you."

"No, not at all. I was just watching a bit of news."

She read each of the emails to him. When she finished, he let out a whistle. "Siler's playing hardball," he observed. "Interesting how he's turning things back on you."

"Yes, I noticed, but *interesting* wasn't the word that came to mind. I'm fuming."

"I'm sure you must be."

"Once last fall, he told me I didn't need to be in college because I had so much experience in the restaurant world. Now he's telling me I don't have basic skills. The dirtbag. What should I do? Should I respond to Dr. Siler? Or Boswell?"

"No, certainly not Siler. He's baiting you, and if you ignore him, you're not giving him anything he can use. As for Boswell, let's sleep on it and give it a couple of days, then we'll talk it over. I would print off both letters, though. The fact they're emails means we have evidence of our attempts and the response. Siler's response in particular can be incriminating, since he's threatening you. You never know if one day we'll need more proof."

"Good idea." She took a long breath. His voice had calmed her. Already, she felt her pulse ease, and her breathing become more even. "I'm so glad you're my lawyer."

"I'll be sure to give you a good rate."

"Gee, thanks. I'm a little short on cash. Would you accept a kiss?"

"I would certainly accept a kiss but may ask you for two. Inflation, you know."

Eden laughed. "I'll start a file with the emails."

"Try to get some sleep, if you can." His voice became tender, like a caress spilling over Eden's agitation.

"Huh. I don't think that'll happen right away."

"I know two things that'll help," he said. "Giving it all over to God, for one. Then a warm mug of hot chocolate."

Chapter Twenty-Two

Hard to believe it had been a full year since Eden had taken a flight. And once again, to attend a wedding. So much had happened since that trip to Wilmington. Colin sat beside her, rubbing her fingers with one thumb. A flight attendant glanced down their row. "Something to drink?"

"Yes, do you have hot chocolate?" Eden asked the perky woman in the navy-blue uniform.

Colin snickered. "I've been meaning to talk to you about your hot chocolate addiction." He looked up at the attendant. "I'll take a Diet Coke."

Once they got their drinks, Eden took a sip. "I can't wait till you meet everyone," she told him. "They'll love you."

He turned a soft expression toward her. "I'm more concerned about *you* than them."

She paused and held his gaze. "I already love you, Colin." She couldn't stop the truth that tumbled out.

He appeared to take in her words for a moment. Then his small smile that melted her insides. "And I love *you*, Eden Godfrey. I'm glad we stuck it out all this time." He brushed her lips with his.

Eden closed her eyes, savoring his touch, however brief. "I almost forgot about how we started when we met at the tapas restaurant," she said after he pulled away. "Back when I thought you were controlling. Makes me laugh now, since I was so wrong about you. In fact, it seems *I'm* the controlling one."

"I wasn't laughing back then. I was bummed that I'd let a smart, beautiful, and very impressive woman get away."

"Oh, you did not." She swatted his arm. "Back then you had no idea how impressive I was."

He joined her laughter. "You're in a frisky mood. I think you needed a break. Getting far away from home and pressure is just the thing."

She settled back in her seat and sighed. "I have to admit, I'm feeling so content being with you, leaving town, and seeing my girlfriends." If only she could capture that state in a bottle, suspended in that happy place, in quarantine against the darker realities that awaited her after their idyllic weekend in Asheville.

"Even though I haven't heard from Dr. Siler in a few weeks, the stress of that whole thing still hovers in the background." She hadn't run into him either, because of her paranoid efforts at hiding. She'd even worn a baseball hat to class a few times to disguise herself, though she'd felt ridiculous. That too was stressful. "I guess he figures he's won, since Dr. Boswell totally believed his made-up explanation."

"We'll let him think it's blown over and he's in the clear."

"Then we'll zap him with Plan B, right?"

"Right. As soon as we figure out what Plan B is."

"Let's not talk about it anymore this weekend. Agreed? I *so* can't wait to get there. Not just to see my girls. I always love that. But wait till you *see* this place. Biltmore Estate is the largest private residence in the country and it's stunning. It's modeled after a French Renaissance château. Eight thousand acres and tons of beautiful historic buildings. I looked it up online since I've never been."

"That's sounds pretty fancy. I thought you said your friends wanted a small, intimate wedding."

"It'll be fairly small, around sixty guests, I think Marissa told me, but the venue is amazing. They host weddings of all sizes. You'll easily see why Marissa and Jarrod chose it."

Colin took her hand again as the plane began its descent. "Can't wait to discover it with you."

An hour later, the shuttle that took Eden and Colin from the airport to the Biltmore Estate drove through the property, affording them views that had not been exaggerated. Eden gawked as she stared out the window. The Biltmore House, more of a castle, rose in the distance like a sparkling mirage from lush clusters of trees. "Wow, look at that," was all she could say. The van continued past the spectacular sight and wound up the road to more modern-looking inn which sprawled over the hillside.

The chauffeur unloaded the passengers' bags, and a porter took them on a cart into the building. Eden and Marissa would share a room prior to the wedding. Not only were they the only single women left in their group for two more days, but Eden and Marissa had always been close, having both experienced widowhood. Eden often thought of her like the sister she never had and regretted the lapse of time she'd allowed to extend between phone calls. Soon, Marissa would be a married woman, and things would change yet again. A tinge of melancholy swept into her contentment.

"There you are! They're here." Eden recognized Sydney's voice right away and turned to see Sydney, Tyler, Julia, and Craig coming through a grand double doorway into the lobby. What handsome couples they made. Sydney was the first to reach Eden and Colin. Eden fell into Sydney's embrace, then repeated the gesture with Julia, holding on to each of them in an extended squeeze. She also hugged Craig and Tyler before hastening back to Colin's side. "This is Colin Taylor. And this is Sydney, her husband Tyler, Julia, and her husband Craig."

Craig, Julia, and Tyler shook hands with Colin. Sydney threw her arms around his neck and gave him a warm hug. "Looks like you're one of us now, Colin. I hope you're prepared for the craziness."

He grinned at her. "I've been thoroughly briefed, don't worry. I have my security clearance and my Xanax."

Sydney laughed aloud and put a hand on Eden's shoulder. "I think he'll fit in just fine. You guys can settle into your rooms now if you want. Then we'll meet back down here at six-thirty to go to dinner." She flung her hands into the air in a celebratory gesture. "Then the par-tay will begin."

Julia, elegant in a fuchsia dress and floral scarf, stepped toward Colin with a shy but sincere smile. "It's good to finally meet you, Colin. I'm glad you could come."

"Thanks, Julia. I'm glad to meet you too. I've heard a lot about all the special friends in Eden's group. She really loves being with you all."

"It's totally mutual. I just wish we all lived closer. But weddings have helped us get more face time."

"Yes, congratulations on *your* recent wedding in Florence," he said.

"It was *amazing*." Eden sidled up beside them. "Both the wedding and our tour through Tuscany afterward. And Julia was such a gorgeous bride." She turned to Julia. "But then, I've never seen you when you *weren't* gorgeous. It's simply not fair."

The four couples drew into a cluster in the lobby and started talking. With relief, Eden noted that Tyler and Craig immediately absorbed Colin into conversation. She knew Colin could certainly hold his own, but badly wanted him to enjoy her friends' husbands and feel a part of everything. The men would help their little group solidify and grow. She didn't know if Colin would become an official member or not. Best not to rush things. No, she'd put all her questions about their future, pressures from school, and Launchpad tensions out of her mind for the next three days.

ରେ ରେ ରେ

"One more day, Marissa," Eden called from the bed where she had perched to fasten her sandals. Marissa finished her makeup at the bathroom counter. "You better enjoy being single while it lasts."

Marissa dusted powder over her face. "I may have told you this already, but I'm over the singleness thing. I'm ready to be a wife again. And Jarrod's ready to have company in his big house."

Her words struck Eden and for a moment, she didn't know what to say. She was there too, almost. "I'm with you. I'm over it too. I've decided that long-term widowhood is overrated."

Marissa came into the bedroom and stood before Eden, still fastening an earring. Her dark wavy hair had grown longer since the last time Eden had seen her and was layered in an attractive cut. Her pale face glowed with beauty and peaceful contentment that seemed to radiate from inside of her, outpacing her makeup by miles.

"I'm so glad to hear you say that, Eden. Took you a while to get there. I like Colin. He seems like a decent guy, and you fit so well together."

"You think so?" Eden couldn't stop a wide grin from blossoming on her face. "I'm so glad you like him. Maybe you all thought I'd never meet someone. I thought so too." Eden shook her head. "I can't believe that God actually gave me a great guy. We're not engaged or anything, but it's going well. I feel blessed." Eden's eyes stung as she spoke. She shifted her gaze away from Marissa's and stood. "Time to go?"

Marissa drew her in for a tight hug. "You deserve a great guy, Eden," she murmured. She pulled back and her expression challenged Eden. "For today, you'll have to entrust him to the men, because this is *our* time, starting now. Ready?"

"Absolutely."

The women had included in the trip an extra full day so they could have their girl time before the wedding. It wasn't as long as the previous year before Sydney's wedding or the week of traveling Italy after Julia's, but Eden was happy for what they could get. Who knew when the next girls' weekend would be?

Marissa took them to an elegant restaurant with a Tahitian vibe, complete with outdoor seating and round-back wicker chairs. Colorful umbrellas stretched out overhead and tall potted palm trees adorned each corner of the large patio. Much of the conversation during lunch centered on Marissa's plans and the honeymoon which would be in London. Jarrod had happily agreed to spend a couple days of their trip helping Marissa do research for her next historical novel.

"This is perfect, Marissa," Julia said, tipping her straw hat to one side. "The food was great too. I've missed all of you. I can't believe we're all sitting here together. We should plan our next gathering before the weekend is over."

"I like the way you think, Julia." Eden took a sip of iced tea. Their empty salad plates sat in a stack near the center of the table, but they took their time with fresh fruit and iced tea.

"Me too." Sydney glanced around at the women. "If we have a plan, the hubbies will accommodate us. We'll simply tell them that's just how it is, married or not."

"How about October?" Julia suggested "That won't get in the way of Thanksgiving."

Eden heard a faint buzz from her purse. She ignored it, but ten minutes later, she heard another one. "My phone keeps buzzing. I wonder if it's Colin or one of the kids." She took it out of her purse and her mouth went dry. Why was Marcus Siler texting her? She shoved it back into her purse as if it were a dirty rodent. He was *not* going to interfere with her special weekend.

"Not Colin or the kids?" Marissa turned her head.

"Who was that, Eden? Suddenly, you look all agitated." Sydney leaned toward her at the table. "Is everything okay? We're your girls, so you can tell us unless you'd rather not talk about it."

"Honestly, I'd rather not, because it's a long, ugly story and I was determined to put it out of my mind for the weekend."

"But if it's bothering you and it would help to talk . . ." Julia's blue eyes invited Eden. "But no pressure, of course."

"Of course, I'd want to tell you. I just don't want to put a pall on our lovely day and time together."

"Nonsense, Eden. We'll have a lovely weekend either way, but you shouldn't shoulder a burden by yourself, unless you prefer to, in which case, we'll respect that." Marissa leaned back.

"Okay, I'll summarize, but we aren't spending a lot of time on this. Deal?" Eden looked around the table as the women nodded. They already knew her context at school and her original concerns about gender discrimination within the Launchpad. That background would be a help. She'd have less to explain.

She outlined her suspicion about intellectual property theft, Joanne and Eric's accounts, and the patent attorney's confirmation of Dr. Siler's involvement. As she spoke, they riveted their attention on her. "So, in his email, Dr. Siler confirmed his original threat about blocking me from taking the last class I need to graduate."

"Slimeball," Sydney said. "I say he's got something to hide."

"It's obvious." Julia took a long sip of tea. "Did the text you just got have something to do with this drama?"

Eden hesitated. "It was from him, but I didn't read it. After we went to the dean, he went to Siler. I wish he hadn't. Anyway, Siler gave the dean some explanation that placated him, so the whole thing was dropped, though Siler retaliated with a nasty email to me. I haven't heard anything new from either Dr. Siler or the dean in about a month. For them, life went on as usual."

"With no justice for the students and their inventions." Sydney frowned.

"Right. But Colin and I aren't planning to give up. After my finals, we'll regroup and maybe go to the college president."

"So, the text was from your professor? The one who threatened you?" Julia asked.

Eden nodded. "There are two texts from him about a minute apart. He probably thought I'd respond, and when I didn't, he texted again. I don't know what about and I won't read it until after the wedding. I can't let this spoil my weekend."

"But it looks like you won't be able to graduate. That was the one thing you really wanted to do, aside from getting justice for the student inventors." Sydney cocked her head, her blue eyes trained on Eden's. "It's so unfair. He shouldn't be capable of blocking your graduation."

"I have an idea," Julia said. "You already have three full years from U.N.C. Then you have two years—the year you went back to Indiana, plus the current one—at your current school. Maybe you could take the class you still need at U.N.C. either online or on campus and transfer it or else transfer all your Indiana classes back to U.N.C. and get your diploma from there. I wonder if that would work."

"Colin had a similar idea. He said I should take the class online with another school and transfer it in. Thing is, it's the last senior class I need, so it's probably particular to my school and program. And it's a higher-level course, so I'm wondering if an equivalent is even out there at a school that could transfer it."

Marissa crossed her arms. "If you did Julia's idea and transferred it all back to U.N.C., they'd likely have slightly different requirements, and you'd have to go longer. It may be an option worth researching, though."

Suddenly, Eden's situation seemed too complicated. She drained her iced tea glass. "It's not the end of the world if I don't have a diploma. I've sort of made peace with that. It's all because I tried to help these students, and that's a more worthy goal for me."

"Absolutely. If you had it to do over, you'd do the same thing. I know you, Eden." Marissa laid her hand on Eden's arm. "You're just that kind of woman. Your heart is so big. You always were for the underdog."

Eden smiled. "Because I *was* the underdog at one time. I appreciate that, Marissa. I do want to help struggling young women. In my head, I know I can do that without a piece of paper saying I graduated."

"But in your heart, you'd like to finish. You've wanted it for years. That's understandable." Julia nodded and swept a thick lock of dark hair from her shoulder. "If you go online or even call the business dean at U.N.C., you can find out if there's a similar course being offered in the summer or fall."

"I will. That's a good idea, if all else fails." Eden smiled at her. Of course, it would fail. What were the chances her program would accept one senior-level course from another school? But what if she tried Julia's original idea and had all her current courses transferred back to U. N. C? Might that work? She'd research their courses online next week.

But first, she'd have to find out what was behind Dr. Siler's repeated messages.

ʘ ʘ ʘ

Marissa's wedding day dawned clear and dry. The ceremony would take place outdoors at the Butterfly Garden of the Conservatory. Eden had expected that, like the rest of the property, the Conservatory would be elegance in a smaller space. But it was beyond elegant as well as dripping with history.

As she settled next to Colin on a folding white chair, her eyes swept back and forth over the scene. "It's lovely, isn't it?" She squeezed his hand. "Now you see why Marissa and Jarrod wanted to do the ceremony here. It's a visual feast."

"A perfect place for a wedding. I'm glad you invited me." He looked down at her with warm eyes. She treasured his presence next to her, leaning against him as their bare arms touched beneath short sleeves. The setting and Colin were enough to chase away any worries she had waiting for her in Indiana. For one more day, they didn't exist.

In front of her, the arched windows of the brick conservatory revealed towering palms and exotic plants inside. Lush trees and flowers grew everywhere outside too. A six-foot tall harp sat near the front, next to an unobtrusive podium. Small lanterns filled with rose petals lined a brick walkway where Marissa would appear any second.

"Marissa told us yesterday at lunch who the guests were," Eden told Colin. "Most of them, of course, are on Jarrod's side, since he's lived in Asheville over thirty years. He has an architecture practice, so I'm sure some of these people are colleagues from his work or even clients. But he's active in his church and known in the community."

Colin listened attentively, his eyes roaming through the clusters of guests. He didn't respond, other than an *un-huh*, so she continued. "Marissa told me she'd made friends at church and among the wives of Jarrod's friends. See that guy over there? That's her long-term literary agent, Randall. Those might be some of her publishing colleagues sitting next to him. The younger guy talking to the pastor is Sean, Marissa's son. He came with the redhead in the front row. And the pretty blond holding the bouquet is Jarrod's daughter, Bethany. She's here with her boyfriend." An older man, Eden guessed was Jarrod's father, occupied a seat near the front.

After Colin murmured another *mm-hmm* Eden laughed. "I guess this is boring for you, isn't it? I find it interesting to know who's here, mostly because I know Marissa's background and some of Jarrod's."

He leaned against her in a brief nudge of affection. "Thanks for the summary of these people I'll never see again. I feel grounded now."

She swatted his arm playfully. "It's a female thing, I guess. Just indulge me." A woman in a flowing floral skirt stood from where she'd sat on the first row and began to play the harp.

"Saved by the harp." Colin chuckled, and Eden joined him.

For the next hour, Eden was mute as the ceremony swept her attention and emotions to another place. Marissa took slow steps in time with the music, giving the impression of royalty, her dark, flower-wreathed head lifted, her eyes fixed on the man waiting at the end of the path. Sean walked beside her, his arm linked in hers. All the guests stood and the clicking of cameras mixed with the notes of the harp. Eden sighed as joy for her friend and a deeper, unnamed emotion swirled inside her. Who said a second wedding couldn't be as sacred, as glorious as the first?

Chapter Twenty-Three

The glow of Eden's weekend in Asheville faded quickly as she sat at her desk in her home office and stared at her phone, where two text messages remained unread. During the trip back to Indianapolis, Colin asked her if she wanted to read them. She hadn't. No way would she cut short her fabulous weekend by exposing herself to unpleasantness.

In retrospect, she should have. Colin would have provided moral support and a warm hug. Here she was, alone on a Monday morning, facing her phone as if it were a tarantula about to spring at her.

She had to read them. The content of Dr. Siler's text messages might give her an idea of where she stood, where the Launchpad stood. And she wouldn't be capable of concentrating on her homework until she'd gotten it over with.

Lord, this thing isn't over yet, but I know you're here. She took a deep breath, let it out slowly. *Sovereign Lord, take over, please.* She sat still for a moment, eyes closed, allowing the tension to drip off her body, replaced by calm.

She put her code into the phone. There were a few calls from the previous day while she'd traveled, though only one message, which was from Jordan. Two attempted calls from Dr. Siler, but no messages. Two texts and two phone calls in a forty-eight-hour period after a month of silence.

She ran her moist palms down the front of her shorts and scrolled to his texts. The first one read, *You've done it now. I warned you, but you couldn't leave this alone. I'll make sure you don't graduate, but I'll also make sure you fail this spring. You think I can't do it. I will. You'll remain an unfinished failure, as you already are.*

Eden froze in her chair. Siler's cruel words were meant to wound her. He was striking out because he was afraid. Knowing this didn't keep her eyes from stinging with tears. *Unfinished failure.* Is that what she'd always be? Maybe.

She read the second text, which was shorter. *I have many contacts in the community. I'll make sure it's impossible for you to start a nonprofit. You won't have any credibility in this county or in the entire state. Was it worth all that just to try to bring me down?*

Eden stared at her phone for several minutes. The tick-tick from the wall clock rang out like repetitive gunshots. Something hot and furious, yet powerful, stirred inside her like a dormant geyser coming to life. She shut her eyes tightly for a moment, then whispered into the silent office, "Yes." She lifted her head and rose from the desk. Still holding the phone, she stared at it and said in a loud voice, "Yes, it was worth it to bring you down, Eugene Marcus Siler, you dirtbag."

Eden called Colin and left a message. Fifteen minutes later, he phoned her. "Sorry for the delay, Eden. I was tied up on a call. Happy Monday, by the way. Can you read me the texts?"

"Gladly." She read both text messages to him and to her surprise, he chuckled. "He's blowing hot air, Eden. Don't you see? He's scared."

"I know he's angry at me for starting all this, but do you really think he's afraid, after Boswell blew the whole thing off?"

"Yes, I do. Think about it, Eden. Suddenly, he's renewing his threats against you after a period of silence. Either he's had more time to stew about it, or something new has happened." He paused. "You aren't taking any classes with him this semester, are you?"

"No, but he seems to think he has power over the entire business faculty and the state of Indiana."

Colin snorted. "I'm fairly certain he has no ability to influence your current semester. How are your grades?"

"Pretty good. All As so far."

"That's better than pretty good. Don't know what he can do with that. You can back up and save those text messages. You could even make copies to add to the others. As for the nonprofit, that's an empty threat too. Something new has made him desperate. I think this may be a good sign."

"I hope you're right." Sure didn't seem like anything *she* would call good.

They chatted for a few more minutes. "I have a client coming in five minutes, so unfortunately I have to hang up," he said. "Try not to let it weigh you down. God's in control. And I'm in your corner. Remember, both of us love you."

Eden smiled. "I love you both too."

Colin's words had a calming effect, but contentment also swelled inside her. His newly expressed love was a secret treasure in the middle of her storm. But now, back to work. She pushed aside her additional pressures to focus on her economics project. Keeping her Mondays free from classes had been a genius move for which she was grateful after each weekend. Two hours later, she took a break and fixed a snack and a mug of hot chocolate. Her addiction, Colin had said. Which made her smile, despite the turmoil hovering on the back shelf of her mind. Felt good to lean on him, after thirteen years of leaning only on herself.

Not finishing her degree was a certainty unless she could find a workaround. Julia's idea drifted into her thoughts. She would spend the next few minutes investigating her options in other schools.

By noon, it was clear there were no online universities, including U. N. C. that offered the specific class she needed. Discouragement pooled inside as her hope drained away. She couldn't let Siler win. Couldn't let him pull that prize out of her reach. She could always call the business department at U. N. C. Maybe there was an equivalent course that had a different name. Then she could ask her outrageous question, whether it was possible to transfer in courses thirty years after the fact.

For the next two weeks, Eden continued to look over her shoulder and survey her surroundings, not wanting to run into Dr. Siler. They'd surely have a showdown, after all the threats he'd launched at her lately. With regret, she told her campus girlfriends she couldn't meet with them at the coffee shop for a couple of weeks. Mariella alone knew why. If Dr. Siler was aware it was a recurring appointment, he'd know where to find her.

As her economics class ended and students rose to leave, her professor, Dr. Evelyn Chambers, called to the front row where Eden sat. "Eden, can I talk to you for a moment?"

As the room emptied, Eden gathered her belongings into her tote and approached the professor. "I don't know how to tell you this, Eden, but there's been an inquiry into your work in the class. I'm aware you have excellent grades, but there's been a question about how you got them."

Eden cocked her head, but inside she bristled. "May I ask where this inquiry is coming from?"

"I'm not at liberty to say, but it's someone in the business department."

"Ah. Dr. Marcus Siler, that's who. We have a, um, conflict between us and he, being a vengeful man willing to exploit his position, is trying to sabotage my semester. He even informed me he'd do just that. I think my grades and work speak for themselves, don't you, Dr. Chambers?"

The woman seemed flustered by Eden's confident response. "I have no idea. Things are not always as they seem." Her tone was dry.

"No, they're not. Dr. Siler, for example, is not what he seems."

The woman's gaze narrowed, but she didn't respond.

Eden's heart pounded but being prepared had made her bold. That and her fervent prayers that morning. "Dr. Siler is my advisor, but I'm not in any of his classes. I don't know how he would have any knowledge of my work habits. Trust what you've seen so far, not what he insinuates, Dr. Chambers. I've given you no reason to distrust me."

Dr. Chambers stared silently at Eden for a moment, then nodded. "As you say, I'll trust what I see. But I'm watching you."

The encounter left Eden shaking, though as she left the room, she held her head high and kept a straight face. She'd expected this. Dr. Siler had warned her, and now he'd made good on his threat. But as Colin had asked, did he really have any power? Or was he fighting like a cornered lion because his crimes were being revealed? He'd been at the school for over ten years and had developed a reputation, had the respect of his colleagues and students. He'd created a completely false persona with the faculty, including the dean. They all believed him. Would anyone believe Eden? Older student, former housewife, showing up three decades later to make trouble?

Probably not. But she had to do what her heart and her God told her to do . Period.

By the time Eden stopped by the grocery store and the gas station on her way home, her pulse had returned to normal. Instead of frayed nerves, peace settled in like a calm lake. Whatever happened, she was solid. God would handle it for her.

She made a light supper, then remembered to grab her phone, which she hadn't consulted in several hours. Her breath hitched when she saw Brent's name on her list of text messages. She wiped crumbs from her mouth and fumbled with the phone. *Hey, Mom. Just want to say I'm sorry for being a jerk recently. After Thanksgiving, I kept thinking about what you said. You probably thought I blew it off, but I didn't. When Kelly broke up with me, I took it out on you. It wasn't your fault. She and I talked a couple times since then and one of our talks was really long. She did most of the talking and I just listened. I tried hard not to tell her how wrong she was. (Smiley face). Not really. She expressed a lot of stuff I totally needed to hear. I told her I want to get back together, and she didn't say no. She's thinking about it, which is progress. We've started hanging out again as friends. Anyway, keep us in your prayers, okay? I'll keep you posted. Love you.*

A wide grin stretched across Eden's face. Tears sprang to her eyes. She held the phone against her heart. "Thank you," she murmured to the ceiling,

She reread his message and a chuckle erupted from her throat. Not only had Brent never said those kinds of things to her before, but it was the longest text she'd ever received from her son.

And the very best.

Chapter Twenty-Four

In May, the town of Wadesboro sprang to life after a long winter. Dogwoods and cherry trees festooned in pink and white bouquets lifted Eden's spirits. She closed her eyes and savored the balmy breeze that caressed her face. Textbooks, notebooks, and her laptop covered the long patio table on her back porch. Final exams had begun the previous day. She'd be submerged for most of that week and wouldn't even have time to see Colin. Then summer break. Blessed relief.

As a reward for her hard work that year, she could relish the prospect of a trip with Colin to Colorado the week after finals. As a destination, it had never piqued her interest in more than a general way. But hearing him rave about it and being able to go there with him boosted her excitement. When they arrived in Denver, Colin's son, Davis, would pick them up. It would be her first visit to the place that had captured Colin's imagination. Maybe it would do the same to hers. She owed it to him to be open to that. And to God's sovereign leading.

Over the past three weeks, Dr. Siler had again gone silent. But what else could he do when she wouldn't respond to him? He might stop her from graduating, but he hadn't succeeded in his threat of sabotaging her semester. Her grades going into finals were strong. The Launchpad remained a question mark in her mind, but she assumed it would continue unchallenged to exploit more unsuspecting students. Maybe she could at least find some way to warn the student applicants to sign a non-disclosure agreement, which is the only protection they could have in lieu of a full patent.

Eden leaned back against the cushion of the wrought-iron patio chair. The turmoil of her year was about to end, but what had she accomplished? Students would still apply to the Launchpad, still have their ideas stolen. Women would still face discrimination in the business world. What had she really done? She'd completed two semesters of her college degree. Without getting the degree itself. She shut her eyes as disappointment surged through her chest. *Lord, what was it all for? Were you testing me, making me stronger? Why wasn't I able to help anyone?*

Yet, her heart had obliged her to take the risk, to step out of her comfort zone even if it meant not getting her coveted college diploma. It hadn't benefited her or the students, but she'd had to risk without knowing. And she'd do it again.

Colin's words from the previous month returned to her. Nothing could stop her, not the lack of a degree or opposition from Siler, from eventually starting a nonprofit and helping women begin as entrepreneurs. Not even her inability to protect students from the Launchpad could stop her. She needed to put a line through the entire experience, knowing it had strengthened her. It had also taught her how to rely on someone besides herself.

On God, her sovereign Lord. And On Colin. Despite her bittersweet musings, she smiled. *That* was a lesson worth learning in the face of any cost she'd have to pay, any sacrifice she'd have to make. Letting God be her very present strength. Letting Colin be her loving partner in life and work.

If she couldn't take Dr. Siler's course in the fall and graduate, what could she take instead? Should she simply withdraw from the university, one course shy of graduation? Maybe she should ask Dr. Boswell to intervene for her in the face of Siler's threats. Show him the copies the text messages and emails. Hmm. She hadn't thought of that before.

Eden knew she ought to get back to studying for her economics final the next day but reached for her laptop. This would only take a minute and might assuage the void that throbbed inside at the thought of dropping out of school.

She pulled up the university website and located the business courses for the fall semester. Preregistration started in a few weeks, if only she could find something to take. Maybe a course related to non-profit management. As she scanned the computer screen, she saw the class she needed, Managerial Economics, but in the space where the professor's name would normally be, it said TBA. To be announced. Siler wasn't teaching the class? Then who was? And why?

Maybe Dr. Siler had decided to quit. Or had been removed.

What else could have happened? On impulse, Eden inserted Business Innovation Launchpad into the top search bar of the university website. The search returned no results. A general search only revealed a marketing company in Oregon and a software app. The Launchpad website didn't appear. Nothing did. A slow smile spread across Eden's lips as she picked up her phone to call Colin.

"No idea how all this came down," she told him after describing her discovery, "But I think that means we've won."

"That's great, Eden. But I'd like to know what happened, wouldn't you? We should make an appointment with Dr. Boswell to make sure. Right now, all we have is some circumstantial evidence. We have proof a member of the faculty threatened you. Boswell needs to know about this. Aside from that, you need closure."

"You're right. There could be some other explanation, but with the Launchpad missing too, I think we both know they're in trouble."

Colin laughed. "Let's hope so. I'll let you call his office. Maybe we can see him before the semester is over. And before our trip."

After they disconnected, Eden called Dr. Boswell's office. She recognized the voice of his receptionist. "I'd like to make an appointment to see Dr. Boswell hopefully before the semester ends. It's Eden Godfrey. I came in to see him—"

"Oh, yes, Eden," Dr. Boswell's receptionist said warmly. "I remember you and your friend. Dr. Boswell wants to see you too but hasn't had the chance to set up a meeting due to some out-of-town travel. How about Friday morning at ten?"

"We'll be there."

ೞ   ೞ   ೞ

Usually, when Colin and Eden finished dinner at his dining room table, they lingered in conversation, bathed in candlelight. This time, Colin cleared the table and spread a map of Colorado across the surface.

"This'll be easier to see than an online map. I can mark it up too." He turned the dimmer switch, and light flooded the room. Eden had turned in her last project that day, so they were celebrating. And the next day, they hoped to fill in the gaps of the mystery during their meeting with Dr. Boswell.

Colin settled into his seat again and pointed to a spot on the map. "Here's the Denver airport. Davis'll pick us up and we'll all have dinner in the city before we go back to his place over here in the northwest suburbs. He's taking that day off."

Eden leaned forward, both elbows on the table as her finger followed the path he'd traced. Excitement grew inside her. "I'm looking forward to meeting your son. You said Denver time is two hours behind us?"

"That's right. We'll get there at three-thirty local time. Depending on what you enjoy doing, some options for the week would be hiking, visiting the city, touring the area. We can go to Boulder and Estes Park or drive in the mountains. Vail, you know the famous ski area, isn't too far, and in summer, they have plenty going on too. It's cute, fixed up like a European village."

"For decades, I didn't go anywhere." She stared down at the map that represented the coming vacation. "Even as a family, we

270

didn't do that much out of the area. There was always the restaurant. And the kids."

"You didn't take the kids on vacations once in a while?"

"Oh, yes, we did once in a while, mostly close by, but the restaurant always came first." Eden smiled. "We had some good times together as a family. But I haven't done as much as you have. You can bring me up to speed."

His hazel eyes caught hers, holding warmth and promise. "This'll be our first adventure together." He added a wink and a squeeze of her hand. "But certainly not our last."

Ԓ Ԓ Ԓ

For the second time that spring, Eden perched on the edge of a wingback chair in Dr. Boswell's office with Colin seated beside her. Gone were the anxious flutters of their first meeting with the dean. Instead, eager anticipation pressed inside her, like a flock of birds eager to break out and fly. She was hungry for answers and hoped Dr. Boswell had them. This time, the man seemed just as eager to see her and Colin as they were to see him.

The campus buildings and open spaces were far less populated since most students were finishing their exams or had already begun their summer break. A weight had been lifted from Eden's mind, not only because she'd taken her last final the previous day, but also the injustice that had preoccupied her thoughts for months was about to be resolved. Hopefully.

The receptionist called them only minutes after their arrival and they entered the dean's office. "Hello, Eden and Colin. Please have a seat." Instead of the detached administrative expression he'd worn the first time, his eyes seemed bright and eager. Eden hoped that signaled good news.

"Thank you for receiving us again, Dr. Boswell." Eden smoothed her knee-length skirt and scooted forward in her seat. "I have some new information as well as a few questions—"

"Yes, I'm sure you do. Well, first allow me to apologize to you both. I jumped to conclusions in support of Dr. Siler and almost let the whole thing go. I'm embarrassed by that because I didn't do my due diligence." He pulled out the file folder that Eden had given him during their previous appointment. "After I spoke with Dr. Siler that day and he gave me his explanation, I dismissed it for a while. Then, for some reason, I recalled your statement about the designs being the same, referring to Siler's designs he submitted for the patent application and the students' designs they'd given in applying to the Launchpad. I don't know why it didn't hit me the first time, but I couldn't imagine how they'd be so similar, unless it had been the same applicant. Or possibly stolen."

Eden and Colin exchanged glances. Eden turned back to Dr. Boswell. "I'm relieved you saw the similarity."

"There's more. I went to Dr. Siler, this was maybe a month or six weeks ago, and asked him if he could tell me more about one of his inventions, the educational toy. That was the most recent. He was incapable of describing his process of inventing it, said it had been too long ago and he'd forgotten the details. I would assume that even after a few years, he'd be able to describe it in detail, if he had been the inventor. That raised my suspicions. Then, a few days after that, a professor in the English department, Dr. Morris, came to me. He had been in the library to get a reference for one of his classes when he overheard a conversation between you and Dr. Siler. Dr. Morris was concerned that Dr. Siler appeared to be threatening you with not graduating. Siler's manner seemed very inappropriate to Dr. Morris, regardless of the situation. He wanted to follow up on it, but didn't know you, Eden, or what program you were in. Sometime later, he saw you talking to one of his students and asked that student who you were and what you were studying. He remembered your blond hair and small stature."

Eden grinned. "Finally, they came in handy."

Colin chuckled and Dr. Boswell smiled. "Yes, in this case, they did. He came to my office and told me about the incident. Of course, he knew Dr. Siler's identity, since they're both on the faculty. Though it was a bit late, I put two and two together."

"What did you do as a result, Dr. Boswell?" Colin asked.

"I'm sure you know how difficult it is to prosecute this kind of thing. I spoke to Dr. Fitch, the university president, about it and showed him all the documents you'd given me. He met with Dr. Siler to ask more questions, in a desire to be fair and hear both sides. He felt the same way I did, that Siler was full of ambiguous explanations he couldn't prove and quite a bit of defensiveness. After consulting with the university attorney and human resources, Dr. Fitch decided to dismiss Dr. Siler, though not pursue any legal measures. It would be difficult to prove, and we don't want the school embroiled in a lawsuit. But at least Siler won't be able to continue to steal ideas or harass students."

Eden took a long breath. Dr. Boswell's questioning was likely the catalyst for Dr. Siler's renewed efforts at intimidating her. "And what about the Launchpad?"

"Ah, the Launchpad. I asked Dr. Siler if he was complicit with someone on their board and he was still denying everything, so we didn't get any names. Dr. Fitch decided that, as a university, we'd end our relationship with this organization. Don't worry, we'll find another one we've vetted thoroughly to take its place. There is a similar nonprofit doing good work down at Bloomington."

"Oh, that's good." Eden nodded.

"So, I hope these explanations will help close this unfortunate chapter in your lives, as well as for the university. Dr. Fitch and I are deeply grateful for your persistence in pursuing this situation."

Eden smiled and rose. "I'm glad it turned out the way it did." She extended her hand to shake the dean's. "Thanks so much, Dr. Boswell. Your support through this means a lot and has helped future students."

"It's my obligation, but also my pleasure." The dean turned to shake Colin's hand.

"I have one last question and a comment before we leave," Eden said. "The class Dr. Siler was going to teach in the fall, Managerial Economics, is the only one I need to graduate. He told me he'd block me from enrolling so I couldn't graduate. Will I now be able to take that class? There wasn't a professor listed in the fall catalogue."

"Yes, that's an important class for seniors, so definitely we'll run the class and of course, you should enroll. There are no barriers now, Eden." He smiled at her.

"Great. Any idea who will teach it?"

"In all likelihood, I will. It'll be a pleasure to have you in class."

"Yes, it'll be great to be there. I also have a comment I want to make to clear my record regarding Dr. Siler. I went on two dates with him, and *I* broke it off with *him*."

Dr. Boswell grinned. "Understood. I stand corrected on your relationship. I'm glad you ended it. You seem like a decent woman, and given what we know now about Dr. Siler, I seriously doubt he's suitable for you."

"No worries, I found someone suitable." She smiled and turned toward Colin, extending her hand to grab his.

They said goodbye to Dr. Boswell and his receptionist, wishing them a pleasant summer. Her break had *finally* begun and the lightness in Eden's chest was indescribable, as though she could simply float upward like a helium balloon. As she and Colin reached the ground floor, he stopped. "So, you think I'm suitable?" An impish smile tugged at his lips.

Eden faced him. She drew closer, so their toes and torsos almost touched. "Yes, you're suitable. And funny, and handsome, and smart, and of course, godly. I think you just might be a keeper."

His hazel eyes burned into hers. "Think so?" His voice was husky. He bent forward and brushed her lips with his.

The same pool of warmth he always stirred in her swept into a small bonfire. Gone were the distractions, the misunderstandings, the questions. God in his sovereignty had been at work behind the scenes doing things that had never occurred to her or Colin.

And Colin. He'd walked through everything with her and was here now, not controlling, but supporting her like a partner. A life partner. Staring at her in a way that made her knees weak. "Yeah." Her voice came out in a whisper.

He leaned his forehead to touch hers, still staring into her eyes. "Well, that makes two of us."

Then he kissed her. His kiss spoke of promises and a future where she could join him unafraid. She leaned against him and linked her hands around his waist. His arms around her felt so good, secure, loving.

"Let's go somewhere for lunch," he said. "We need to get this summer started."

She reached out and curled her fingers around his. They left the building and walked out into the late morning sunshine.

I hope you enjoyed reading *Eden Redefined*. If you did, please consider leaving a review at the online store where you bought it. It would help other readers discover my books and be encouraged by their inspiring truths. You can also sign up to receive updates about new books at www.Kyle-Hunter.com where you'll receive *Marissa Rewritten* (first book in this series) free just for signing up!

For more romantic stories that take you places . . .

Romance in Provence Series

The Provence Series takes you with Bree and Lauren, best friends and business partners, to one of the loveliest regions of France. It's not always idyllic in the land of lavender fields and cliffside villages. Join Bree and Lauren as each woman discovers her unique journey—and surprising romance.

Prodigals in Provence (Bree's story) #1

Bree and her friend Lauren own Le Bon Voyage, a travel company specializing in tours to charming Provence, France. Bree battles anxiety before each trip, sure some detail will fall between the cracks.

Travis is a TV travel critic who crosses the globe to film documentaries. But he's been in a spiritual desert ever since losing his marriage and ministry five years earlier.

Between film projects, Travis plans to accompany his elderly mother on a tour to Provence, a long-term dream for her. Bree tries unsuccessfully to block him, sure he's coming to spy on the struggling company for an exposé article.

A diverse group of tourists arrives at the rented villa to spend the week and discover the spectacular villages, vineyards, and history of the Luberon mountain region of Provence. Amidst a series of problems and relational tensions, Bree thinks she has all she can handle . . . until she becomes attracted to Travis.

As Bree and Travis are drawn together, will their hidden wounds drive them apart?

A Promise in Provence (Lauren's story) #2

Lauren is at a turning point. If only she knew *where* to turn. Her long-term relationship with Mark is fading fast. Instead, she feels drawn to Jean-Pierre, an attractive Frenchman she'd met the previous summer. When she's laid off from her job as a chef, she decides to go see him in Provence, France.

Mark can't get Lauren out of his heart, even though it's been close to a year since she asked him to give her space. When she goes to France, he's afraid he'll lose her for good. That is, until he decides to go there, too, as a last-ditch effort to win her back.

At first, Lauren is angry that Mark follows her to France. But a joint desire to help a young refugee boy leads them to work together. Lauren finds herself torn between the two men. Worse, she's confronted with obstacles in helping the boy and even greater obstacles within herself.

Stand Alone Novels that take you places . . .

One December

Is there any way to recapture what happened under the moon one December?

Nikki has loved Mike for as long as she can remember. Mike has his own past hurts to resolve, having lost both parents when he was fourteen. He's tried to escape the memories by starting a new life on the West Coast.

At Christmas, he comes back to New York for the first time in three years. He and Nikki rekindle the friendship they had as children and share their newfound faith. Under a Christmas moon, romantic sparks fly...but their mutual attraction takes an unexpected detour.

Nikki is devastated, believing the romance is over. She impulsively takes a one-year teaching opportunity in Paris to face her own fears and to get over Mike.

If they think they can run away from each other, they'd better think again.

"*One December* sizzles with romantic tension, taking the reader on a roller-coaster ride from New York to San Francisco, with a delightful detour in Paris. I couldn't put it down!"

– Elizabeth Musser, author of *The Secrets of the Cross* trilogy and *The Swan House*.

Circle Back Around

Hailey and her father haven't always seen eye to eye, especially in running the failing family textile mill. Frustrated, Hailey leaves the mill and her hometown in North Carolina to start a new life near her sister in Colorado. Only months later her father calls to ask a special favor. He needs heart surgery and asks Hailey to run the mill in his place.

Moving back would devastate Hailey's sister, Hope. Yet Hailey would have an opportunity to possibly save the mill, and at a time when her father needs her most. And maybe he'd even approve of her for the first time in her life.

Filled with self-doubt, Hailey returns to North Carolina and struggles to make a difference at the mill, facing more challenges than she bargained for. Her attractive neighbor, Alex, is almost enough to outweigh the difficulties, but she doesn't know that in the shadows lurks someone who wants to destroy both her *and* the mill.

Second Chance Series

In *The Second Chance Series*, you'll meet Marissa, Julia, Sydney, and Eden, four college friends who, twenty-five years later, renew their friendships as they find themselves empty nesters and single again. You'll love getting to know these women and following each one in her own book.

Marissa Rewritten (Book 1) A Novella

Author Marissa Thompson has had a writer's block since her husband died almost two years earlier. Her three closest friends are a comfort. Despite this, things are getting urgent as her career hangs by a thread and repairs on her historic home mount up. Prodded by desperation, Marissa heads to Wilmington, North Carolina for a Civil War research trip. She hopes for inspiration, but receives encouragement from a surprising source, a feisty character from her last novel.

Jarrod Lambert has already lost his wife. He's always been close with his college-age daughter, but she seems to be slipping further away from him. In an effort to reconnect with her, he makes an impulsive trip to see her in Wilmington.

Through an accident, Marissa and Jarrod meet and discover common ground. Will it be enough to overcome the obstacles standing between them?

Julia Redesigned (Book 2)

Can a stack of letters provide clues to an age-old conflict and a doorway to a new family?

For the last three years, Julia De Luca has juggled her successful interior design business with caring for her elderly mother. Following her mother's death, Julia finds old letters from distant relatives in Italy. They remind her of visits she and her mother made when Julia was a child. Could these letters hold the answer to why their trips to Italy ended abruptly when she was ten years old?

These people whose names she's forgotten are the only family Julia has left on earth. How can she reconnect with them after so many years? Would it be crazy to try?

Her compelling desire to locate her distant family leads Julia on an impulsive trip to Florence, Italy. Along with savoring the sights and flavors of Florence, Julia discovers that families can be messy, that it's not too late to fall in love, and that there's more to Julia De Luca than she ever knew.

Sydney Rewound # 3

Sydney Bennett's life is anything but calm. She's a high-school teacher and the single parent of a teenager. An unexpected event shakes her pressured but predictable routine. As she tries to regain her balance, she's drawn to a secret that even her daughter doesn't know. Nor do her three best friends.

Her private quest leads her to the beach town where she grew up, and her strained relationship with her mother. The last thing she expects is to cross paths with the man who once upended her life, a man she's never forgotten.

As Sydney's past collides with her present, she's forced to reveal her secrets and encounters the surprising power of letting go.

Read Chapter One of all books at
www.Kyle-Hunter.com

Kyle Hunter writes inspirational romance and women's fiction that sometimes take her characters to faraway places. She lived in France for thirteen years. Currently, she lives in North Carolina where she writes fiction, non-fiction (under the pen name K. B. Oliver) and the travel blog OliversFrance.com and teaches French to adults.

www.ingramcontent.com/pod-product-compliance
Lightning Source LLC
Chambersburg PA
CBHW051509150726

47997CB00001B/181